Earl

CW00822411

"Web

84,586 words June 16th 2016

©

Thanks and love to Joy Jackson
Hurst.
And Dawn Jackson Golding
For Fine art work.

Thanks to Paul for Technical
Assistance.

Happy days to all at Scribblers

Love as always to my Son's.

All my work comes with dedication
and Love.

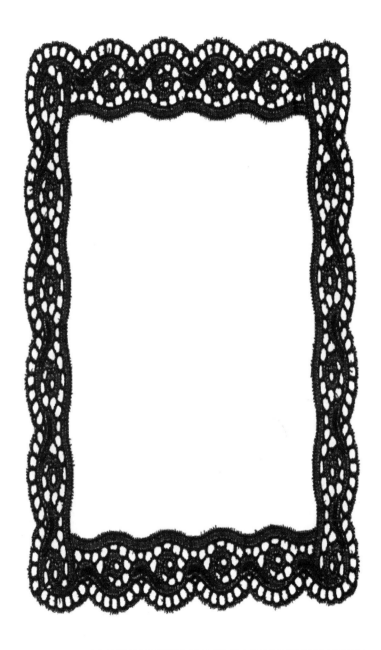

Prologue

This book will test your many senses
and it will give you insight into a
marriage that is hitting the rocks. The
couple are not seeing the other's point of
view. Who do you agree with Harry or
Lilly? Who will gain and who will lose,
for there are things to be gained or lost.
The era is depicted during the time a
man's word was his law and the wife had
to adhere to his kind of justice.
Some scenes are described and may be
disturbing... not for the faint of heart. I
leave you to discover a world you would
not normally enter. It is in fact the world
we live in, where sometimes fact is
stranger than fiction.
If you can review this book on Amazon I
would invite your opinion.

Thank you, Sylvia Jackson Clark.

Web of Secrets

Chapter one

Lilly never thought she would have children when at the age of forty five she found herself with child. Both she and her husband Harry thought it was the change of life that had stopped Lilies monthly cycle. It was the sickness that had sent her to see the Doctor. The news of the baby had come as quite a shock. When she told Harry he thought the Doctor had got it wrong, in fact it was not to Harry's advantage for Lilly to have a child. He was used to Lilly tending his every beck and call he liked her in sole attendance to his needs. Lilly had told his Lordship (as she often addressed her husband) after they had ate a good meal and were sitting together in the evening.
"I have some news for you Harry dear."
"Good news I hope Lilly I have enough problems to attend to already." Harry lit his pipe and sat back ready to listen.
"You know dear of me going to the Doctors? Annie went with me."Harry rudely interrupted,
"Get to the point Lilly I don't want to hear

about Annie".

"Alright Harry well the thing is, Lilly hesitated again. The thing is Harry I am going to have a baby, or I should say we are going to have a baby." Lilly watched as Harry's face changed he said,

"Is that Doctor stupid you have gone by your time to have a child?" He glared at Lilly with no respect Lilly next to tears said,

"But Harry I thought you would be delighted, the Doctor says sometimes this happens during the change of life and I am not alone there are other ladies he tends and the same situation has occurred."

"Lilly a child at this time of my life is a child too many, you can get it seen to can't you? We don't want a child, well I certainly don't anyway." Lilly looked disdainful she had hoped Harry would share her experience she needed his support. It was as much a shock to her as it had been to Harry but now the child was growing within her womb and she cherished the feeling she replied,

"No Harry I can't have this child seen to, it is what destiny has seen fit for me to do, you will see things differently as time goes on and you turn out to be a good father you'll see."

"No Lilly you will see, I want no part in this mess you have landed yourself in. Good Lord

woman I am fifty years old what would I do with a child?" Lilly cowered down in her chair thinking…this was not my doing it was more yours than mine, you would insist on regular visits to my bedroom for your own satisfaction and be angry if I didn't adhere to your demands. How can this be my fault alone?" Harry realised how quiet Lilly had gone he said,

"Busy yourself about woman and fetch me a glass of whiskey and a cheese sandwich before I go to bed." Lilly decided more argument would not get her the answer she needed so went to do Harry's bidding all the time trying to accustom her mind to her new status and wondering how she could make Harry see sense and this baby a joy to be looked forward to.

Next day Harry's mood had not improved, in fact Lilly thought he was dead ignorant towards her and the baby was not mentioned. The atmosphere in the house was heavy and laden with annoyance. Lilly needed Harry more than anything in her life right now. She was full of apprehension and fear at actually giving birth in her forty-fifth year, the future looked bleak without Harry's support. Annie was a good friend so Lilly decided to find a little solace when Annie was with her she often popped in for a cup of tea when she knew Harry would not be in the house. Annie could do without Harry anytime, he made snide remarks and was brusque and unyielding in his manner. As soon as he returned home Annie left, not staying long enough for Harry to get his social dig about Lilly and herself, this was usually about Lilly and her having time to sit around drinking tea. When first meeting Harry Annie tried to be a friend to him as well as Lilly but he soon nipped that in the bud, stating things that were downright insulting and leaving a sting instead of a pleasure. Never the less Lilly and Annie had cultivated pleasurable company and met when Harry wasn't around, or chatted in town having a pot of tea for two at a smart teashop of their own choice. A bond soon developed as Lilly could confide in Annie telling her things personal and deep they trusted each other. At this moment Lilly could find no better way than to turn to Annie knowing she would share this burden and help all she could.

Chapter two

Harry came home from his club still unsympathetic towards Lilly. Thinking that her husband would mellow Lilly had his favourite meal ready. Harry put his coat and bowler hat on the hall stand and placed a black furled umbrella in its intended place. He went in to see Lilly saying,
"Is that my tea Lilly?"
"Yes Harry your favourite."
"Well you can eat it; I am going out again very shortly and will have my meal with a companion." His manner was again brusque. Lilly didn't argue she didn't dare. Harry spoke,
"You can give my better shoes a polish I need to look smart tonight. I will also need a fresh white shirt the one with the pearl buttons, lay it on the bed ready for me to put on." Lilly cringed how cruel Harry could be, she had done nothing wrong but he was punishing her as if she had. How could she carry this man's child if he wouldn't even recognize she was in fact with child? Pinning her hopes on a future after Harry had got over the shock. Lilly humoured him laying his shirt out ready and polishing his shoes, he looked smart as

he left the house, sprightly and singular but where on earth was she going to fit in? The tea she had made especially for Harry had gone cold and stale, she sat and picked at it and then threw it away. Lilly cleared the table and then sat down heavily on to an armchair. Harry's behaviour was beyond reason, she needed his support more than ever before, but he was letting her down. Tears came readily to her eyes and anger to her mind. This was not her baby it was their baby and she dreaded the long haul ahead even though Annie would be steadfast it was not the same as Harry beside her sharing this oh so new experience.

A couple of months later there was still no change in Harry's attitude, he had kept away from Lilly's bed and only spoke if it was necessary Lilly was beginning to show in her changing figure, she approached Harry with caution saying,

"Harry dear I must ask you to give me an allowance to buy baby clothes and a cot, the perambulator I can get later but the essentials I must get now to give me peace of mind. Annie says you are duty bound to help me with the costs." That did it, Harry was furious he said,

"Oh! Now we have it Annie's word is as good

as law is it? No you want the baby and you can pay for its needs. I give you housekeeping and food money as it is. I have thought of late of the money your father left you use that, I told you to rid yourself of this child and you didn't so it is up to you to provide for it. I want nothing more to do with this situation you will keep this child a secret and don't name me as its father. Lilly felt her strength weaken but tried once more saying,

"How can you sit on the fence and watch my anguish? Haven't I been a good wife all the years of our marriage? Why can't you see what is needed from you? This baby may be a boy…your Son Harry will you not stand beside me until the happy day of your Son's birth?" Lilly saw a spark in Harry's eyes when she mentioned a son but he said, "Don't come here with your tricks and suggestions my mind is made up, I can eat at my club and there are women a plenty to satisfy my personal needs. Look at yourself, hair greying, skin wrinkling, and a belly that should be well hidden to disguise the fact that you are laden with child. I find you repulsive and would have rid of you if I could."

"Have rid of me Harry what a terrible thing to say, I have given you no cause to justify how you are treating me I would never have

believed it of you. Daily you have given me cause to think you are being downright cruel with intention to disgrace my condition. I will not be put aside because of your whim and by the way you are not such a catch yourself these days. Alcohol has given you paunches in your belly equal to that of my own, your hair is also greying and your own skin is wrinkling. You must pay a pretty penny to those ladies of the town to pamper your every whim. I am glad it is no longer my duty to satisfy you and considering your venomous treatment I am only too sorry it was an act of your own that has placed me in the family way." Lilly burst into tears and ran upstairs once more considering her bedroom a haven of retreat. The very sight of Harry made her feel sick. The front door banged and resounded through the house as Harry left. Lilly's reminders of the home truth had rather dampened Harry's ardour, the image Lilly had portrayed didn't fit in with the image Harry had of himself. He liked to think he was full of charm and that the ladies that tended him in town did so because he had excellent style and pizzazz. If Lilly thought she could get her own way by insulting him she had another think coming, blasted inconvenient woman and the thought of her

having this child at her age was laughable.
Harry felt bitter as these thoughts trickled
through his mind. He was now near to the
destination he was heading for and girls of
all shapes and sizes tried to accost him as he
walked, but these girls were not good enough
for Harry, he wanted pampering on a soft bed
or couch with a pretty face to look upon. He
didn't care he could afford to pay for such
treatment. Reaching the building Harry
tapped the door, almost at once a grid was
opened to see who was there. A lady called
Victoria in a red and black dress appeared
she said
"Hello Harry, good to see you dear." The
bolts and locks on this heavy door were
opened and Harry entered. Victoria said
"Is it the full treatment? Or just a glass of
wine with my girls you are wanting dear?"
" I will have a glass of wine with my pretties,
then after I will have the full treatment.
Victoria please make quite sure the new girl
is in attendance I would like to try her out."
"She's a pretty one Harry and no mistake
young too, I will select her for you but it is
going to cost you more my dear."
"Money is of no object, I will have just what I
want, now take my top coat and my brolly and
I will go and feast my eyes on the fair skinned

maidens. The new one is she in the parlour with the others?"

"Oh no Harry she is treated separately her charms are expensive, she is a one off so to speak." Harry's excitement was mounting but he didn't want to miss the chance of sitting first with the other girls, they would look after his every whim and feed him with exotic fruits while sitting on his lap whispering into his ear. Things that were whispered would be obscene and unrepeatable but Harry liked to get down and dirty after all, this entire visit would cost him quite a penny and he wanted his money's worth. Into the parlour he went, as soon as his presence was felt the girls greeted him.

"Hello Harry sit down here beside me and I will make you comfortable. Harry sidestepped this girl and went over to a buxom blonde who was sitting on a chaise longue, the seat was covered in bright red velvet and the girl dressed in black lace with bosoms almost hanging loose at the top. Harry knew this bitch, she would give him an obscene earful. Harry's mouth watered at the thought. As he sat down in the space made for him he saw her eyes glint she said,

"Well my handsome man it's me you want is it?" Her hands caressed his chest and his *manly body parts. Harry felt the delight run through him.*

"Are we going to the bedroom shortly Harry? I am panting with desire for you." She kissed his face, eyes and lips as her hand tugged at his belt.

"Now now my dear you are going too fast for me, first I shall desire some petting and you can feed me some of those black grapes along with the red wine." Harry nodded his head towards the wine decanter and the huge bunch of black grapes that lay before them. "Is my darling holding back his passion just to drink wine and eat grapes? In the bedroom I could show you far more exotic fruits to taste and enjoy, let us go upstairs now." Harry knew precisely where this lady was leading him and what she was referring to but upstairs he had the new girl waiting for him, she could be a virgin and again his mouth watered.

Chapter Three

Back in her own home was Lilly red eyed and downcast, she had run all the immediate events through her mind and realised she was losing Harry he hadn't had a kind word to say to her since the baby was mentioned, now the last recent blow telling her she must pay for the baby's needs out of her own pocket. Insult after insult she had suffered always hoping one of these days he would see he was wrong and apologise so that their lives could be set on a true course again. No it wasn't happening, as the days passed by he was even more arrogant and dismissive. Lilly even questioned her own capacity as regards loving him, how could she love such a qualified bounder? So she took a back seat to avoid Harry's flailing tongue relying on Annie to give her the comforting words she so badly needed to hear. Together they started to buy baby clothes choosing white to accommodate either boy or girl, but Harry had knocked the stuffing out of Lilly and her enthusiasm was suffering. Annie was very sorry for Lilly for she had felt the whiplash of Harry's harsh tongue and tried to balance his insane remarks by comforting Lilly. Harry's terrible behaviour had left a void that couldn't be filled Lilly was trying to understand him but it proved to be a thankless task Annie knew she couldn't fill the void no matter how she tried.

Lilly was looking bedraggled and tired and her baby bump got bigger each day, her back ached and her feet were sore, she no longer got Harry a meal she felt defeated, when she recently had put a meal before Harry he would not eat it, so having thrown away so many carefully prepared meals she stopped cooking at all she was so disheartened. At certain times she even wondered about her own desire to bring this baby into the world, it had caused nothing but grief and anguish and pain and it was of Harry's blood. It made her shudder at the thought. How would Harry treat this child? Would Lilly have to keep the child out of Harry's sight? What would the child think living with a parent who despised his very existence? Babies don't stay babies for very long, during the child's growing up years there would be a time when questions were bound to be asked, how was Lilly going to answer?

Chapter four

Harry had seen the new girl that he was promised and was now on his way to bed her for a second time, never giving a thought towards Lilly. He could see this new girl in his mind's eye, slender with skin like silk, flowing blonde hair and very little covering her statue like pose. Harry was intense, his step quickening as he approached the house. Knocking the door Victoria answered and opened the grid. They went into the parlour. The girls lying and sitting around expectantly looked up as Harry walked in they had heard that Harry tipped the girl of his choice generously so they vied for prime position. More flesh was exposed by slipping the sparse top further down, or the skirt would be lifted to show bare thighs. Harry sat down conversation was rude and even to the point of being dirty but Harry liked this kind of banter and he liked the girls contesting for a place beside him, he was in control and enjoyed this position.

The air was scented and thick with the smoke from the dainty cigarettes smoked from a holder, a heavy scent from stale perfume mingled in. Harry was in the place he wanted to be and what is more his darling

*new girl who he had named Angel was
waiting for his company upstairs. He had
promised himself a lively romp with her
today, last time she was so new at the game
he had to be gentle with her but the visit was
very special, as he penetrated her deeply and
took her virginity, he heard her cry out with
pleasure. Harry slipped away from Victoria
and the parlour and went straight upstairs he
tapped on Angel's door it was open so he
went straight in. There she lay this beautiful
specimen of a woman, the only garment that
covered her nakedness was a slip made from
white satin it emphasised the pale pink of her
bosoms, it made Harry drool , he drew in a
sharp breath, how lovely she was! He said
"I am here my love have you waited for me?"
Angel replied,
"Come Harry lie beside me and we will be
transported into the heavens, are you ready
for me?" Harry was ripping off his shirt and
flinging his trousers to land on the floor, how
he wanted her he had planned to make this
session a long one but his desire overpowered
his intent as he penetrated her with force.
The sweat ran down his face as he tried to
imitate a much younger man needing his
thrust to be strong and powerful but he was
not a young man anymore and his agility was*

failing him. With one last thrust his seed left his body and was deposited into Angel's vagina he gasped for breath. "Blast!" the word escaped from his lips, this was not supposed to happen, it was too quick, he had planned to play with his Angel until she was begging him to enter her. Control that is what he needed, at best this session had lasted all of fifteen minutes now he would have to pay dearly for that short time. Angel languishing on the pillow she was pleased, she only had to play act and tell Harry she had found a wonderful satisfaction then her money would have been easily earned, she would be reluctant to see Harry leave but that also was pretence so that he would be back to see her again. Harry said,

"Did I satisfy you my darling Angel? She replied,

"Of course Harry why do you ask?

"I felt I did a hasty penetration and I so wanted you to feel the same ecstasy as I did, I didn't give you enough time. Sorry, I promise next time I will make love to you before things get out of hand."

"Don't worry Harry, but do make another appointment before you leave I will be here for you." In Harry's mind this reply led him to believe he had awakened a real love and

desire inside of his mistress, but the truth was far from that description Angel smiled to herself she had Harry hook line and sinker and she would play her part well while he had money to spend. He called her "Angel! What! Maggie was her real name and she was certainly No Angel. Some men were such fools and Angel was a good actress, growing up in the slums with good for nothing parents had been leading her to find where money was readily available. At the tender age of twelve she had already began to entertain men. At first it was a quick fumble under her skirts with the touch of her bare thigh thrown in. Angel could earn enough in one night to feed her starving siblings for a month. As she grew older she had a few tricks up her sleeve and could satisfy any man as long as he gave her money. Victoria had named her "the new girl" but Angel was anything but new, Victoria had seen prospects in this girl her figure suggested youth and her bosoms were full and inviting, a sweet smile and portraying a feeling of hard to get, all of this appeal was close to a young girl's attitude. Her longing (albeit false) was in her eyes and she pretended to be shy. Underneath she was as hard as nails and sniggered to herself after the paying client left; if she had been real nice to the fellow he would give her a personal tip on top of what he paid to Victoria for the privilege of spending time in her bedroom. Of course Angel was especially nice and so made more money in tips than Victoria actually paid her. It was so easy to flatter a man especially in his middle age with his belly paunch and his hair thinning… "Come to Momma" was Angel's thoughts as she plied her trade and the men kept coming.

Harry hated returning home, very often he would stop at his club and drink more wine or whisky to fortify him lest he had to face Lilly, darned woman the very thought of her turned Harry's stomach, sick of the thought of the coming baby, it was laughable he had no desire to become a father. Maybe Lilly would die giving birth? After all she was bearing this child very late in life, this was one way of getting rid of her but what if the baby lived? He casually dismissed this thought quickly; anyway he could get the baby adopted he had no sentiment in that way at all, it interfered with his lifestyle and he was not going to tolerate that happening.

Arriving home Lilly was not there, another damned inconvenience, she should be here to get my food cooked and welcome me home to a warm house. Harry mumbled something to *himself thinking …she is round at Annie's place that is where she is, probably moaning about me as usual. The sound of a key in the locked front door interrupted Harry's thoughts. Lilly came in took off her hat and coat without saying a word and went directly upstairs. She knew Harry was in, the smell of pipe smoke was in the air and the light was on. Harry grimaced a distorted look crept across his face. Lilly was ignoring him! It made him very angry, Lilly had a duty to perform and if he wanted something to eat it was up to her to provide it. He called upstairs, "Lilly Lilly, get down here woman I want some supper." Silence fell, Harry called again still no reply he went up the stairs two at a time his anger driving him on. Arriving on the landing he went to the bedroom he had previously shared with Lilly on the nights of his choice. Turning the knob to go in he found the door was locked. He heard Lilly say,*

"Go away Harry you have turned your back on me once too often and I don't want to set eyes on you. Pity is all I feel for you. Pity is not enough. I consider you should get your own meals; I have had enough of preparing a meal for you to declare that you do not want what I have cooked. Get your own meal I

have had enough of rejection and waste, who do you think you are to lay down the law?" Harry was taken aback, he was livid! Lilly answering him like that, he would put her in her place, but he couldn't get at her which infuriated him even more. He thumped the bedroom door with clenched fists but it made no difference, he gave her a mouthful of disgusting abuse and went downstairs again. Back in the kitchen as he was hungry he was forced to get something to eat. He made much ado about making a plain cheese sandwich as Lilly had made cooking a complete meal. He didn't have to use pots and pans but he rattled them about purposely making a noise for Lilly to hear and fully letting her know he was not best pleased. In her room Lilly was smiling to herself knowing Harry was missing her presence. Lilly thought…get on with it Harry and wait until you want your white shirts laundered ironed and delivered crisp and clean every day… then you will miss me and no mistake!

Harry had a rude awakening coming, because Lilly was withdrawing her wifely duties not only in the bedroom but in day to day life. Harry was feeling very sorry for himself, had Lilly taken leave of her senses? On arriving home the following day Lilly was nowhere to be found. The fire had gone out and there was still no food to be had. Harry searched in the pantry and the cupboards and all he found were scanty bits of leftover food and these all had mould growing on them. Harry thought …Lilly should clean out these cupboards and get fresh stock, where are the vegetables and the meat? Harry looked in the meat safe that sat on the thrall in the pantry. There were flies buzzing around it but nothing in it except a steak that had mould and white maggots wriggling on it Harry jumped back in disgust. Lilly had clearly planned this situation Harry knew this was meant to disturb him and he was full of condemnation towards Lilly he thought…I must take Lilly to task and give her a good dressing down what does she think she is playing at stupid woman. I pay her food allowance so food should be here when I want it. Meanwhile he scraped the mould off the jam and put it on a half decent crust he had found then sat heavily on his armchair to eat it. Very soon he realised how cold this room was without the fire, he shivered, gulped his sandwich down and went straight to his empty bed. His fancy piece Angel never crossed his mind it was no good going to her for necessities and daily duties. Lilly should be here, it was Lilly's duty without a doubt. The word "Duty" came easily to Harry's tongue in regard to Lilly, what about his own "Duty" towards Lilly he had no qualms of conscience, he was master in this house and always would be.

Chapter five

Lilly turned over in her bed with a satisfactory sigh, men would be men but this time Lilly had the upper hand, she despised Harry for not wanting this baby that grew daily bigger inside of her. Always she had been faithful to Harry, always his demands were dealt with, but this time he had gone too far. It had done her good to leave Harry, a taste of his own medicine. Lilly got up quite brightly, this was Annie's house and knowing Harry was not going to see her until she decided the time was right had lightened her mood. Annie had thought this ploy up, together they had found quite an innocent way of disturbing Harry's well planned life. Soon he would know just how much Lilly had put into his daily welfare. Harry had taken it all for granted, but not anymore. He had brought this on to himself and he still couldn't see it. In his view a wife's place was in the home and to grace his bed whenever he decided he needed her also to cook his food whenever he was hungry. To keep his appearance pristine each day, shine his shoes and wash his shirts, the reward Lilly got was a smile now and again. In fact Lilly existed to cook clean bottle wash and pander his every whim. Yes Lilly had done that and more, now because this child had been conceived very late in life Harry wanted no part of it, he disgusted Lilly so it was in defence she was going to let him know that her services had been withdrawn. Lilly went to join Annie downstairs Annie said,

"Mornin' Lilly, how did you sleep last night?"

"Very well thank you Annie, is the kettle on? I would love a cup of tea."

"You should know by now Lilly the kettle is always on in this house, sit yourself down in the rocking chair by the fire and I will make toast, do you want an egg Lilly?"

"No thanks tea and toast will be just right for me. I am wondering how Harry is getting on there is absolutely nothing in my pantry he will be starving."

"That is how it should be Lilly, all part of our well devised plan. It won't be long before Harry gets the message and I shall not let you starve we have your little one to consider as well as yourself I am well aware of that."

"Thanks Annie you are a true friend, I shouldn't really say this but since your husband passed on and your family left home it has been to my advantage, it is good to know you don't mind when I come to you

with my troubles. Don't get me wrong though I have no intention of putting on you. At the moment your help is regarded by me as being so needed, carrying this baby is more than I bargained for at this stage of my life and Harry's attitude has appalled me. Do you think he will ever see my point of view?"

"I really don't know Lilly he is a stubborn man, maybe when the baby arrives and he sees his own flesh and blood he will change his mind and welcome you home. Meanwhile you are very welcome to share my abode and a new baby to look after will be wonderful. How far have you gone Lilly? Is it time to see a Doctor on a regular basis? Or if you don't want a Doctor maybe you should see a Midwife?"

"I have been thinking about that myself Annie, but I was hoping Harry would have seen sense by now, I don't want to tell a Doctor of how Harry has treated me after the news of our child, I am ashamed and to tell you a fine point Harry is without question the father of this baby"

"Of course I know that Lilly, Harry is just sulking about having his wings clipped and your attention being taken by baby's needs instead of his own. I have heard of this happening but never thought I would witness

it at such close quarters he is in fact jealous. Don't you worry when he realises he is on his own in your house he will soon make an effort to get you back."

"I do hope you are right Annie, I am full of personal anxiety about birthing my baby the last thing I wanted to see is Harry as he is now, it is very selfish of him."

"Just bide your time Lilly that's all I can say. As regards birthing your baby I shall be right by your side." Lilly had to settle for that arrangement otherwise she didn't know where to turn.

The house that was Lilly's home was detached and set in a very quiet area, when she and Harry had first wed they were very happy, as time went on and no baby arrived they had time in abundance for each other. It was only just of late that Harry had shunned Lilly and obviously she knew why. Inside this same house this morning was Harry disgruntled and angry that Lilly was not there to get his breakfast. He went to the kitchen as usual but the kitchen was bare and cold, because Lilly was not there the fire had not been lit and the grate needed a good rake out to rid it of grey ash which in turn would have to be taken out into the garden to be exposed of. Harry was not a happy man, he expected to be obeyed in his own house, it had been said in the marriage vows "To love honour and obey". The more he thought about it the more furious he became. He knew from his scavenge last night there was no food in the house, by now he had expected to see Lilly back, cap in hand and with groceries to fill the cupboards. There was certainly no evidence of that, at this early hour Harry did not like showing up at his club, he knew it would set tongues wagging, so he dressed and went to a small place in town where they served breakfast, it made him feel an idiot ordering breakfast as a solitary person, sort of left out so to speak. Wait till he got hold of Lilly she would have a lengthy scolding from his angry tongue. Where was she anyway? Again he could only think she was at Annie's. Darn the woman, probably right at this moment Annie was serving Lilly her breakfast beside a warm glowing fire. Eggs and bacon came to mind, the thought made him even angrier and indeed hungrier. He didn't want to order eggs and bacon, café's did a greasy version of this dish so he ordered tea and toast and played safe. The waitress was a pretty girl wearing a red gingham pinney with a matching cap, she took Harry's order and as she left the table Harry noticed

*her trim figure, a winning smile had been
another feature it set Harry thinking. … I
wonder if the girl would meet me after work.
She wouldn't cost me much, not nearly as
much as Angel. The very thought of Angel set
his pulses racing and even though it was
early morning he wished he was in bed beside
her caressing her warm body. The waitress
broke his thought pattern returning to his
table with tea and toast, she leaned over to set
the tray down and Harry thought her bosoms
were creamy skinned and voluptuous. The
thought of Lilly and Annie sped far from his
mind. He was going to try his luck with this
girl he said,*
*"Thank you very much my dear would you
like to sit with me while I eat?"*
*"Oh no Sir I am not allowed to do that." A
frown replaced the earlier smile.*
"What time do you finish work here?"
*"5pm. Sir but I have to go straight home to
tend my ailing mother."*
*"That's a pity, I could show you a good time
if you came home with me." The waitress
looked at Harry thinking… go home with this
man he is old enough to be my father such
cheek! She said politely,*
*"Thank you Sir but no thank you I am
keeping company with my own childhood*

sweetheart, he would surely have something to say about your proposition and he is six foot tall and built well, he would very soon put you well into your place." Harry looked disdainful was she telling him the truth? He knew anyway his plan had been scuppered. After paying his bill he left the café thinking…refusal eh, am I losing my charm? Angel doesn't think so, I can please her. Harry walked around until twelve of the clock and then went to his club where he could exchange views with other stray men. Having settled into a chair with the newspaper Harry did not want to be interrupted. James came over and said,

"You are here early today Harry, had a row with the misses have you?"

"You could say that James, I am furious with Lilly, can't think just what she is playing at but I shall have the last word and no mistake."

"I heard Lilly is to have a baby is that right old man?"

"Yes I must admit it is. I told her to have rid of the brat but she wants to bring it to term, stupid it is, she is acting in the most peculiar way I just don't understand her, I ask you a baby at my age, it will be nothing but a pest I have told her so too. I also told her to keep it

all a secret, you know old man I don't want all and sundry knowing my business, I would ask you not to mention it to anyone and if I have my way the state of affairs will be reviewed and there will be no baby."

"Oh dear Harry you won't beat this one women go bats when a late pregnancy occurs, and to follow their mind pattern is beyond all reason. Best grin and bear it if you ask me."

"I do not want to grin and bear it as you say James. Lilly's first concern should be me. I think she should honour what I want and if it is too late to get rid of it have the brat adopted."

"Can't see her doing that Harry I think you should bend with the wind, she might give you a Son and he would be your heir, surely some good would come of that."

"No good can come of anything, I feel trapped, I could strangle Lilly, and drown her brat given half a chance."

"I say steady on old chap, surely you had something to do with this child's conception?"

"Don't say another word James I shall do as I think fit." Harry picked up his newspaper and obliterated the disagreeable James. Feeling put out by Harry's dismissal James walked away. Harry was right it was none of

his business he must forget the conversation ever happened. He would honour Harry's request and keep his knowledge a secret. This was an understanding for all the club members it was a way to offload anything that was troubling the particular member and keep the knowledge to oneself. James only wished he could have seen Harry's side of things but his sympathies lay with Lilly.

Chapter Six

Lilly was of course by now getting the layette together, knitting bootees and crocheting a perambulator rug, a little strand of blue and one of pink were being woven in with the white to make the cover a bit more interesting. Both Lilly and Annie marvelled at the tiny items of clothing, it shot a pang through Lilly's heart realising these items were meant for her very own child. A love had developed even before the child was born. Lilly was quite happy living with Annie and indeed they had been places that Lilly would never have seen if she had stayed with Harry Annie said,
"Shall we go and have a look around the Emporium tomorrow Lilly?"
"I have never been in an Emporium Annie is it a shop?"
"It is a huge shop with many individual shops within its walls, something for everyone; we could look at your baby's perambulator and maybe choose a cradle. A look around does not entail buying, so go with an open mind and enjoy an hour or two eh?" The next day Lily was quite excited saying
"Are we going this morning Annie? To the Emporium I mean."

"No this afternoon would be better Lilly"

"I shall just be practical Annie and you must curb my enthusiasm by not letting me buy things I don't really need."

"Yes we have nothing spoiling this afternoon and we could bring back something for tea." As the time we do things is entirely up to us we have no need to keep looking at the clock." After lunch they got themselves ready Annie went to get her coat and hat calling to Lilly,

"Bring your basket Lilly we can pick up a few bargains from the fruit and vegetable stalls." Complete with their baskets they locked up and went out. Harry had given Lilly very little free time so this outing was very special. Lilly always had been there catering for Harry and all his whims it was novel to her to actually choose where to go and what to do.

The Emporium loomed into sight and very impressive it looked, even though Lilly had the weight of her baby bump she did not feel tired, her enthusiastic approach rubbed off on to Annie and Annie said

"I doubt if we see all there is to see today, just tell me the kind of things you would like to see and we will single out the shops that have that type of merchandise." At once Lilly said

"Look Annie there is a shop selling

perambulators can we look?"

"Of course we can but do you want a perambulator at this stage Lilly?"

"To tell you the truth I have wanted to look at them right from the word go, it has been Harry's behaviour that has pushed it to the back of my mind. Don't worry Annie I shall have it stored for me should I be tempted enough to buy one. It would be too much for you to store it for me. I have to admit though I can't wait to have baby in the stroller no matter what Harry says."

As they approached the shop although it was in the Emporium it had its own windows and the perambulators were placed in front of the shop and locked together for safe keeping, Lilly was soon engrossed in the why's and wherefore's of each stroller that were displayed. Not expecting such a choice, it excited Lilly all the more, after about twenty minutes deliberation Lilly chose one in particular saying

"I think this one is very dashing, look Annie isn't this one the best designs you have ever seen?" Annie went to join Lilly to see just what she had chosen. Lilly stood beside the perambulator she said

"Look at the wicker work Annie and it has a collapsible hood. I really like it."

"Have you looked at the price Lilly?" At this point a smart young man came over to offer his services he spoke in a soft tone saying "Can I be of any assistance to you Madam?" "Yes please we want to know the price of this perambulator, I shall need one very shortly but I am not buying today." Lilly's face was flushed with excitement. The assistant took up his place and commenced to bring the chosen baby carriage out single so that it could be seen on all sides saying "There you are you can try pushing it if you would like to." Oh yes Lilly would certainly like to, she set her stance at the head of the carriage and felt the handle, as she put two hands on it to push she full well knew this was the one she wanted she said "This is the one, I think it is lovely and I can't wait to put my baby to lie in it, Look Annie it has everything I want, it is elegant and sophisticated." The salesman stepped forward to say "Would Madam like to secure this one with a small deposit? We never know if the design will be repeated, this way you would be sure to have the perambulator of your choice. We would keep it for you until the birth is imminent we don't charge storage, I urge you to take up this offer I have seen many ladies

*that have been disappointed when their
personal choice has sold out." He got out his
counter book and patiently waited.*

*"Annie that is a good idea, I won't have to
ask you to store it and I can pay in full as
soon as I need it."*

*"If that is what you want to do Lilly by all
means get on with it, but make a deal with
this store just in case anything untoward
happens and after all the waiting you don't
need it."*

*"What do you mean Annie I know I will need
it, don't be so pessimistic?" The salesman
again got out his book but this time he
opened it ready to take Lilly's details, he was
a happy man he had made a sale. He said
"How much would you like to leave as
deposit Madam?"*

*"I know the perambulator is expensive so I
will leave £20 is that all right?"*

*"Quite so Madam." He began to write details
while Lilly dived into her purse to find the
£20 she said*

*"Here you are four five pound notes." It
looked an awful lot of money to part with the
size and the look of the large bright white,
five pound notes made it seem even more
valuable.*

Lilly was elated she had chosen a

*perambulator the whole idea of her
pregnancy was coming into life, for once she
felt this was real. Harry had taken the shine
off the early days but now Lilly was truly
taking over, this was her baby and Harry
could go to hell. Annie said
"Well now you have done it Lilly! You will
have to keep the baby now or there will be
nothing to put in your pram." Lilly knew this
was not a vindictive dig it was a cause to give
both Lilly and Annie a general look of
happiness, laughing together because of
Lilly's courage, this decision had took guts
and she hadn't even consulted Harry!
"Well Lilly where do we go next? I bet your
purse is almost empty."
"I still have money left Annie as long as it is
not paper money, I must confess my purchase
has taken all my notes."
"Don't worry I have money to lend you."
"Thank you Annie but I don't think I will
need to borrow."
 Being in the part of the Emporium that dealt
mainly with baby clothes it was not long
before Lilly had spotted a stall to look at, she
said
"Look Annie over there." Lilly stood on tiptoe
and pointed,
"Do you see? It is a baby stall let us go and*

see what there is to buy." Arriving at the stall
Lilly asked

"Would you tell me please how I buy sensibly
for a new born baby?" The stall holder
replied

"Beggin yor pardon Mam, I can see tis ya
that is avin the baby, how far along ar ya?"
Lilly was taken aback by the question saying
"That is really none of your business my dear
lady"

"Oh that's a larf don't call me a Lady Missis,
I aint no Lady I work hard for my livin. I
makes most of the items ere on me stall, up
arf the night I am stitchin and putin together,
I makes me goods prettier than all the rest."
Lilly could see the pieces for sale were
practical as well as pretty so she lowered her
tone and picked up a tiny matinee coat in
white saying

"I didn't mean to offend, I am very easily
upset at the moment, could you tell me the
price please?" She passed the garment over
the stall to be appraised.

"That will be sixpunce; do you want to buy
it?" Lilly took the tiny baby coat into her own
hands and examined the seams and the size
saying

"What do you think Annie? You have more
idea of baby clothes than me." Annie took the

tiny coat into her hands saying
"It is well made Lilly, but I must suggest you
have enough of this size, baby will grow quite
quickly so you need the next size for baby to
grow into." The stall holder overheard the
conversation and said
"That be gud advice, I do av the next size,
and I av blue and pink other than the white."
Buy two and I will giv you a discount buy
three and I will giv you even a better price a
bargain no less. I av the bigger size ere." She
delved under the stall top and brought out
three matinee coats saying
"Na lisen, all three for one and thrupence.
One of each colour, ya will be able ta chose
what baby will wear ya will and I da declare it
is a bargin!" Lilly and Annie were by now
mesmerised with this lady's banter it took
them all their time to decipher what she was
saying Annie put matters right and said
"It is a good price Lilly and girls do wear
blue as well as pink so if you think you want
them buy them." Lilly also would be glad to
get away from this stall so smiling nicely at
stall holder said
" I will give you one and two pence for all
three, take it and put my purchase in a bag
we want to hurry home for tea."
"Ya drive an ard bargin mississ, all right

then, one and tupence it is. The purchase was handed over and Lilly and Annie made their escape. They just had time to get some fresh vegetables on the way home. Both of them were quite exhausted. Lilly would count this outing as an experience, at least she would be a little more world wise next time.

Arriving home they quickly put the kettle over the fire to boil. Sinking down into a well worn chair Lilly said

"Thank you Annie for your advice and your company I have enjoyed the Emporium. Harry would never have let me go to such a place he would say it is far too undignified. You know Annie I am not missing Harry, I feel a bit guilty saying that but he was giving me such a hard time over my baby coming into the world at this late stage of my life. I must admit I had reservations, but now I can't wait for baby to be born. Talking about Harry I wonder how he is getting along without me?"

Chapter Seven

Harry getting on without Lilly? He just wasn't. He was used to being waited on, his meal ready, his shirts washed and ironed to perfection and his bedtime requirements generously being dealt with. He was a soul of aggravation. Using his shirts day by day he had a dozen or more piled up ready to be washed and ironed. Never in his life had he washed a shirt, and ironing well he wouldn't know where to begin. This was Lilly's job, drat the woman. Soon he would have to buy more shirts or pick up from the floor those that had been soiled to a lesser degree but even then they had the smell of stale cigar smoke. He needed to look his best so that he could readily mix with his club members and of course "Angel". The truth be told he was finding visiting Angel so frequently was sapping his strength and costing him a fortune, but his needs had to be met, without Lilly to tend him when needed her he found life without her was not nearly so pleasant as life with her. No he would not think of Lilly it was her own fault she should have got rid of the baby when he offered her the opportunity. Harry's face clouded over whenever he thought of Lilly and how she had made him suffer drat the women. Harry wanted to use Lilly when the time was right for him and keep Angel as a special treat. That was another thing visiting Angel more and more wasn't as much of a thrill as it had been. He had come to expect Angel to give him the excitement he craved for, it was getting too regular and he didn't have Lilly back at home to pander his ego. Harry tried to think of a way out of this syndrome without losing face but a solution hadn't as yet presented itself. Harry wanted all that Harry wants without question. He was the master, Lilly would have to come back to him cap in hand and full of regret and hopefully without the baby. Why couldn't she see sense? It was beyond Harry's comprehension stupid woman. He could think on this no more so he continued to make his appearance as attractive as he was able, finishing with his top hat on and his cane in hand he proceeded to his club. Arriving he was joined by other friends "Good evening Harry are you well?" This was a close friend Harry had known for years John was his name "Yes John and yourself?" "I am good Harry my youngest Son has gone off to College and my elder boy has joined the Navy so it is just Agnes and I at home now.

Actually we are both delighted, like a pair of love birds again. We have enjoyed bringing our family up to now stand on their own feet. They have turned out to be men of purpose and of course they will always be welcome back to our home but I must say this new found freedom is excellent. How is Lilly these days? Harry didn't know how to reply he hesitated then said

"Lilly is good, at the moment she is having a break and staying with her friend Annie." With that he closed the conversation without a mention of the coming baby, Lilly had landed him in such a fix and he couldn't admit Lilly was pregnant, that would leave him in such a tight spot. Harry had never thought of this baby as his own, it was Lilly's fault and he still did not want to know. He turned to John and said

"Will you have a drink with me John? Harry wanted to change the subject. John replied "Thank you Harry but I must decline I want to get back home very shortly. Agnes is cooking something special and I don't want my appetite spoiled. I will see you again sometime then I will buy you a drink for now I must be off. It was nice to see you Harry." With that John put on his coat and left. Harry was searing with envy John had his

family all grown up and still loved and respected his wife Agnes. Harry stood by the bar and downed a couple of whiskey's his thoughts rambled on…I think I will go and see my darling Angel before I go home, ha that's a laugh, four walls and a roof that is my home, a sickening prospect!

The Madam of the establishment Victoria peered at Harry through the grid in the street door
"Well if it isn't my Harry again come right in my love your princess awaits you." Why couldn't Harry see the gleam in her eye? He thought this service was genuine and the love the ladies gave him a true entity. I could almost feel pity for Harry he is such a foolish man and these money grabbing girls treated him as they did because he paid a good sum of money, he always left Angel with a generous tip as well, smile yes it makes me smile, what a diabolical state of affairs. Harry willingly puts his own neck in the noose and tightens the knot all by himself.

After spending a little more time with the girls in general, Harry had his self esteem back and was ready to go upstairs to his favourite Angel. Esteem yes but control no, Harry had been to his club earlier and had tipped back a few whiskey's the drink had satisfied him so he hadn't ate. A spiral was forming as when downstairs with the girls mingling with a room full of heavy bosoms and tight arses he had been coached into a sense of false security, tipping the girls liberally while his hands went up their skirts. Again he was plied with alcoholic drinks at this moment cheap wine. His senses were far from reality, he went upstairs hanging on to the banister for balance. He almost stumbled when going into Angel's room. Angel sat at her dressing table brushing her long hair, sliding the brush slowly and sensuously. She got up on to her bed, she had seen Harry through her mirror she spoke first

"What do you think you are doing Harry? Are you ill or worse for drink?" Slurring his words Harry said

"I am perfectly alright my Angel." His arm went around Angel and she got the full scent of his foul breath, she turned away angry. To come to her bed in this state was an insult

"Harry you are drunk." He began to laugh and said

"No my Angel, just a little tipsy, I will perform all the better you will see. Come here my darling let me hold you, I need your bodily charms, his hand clawed at her scarlet bodice which was still done up tightly she

said

"Stop it at once Harry how dare you come to my bed worse for drink! I will not entertain a man who is full of liqueur." Harry was shocked he said

"But I love you my Angel you are my very special girl come kiss me." Harry slobbered spittle while attempting to kiss Angel, she drew back Harry's heavy laden breath was revolting, his clothes were dishevelled and his skin swarthy. Cigar smoke twirling up to the ceiling from the cigar still in his hand, beads of sweat on his forehead. So Angel treated him as she treated other men that came to her uncouth and unwashed. Angel slipped out of Harry's grasp and went across the room to the drinks cabinet, she poured a large mixed drink into a tall blue glass, then she poured water into her own glass. Over to the bed she carried the wine tray saying

"Very well Harry dear I will lie with you but first let us have a drink together."She pulled up the pillows behind Harry and helped him to a sitting position, she offered her drink and with both hands Harry took the drink murmuring

"Hmm this is more like it, this is a tasty beverage and no mistake." Angel replied

"Yes Harry tip it back we will drink

together." While Harry drank his concoction Angel sipped her water all the while keeping a happy banter of words and laughter. He had almost empted all that was in the glass when suddenly his head dropped forward and he laid a useless mess and a pitiable sight. Angel would concoct a story of the wonderful time she had given Harry next morning because Harry wouldn't remember anything. Into his alcoholic drink Angel had tipped a generous measure of Laudanum. She would sleep well this night on her couch, not with this drunken piece of work then in the morning slide into bed beside him dishevelling her clothes, opening his buttons pulling out his shirt, rough the bed as though there had been a good tussle of the sheets. In the morning Harry would give her a generous tip as always. Angel had the upper hand and played her cards very well…Money for nothing? Exactly! Morning came and Angel tossed her red laced corset on to the floor to indicate Harry had ripped it off and flung it to the floor in a passionate moment. All Harry's buttons were undone and gaping, his flesh appearing bare. Angel roughed up her own hair and slipped into a red negligee over her naked body laying beside Harry one leg sprawling across his chest as though she had slept like that all night. It was Harry's exhausting love making to be blamed and Angel knew the scene was set. Now she must wake Harry, Angel did not want this big buffoon in her bedroom one minute longer. She wriggled about with the intent to wake him, but he still slept so she put her cold hand on to his private parts, he had sweat and dribbled urine but this scene had to be convincing. It did the trick it shocked Harry enough for him to open his eyes. He looked around and saw Angel her leg over his chest. Still she was feigning sleep so he spoke in a whisper

"Come wake up my love it is time to get dressed." As he spoke Angel moved just enough for her red satin negligee to fall to one side and expose her bare breast. Harry's eyes were eager and his hand went under her red garment caressing and feeling the smooth flesh of her skin. Angel pretended to be just waking up she said

"Oh it is you Harry dear is it morning already?"

"Yes my peach we must have fallen asleep together your leg was over me and you were still asleep." Angel saw her chance and took it saying

"You were such an ardent lover last night

Harry I could refuse you nothing." Harry grinned and said

"Hmm ardent eh? Did I get all that I asked of you my love?"

"Yes Harry everything and more, I don't like to mention this but you stayed all night you know there is an extra charge for that don't you Harry? The antics you had me perform are expensive too. As it was you Harry I knew my payment would be met with, so I let you go on until exhaustion overtook the two of us. We have spent the night but there has not been much sleep. Did you get satisfaction my Harry?" Angel stroked his cheek while talking, looking straight into his eyes. When Harry was just about to say he didn't remember a thing he realised this was not good to say, it would insult Angel so he said "Of course I did, your body is so warm and inviting, I think I am falling in love with you." Angel gave him the broadest smile, at the same time sliding from his grasp and out of the bed. Angel thought…Harry…love? He is out of his mind I can't wait for him to go that is after he has paid my fee, a tidy sum. Harry! A tidy sum you stupid man. Her quick assessment of Harry was…Middle aged, almost bald a bend in his walking and muscles already wasting. Hardly loves young

dream. Harry saw himself very different he prided his self esteem. He knew how to handle a woman and paid his fees to Angel thinking he had delighted her, how wrong he was, it was his money that Angel wanted and she knew she could drain Harry dry.

Chapter Eight

Harry's step was light on the way home, he felt youthful and delighted with his own performance. Then a thought crossed his mind… we must have had a right tussle of love, I only wish I could remember it. I could go over every move we made, it would be a delight in my mind's eye… he frowned next time I must have less to drink I fear it was the alcohol that has blurred my memory. Ah well I know by Angel's attitude I did the job well. I like to think the girls are still delighted in my amorous moments. Must say my pocket is a lot lighter, the whole night is expensive how could I have forgotten it all, truth is I don't remember one detail.

Harry entered his own front door, nothing had changed the hall felt cold and dank. There wasn't the appetising smell of cooking going on in the kitchen, and there were no groceries in the pantry. No help for it Harry had to go shopping. Drat Lilly and her baby she had gone too far why he should suffer while she was comfortable in Annie's house? He went out again banging the door almost off its hinges. Where can I go shopping Harry thought, where did Lilly shop? Never speaking about her shopping trips left Harry blank, the shopping was Lilly's responsibility. All Harry knew about food was when it was placed on the table before him on a plate. Shopping indeed…now somewhere they don't recognise me? He headed for the quieter region of the town.

It was hard for a former accountant not to be recognised, Harry found himself being greeted by many people he didn't know they obviously knew him how could he possibly carry shopping? Stopping and looking into a shop window he pretended to look at the display, while still thinking…Now what do I prefer to eat? Lilly used to cook me a good thick piece of steak with sliced tomatoes I think I could cook that. Ah I see a Butcher's shop. Crossing the road was not easy the horse carriages followed one after the other he weaved and dodged until he was on the other side, right in front of the Butcher's shop. Going straight in he spoke to the assistant still with his own bombastic attitude "Good morning my man, do you deliver?"
"Yes we can deliver but the delivery boy's wage has to be added to the expense of your order. What can I help you with Sir?
"A pound of thick rump steak and some gravy please."
"We don't sell gravy you will have to make

your own, it is very easy to do just add thickening to the meat juices when the steak is ready to be served. Anyone can do it Sir."
"Thank you I will remember that, do you sell the thickening?"
"Yes it comes in a packet shall I add it to the package?" Harry began to fidget he was out of his depth and feeling he must get out of this shop and back home. At least the errand boy was delivering his order so he had no bags to carry he made his escape and hurried home. As he walked he thought of Lilly but not in a good way... Blast the woman I will show her I don't need her, he carried on despising Lilly and the unwanted baby.

Until Lilly had announced there was this baby coming they had got along quite well. Lilly had done everything in her power to please Harry he had been waited on hand foot and finger and he had taken all her adoration as his rights, she was his wife after all. Now this blithering baby was going to be born it was a downright imposition and Lilly staying with Annie diabolical. Arriving home Harry poured a glass of whiskey and sat down in his favourite chair, he was getting really hungry and his eye kept glancing to the window to see if the errand boy was coming. It was two whiskeys later and a good hour before Harry's order arrived. He went to the door to collect his parcel. When he looked at the cost written on the bill under the butcher's heading Harry nearly had a fit…two and sixpence. The butcher's boy stood waiting on the step until Harry asked "What are you waiting for? I have given you the money to cover the cost of the meat and I don't tip errand boys." With that the door was shut. In the kitchen Harry sorted out a frying pan, it was heavy enough to be placed on the top of the glowing coals. He had seen Lilly do it many times. Now how did he cook his steak? He really didn't have a clue. The fire in the black range would have to have coal on it and be brought to a good heat. Then a small quantity of lard used for it to fry. Harry placed the steak into the frying pan and then went to the coal house to bring in coal Ugh! Coal now he had his hands all black and his thought once more turned to Lilly…I could strangle Lilly leaving me all these mundane things to do. He had to get on with it though he was starving. The steak in the frying pan, the fire steadily burning Harry began to feel better, this was a blow for freedom he could do without Lilly he preened himself thinking… I have Angel to go to. I could become self efficient in no time at all. I am *not old and I have a reasonable amount of money. I might even meet up with another lady, and she could keep house for me. Yes the aroma of the cooking had tipped Harry's balance, there was nothing to this cooking malarkey and he could have all his provisions brought to the door. He didn't pay Lilly her allowance so that would balance the books somewhat. Good idea he thought Lilly and the brat could keep out of his way. He turned his thoughts to the steak once more, he lifted the knife to turn the steak over, but it wouldn't budge, the steak had stuck solid to the base of the pan and the top was still blood red, he tried more than once but it needed a hammer and a chisel to move it at all. Not a catastrophe but Harry thought it was! He ran his mind through to find just what he had done wrong. He had seen Lilly do steaks many times. He tried a poke and a prod but the steak was burned solid. He decided to try again and cut a bigger lump of lard that had to be placed into the frying pan realising the frying pan needed to be well greased. Alright he could deal with that, so he took the pan from the fire and scraped the contents into the fire. The pan was no longer useable. Now he was not so smug and he had lost his taste for more whiskey. He thought…what I need*

*to do is pop some fresh steak into the oven
and this time the lard will accompany it. He
peered into the oven and found a tin dish it
was already warm. Without hesitation the
second steak went into the dish and into the
oven. Now he had to clear the air which was
choking, the burnt steak had filled the
kitchen with black smoke and all Harry could
smell was pungent and acrid instead of
inviting and promising. He plonked down
into the rocking chair feeling thoroughly fed
up. Closing his eyes he tried to sleep while
giving the steak chance to cook, but his
hunger would not give his mind chance to
settle. He gave the steak a full half hour to
cook, then busied around getting his knife
and fork and setting the place on the table. It
was then he realised he had no bread and the
tomato slices would be missing. Never mind
the steak alone would be enjoyed. Harry
carefully lifted the steak from the oven, it
smelt good, his mouth watered at last it was
on his plate. That is when his temper got the
better of him because the steak was as tough
as old boot leather. It should have fallen
apart at the touch of his knife it always did
when Lilly cooked it!*

"Now my dear reader don't you laugh, Harry

was upset and even hungrier than he was two hours ago. He didn't stay to clear up the mess he had made, the pots and pans were left unwashed. He upped put his coat and hat on and went out heading for his club. Knowing there would be something he could buy to eat. Harry was absolutely useless without Lilly!"

Chapter Nine

Lilly was quite happy without Harry he had insulted her once too often. Living alongside of Annie was just what Lilly wanted in fact she did not look forward to the day that Harry might eat humble pie and ask her to return to him. Lilly tried to keep an open mind Harry was after all the man that she had married. Her baby bump grew ever larger sometimes she could joke about it, and other times, when she found it all too much to endure her enthusiasm dipped very low. She had seen most of her lady companions carry their children never realising the enormity of it all. Annie was a brick steadfast and strong her advice was acted upon more than once.

Lilly sat in the chair beside the fire, Annie was making tea Lilly called
"When the tea is made Annie would you bring in the biscuit tin please?"
"Is there anything else Lilly before I sit down?"
"No Annie but do come as soon as you can I am parched." Annie bustled in from the kitchen tin tray in hands saying
"Here I am Lilly, the fire was low the water took a long while to boil, it seems ages when you wait for it doesn't it? Do you want milk

and sugar dear?"

"Yes please I think my spirits need lifting, what sort of biscuits have we?"

"Nothing very fancy Lilly but you can dip these into your tea." They settled down together, the afternoon was dull and grey outside but here beside a glowing fire they enjoyed each other's company.

"Have you heard anything from Harry Lilly? I know he hasn't sent you mail but there are always rumours about, have any of them come to your ears?"

"Annie I don't want to talk about Harry, I just want to sit quiet and drink my tea while it is hot. Why ask me anyway? You are more likely than me to pick up local gossip."

"Let's drop the subject as you suggested Lilly, we will discuss your baby plans, how long have you got to go now?"

"I am hoping the next eight weeks will deliver baby into my arms, time is dragging now my back and my legs and feet are playing me up. I dare say it is the extra weight I have to carry. I would sooner have baby in the perambulator than kicking my ribs till they are sore. Another reality I hadn't recognised Annie, yes it is alright as an outsider looking at someone else and sympathising. A totally different thing when you yourself are that

someone, Sorry Annie I do try not to moan."
"At your time of life Lilly you are allowed a
little moan now and again. Would you like
more tea dear?"
Lilly poured her tea dregs into a vessel
especially made for this purpose, it left the
cup clean and ready for pouring tea the
second time. Annie used a tea strainer, but
inevitably a few leaves got through to the cup.
Annie said
"Shall I read your fortune in the tealeaves
Lilly?"
"Didn't know you could do that Annie will
there be enough tealeaves in the cup?"
"Never seen an empty cup without a few
tealeaves Lilly."
"I am three parts down this second cup what
do you want me to do?"
"Drink to the bottom Lilly, then turn your
cup upside down on to the saucer." Lilly did
this, Annie went on
"Now turn your cup around three times, and
tap the bottom once."
"Oh Annie what drivel, Lilly smiled."
"Now I will look at the remainder of the
tealeaves sticking on to the side of your cup.
The pattern that the tealeaves make will help
me decide what the future holds." Lilly
laughed and said

"Well as long as this is only a bit of fun I will do it." She gave Annie her now ready cup saying

"There I have drunk to the dregs and turned it three times, what else did you tell me? Yes I know tap the bottom of the cup." This Lilly did and passed her cup over. Annie then turned the cup three more times and chinked the china on the saucer. Now she was serious. Placing her two hands around Lilly's cup she gazed into the interior saying

"Ah, oh yes what is this I see, your future Lilly is full of mystery, the fates have not yet decided which way to lead you. I see a very dark sky and pouring rain… she paused, there is an umbrella and someone is holding it over your head."

"Oh come on Annie if it is raining the umbrella would obviously be needed over my head."

"Let me go on Lilly and don't interrupt."
"You are agitated Annie and in a hurry."
Annie turned the cup around again and again and then went on with her tale
"Oh Lilly I see one thing very clearly."
"Do tell me Annie you have got me mesmerised I have to know."
"Alright Lilly are you sure you are ready for this?"

"Goodness Annie get to the point of course I want to know." Annie again went into her mystic mood saying

"Lilly dear I have every indication that your baby will be a girl, are you pleased?"

"Yes Annie yes, I am excited at the news, now are you having me on? Or can you really see all that in my tealeaves?"

"You can deliberate on my words all you like but when the time comes we will see, all will be revealed. Lilly said

"I must say Annie that has made a dull day much brighter. You could take up this gift and make yourself a name and a fortune, money Annie Money! You are very convincing tell me how you do it?"

"It comes quite naturally Lilly and the truth be told I cannot tell you how I do it because I don't really know myself."

"Oh Annie you must have some idea in your head before you tell some ones fortune."

"That is just it Lilly I don't know a thing before I have consulted the tea leaves."

"It is a wonder you haven't told me about your fortune telling before Annie, why today?"

"You may well ask Lilly but I honestly don't know, this afternoon gave us the right atmosphere and we were comfortable in each *other's company. The mood came on me without warning, I hope I haven't upset you my dear."*

"No not upset but you have got me wondering am I really going to have a daughter Annie did you see it clearly?"

"As far as I am concerned the reading was true, only time will tell Lilly. I will take the china to wash up the cups, we have to decide what we will have for tea Lilly?"

"Nothing yet Annie, perhaps about seven we will have a sandwich, then do our needlework how are you getting along with your table cloth? We have neglected our sewing of late but now the nights are drawing in we will be glad enough to continue. You know what I would like to do when I have finished my sampler?"

"You already have something in mind then?"

"I would like to do a needle point tapestry, if it turns out well I could have it framed to hang on the wall Annie."

"It is a bit ambitious Lilly but why not, you must take your time deciding what coloured silks to have and the design must be just what you want, then you could turn out a piece of real art, have you done anything like that before? Are you good at that Lilly?"

"It is many years since I did any, but I did

complete a small picture and Mother had it framed, after framing they take on quite a classical appeal I had it in my bedroom for ages but now I don't know where it is."

"I wouldn't mind learning how to do one myself Lilly is it difficult?"

"All I am saying Annie is you will need a strong pair of glasses, or a magnifier on your work. Needlepoint is fine and commands your full attention. On the other hand it is interesting to see your picture develop. Yes I will show you how to get started if you like, the next time we go out of town we will look what canvasses there are to choose from, I think I shall look for one with a nursery scene on it then it will go into baby's room, even if I did make a mistake it wouldn't matter shown in the nursery would it?"

"Knowing you there will be no mistake, now I only wish I could say that for myself Lilly."

"We will go early one morning while the light is good, we then could take the skeins of silk to the shop door where the colour will be true. I am getting excited already. Do you know of a shop in another town that stocks the kind of things that we are after Annie?"

"I believe I do a quaint little shop in the main street, I have never been in but I have always thought how interesting it looks. I have often *stood and looked into the window there is a variety of ideas and a pallet of colour. The skeins of embroidery silks all laid out in a rainbow always fascinate me, spoilt for choice I have always walked away not going into the shop at all, but with you by my side I am looking forward to at last purchasing at least one canvass and a few silks to start me off.*

"It sounds just what we are looking for Annie, now I can't wait to go shopping there."

Chapter Ten

Harry was a miserable man, oh yes he had his fancy girls and of course his Angel, but he needed drink to perform in those quarters. His life had taken a dip dive and he was stunned at his lack of self esteem. While Lilly was waiting on him hand and foot he felt Lord of the Manner, pompous thinking a lot of his conquests and quite rightly so he exclaimed! He kidded himself he was the one that had taught Lilly all that she knew, she was bound to be grateful and he took every opportunity that came along to see that she knew that fact. Almost belittling her image daily he would deliver a blow to her pride. Lilly cooked very well, but the slightest chance Harry got he would point out that the dish needed this or that and the gravy must not be too thin or too thick. Lilly found all his criticism hard to take because she had put her whole self into the preparation and presentation of the meal. Many times she found herself in a disheartening position and didn't enjoy her own meal because of it. Only now with Lilly gone did Harry begin to assess the worth of Lilly.

Harry sat totting up his recent expenses and didn't like the look of the outcome, he frowned and thought…This can't be right my money is melting away like snow in June. He started again seeing that every penny was accounted for, the final total was just the same as it was the first time he was annoyed. Soon at this rate of spending his money would rapidly decrease, he would not be able to pay the ladies of the night to keep his ego going, it was a very expensive way to live. Thinking again his mind went to his Angel and he persuaded his conscience that she would never turn him away money or no money!

Dear Reader I question? Are all men as silly as Harry? No I think not. All his life Harry had been cushioned and he dominated women and he expected this to continue, his status as an accountant in the bank had given him prestige and he confidently thought now as he grew older this esteem would continue. I am by your side dear reader and want to know just what Harry will do, let us read on.

For the moment realising a few sharp facts Harry was at low ebb, everything he touched cost money, he had never spent so much money in his entire life. How could he get Lilly back? The amount of money he had given her while they lived together was paltry compared with his expensive living today. He pulled up an armchair closer to the few embers that were still burning in the grate and breathed a heavy sigh. Nothing pleased him and strange as it may seem he wanted nothing other than to sit and sulk and sigh feeling very sorry for himself. The fire wanted making up as it dropped a fall of grey ash and there was no coal for it to continue burning. Harry's thoughts were still venomous towards Lilly it was her job to keep feeding the fire with coal. Harry hated getting his hands dirty and what is more the coal scuttle was empty he would have to go into the back yard and actually fill the scuttle from the coal shed, that would entail lighting a candle because the daylight had almost gone. Harry pulled a rug over his knees and plumped the pillow behind his back trying to get comfortable. He sat for a while, shut his eyes and tried to doze but the room was dropping very cold his nose was like a block of ice. What a sad state of affairs, he couldn't even call Lilly to fetch the coal in and bring him a nice hot cup of tea. He looked disdainfully at the whiskey decanter frowning at the shallow liquid at the bottom of it. Blast Lilly she should be here in his hour of need

*and where was she? To Harry's dismay at
Annie's house with her feet up no doubt!
Harry's lip curled into a grimace he was not
feeling good. Lilly should be here to see to his
needs. Never once did Harry have a thought
about how Lilly was feeling, or how the time
for the baby was drawing closer each day.
Disgruntled he sat utterly swamped in self
pity thinking of his rotten luck.*

*He sat for about two hours getting colder
by the minute, then deciding he was not going
to fetch coal in, he got up took one quick look
in the mirror and went out slamming the door
as he left. Harry headed once more to his
club, it was not the thing he really wanted to
do because the staff at the club had already
commented on the increasing regularity of
his visits, it would not be long before they put
two and two together and got to know about
Harry and his awkward situation, what is
more the secret that Harry was trying so hard
to keep, the coming baby! If they cottoned on
to that he would become withdrawn. Lilly was
no longer living with him he would be the
laughing stock of the club!
By God! Harry thought, yes that is the reality
of the matter I will really be the laughing
stock of all time, they will be whispering
behind my back about the mess I am in,*

sniggering at the image of me pushing a perambulator, oh dear Lord! I mustn't drop to that level, I will give the club a miss tonight and go over to Victoria's place she will welcome me. I won't disturb Angel tonight the downstairs girls will get me warm and fed they have been waiting for the chance, they are not so costly, I will say I have been looking forward to an evening in their company, that will please them and yes I could do with losing myself amongst their bosoms and skirts. His step quickened as this was decided, he wanted to be pampered and given food.

Through the grid in the door Victoria greeted him always pleased to see a good paying client. On opening the door Victoria said

"Come to see Angel tonight Harry?"

"No not tonight I am in a foul mood and need the pretties in the parlour, I am hungry too are there any sweetmeats and grapes to be enjoyed?"

"Of course Harry my girls will look after you."

Harry went in to the dimly lit smoke filled room. "Here Harry come and sit by me are you staying with us tonight?"

"Yes my petal you can all have a share of me

*tonight, I shall be here a few hours. I
purposely have come to see if you have
invented new tricks or games to play, I am
willing to partake in your inventions." Now
two girls were petting Harry and a third
approaching ready to transport Harry into
bliss, but Harry was hungry for food before
he would let the girls lead him to paradise.
He said in the most whimsical manner
"Have you girls eaten tonight? I am feeling a
bit peckish."
"Yes we had the most succulent chicken
breast moist and white shall I bring you some
Harry?"
"Feed me my darlings I find that man cannot
live on bread alone, fortify my inner being so
that my love making will be strong and
pleasing." Chicken breast was delicately put
into Harry's eager mouth, while the third girl
plied him with luscious delicacies and red
wine. Ah! Thought Harry this is the life. His
hand was stroking a plump gartered thigh as
he ate, bliss. Smoking and eating and petting
until the light of dawn. Satisfaction to every
degree and he was going to remember this
time he would make sure he did, his manly
charms would be delivered with purpose, he
would take these girls one at a time never
stopping for breath. For all these girls could*

give Harry the power to express his manhood. Their breath stank, the odour of unwashed flesh and stale linen did not put Harry off, and indeed it was all part of this façade a brothel no matter what one called the girls was just indeed a brothel, with filth and undetected disease to be encountered. This did not bother Harry he was living in an unreal dimension for when Lilly left if he had but known his life was over. There had been too much water travelling under the bridge for Harry to contemplate any sort of reconciliation as regards Lilly.

Chapter Eleven

It was a fine morning so Lilly and Annie decided to go and choose silks and canvass, intending to use a back stitch to bring the picture to life. Lilly while pulling on her hat said

"I just want reassurance Annie, we are not staying in this town are we?"

"The thought hadn't crossed my mind Lilly but the shop I described to you is not in this town. Is that the one you have chosen to visit? Where is it you want to go then? I don't mind where we go."

"I am sorry to be a nuisance Annie but Harry insists I keep this child a secret. A town other than this one would be best."

"Hell's Teeth! Lilly how can you possibly keep your baby a secret? Surely it can't be done, babies don't come out of thin air, and this is Harry's baby he should be taking responsibility for it. Why are you even trying to comply with his request, he wants a wakeup call does your Harry."

"I thought if I wasn't a burden to him carrying and bringing baby into the world he might eventually see sense and start over again."

"Do you still want him Lilly after how he has

belittled you? You must be looking for trouble. Anyway this conversation has gone on too long have you got money and your house keys Lilly? It is time we were off. The front door was pulled shut and as they walked along Annie caught the look in Lilly's eyes so she decided to humour her saying

"Lilly I suppose you have your reasons and far be it from me to come between husband and wife. I know how I felt when I lost my husband and I understand, ideally you would like to have Harry's support in the future, how can you forgive him though for all the hurt he has put before you? It is beyond me. Today we will go to the other town partly because of your wish and secondly because my quant little sewing shop is not in this town so it will suit us both. Before we close this subject I am telling you now what I foresee as your future with Harry, he will take you on a merry dance and you will be a slave to his every desire, in fact it is highly unlikely to come to pass, you're a fool Lilly."

The two of them walked on in complete silence only picking up conversation when they got into the buggy that was taking them to town.

"Make yourself comfortable Lilly, we haven't far to go, it is a little place I know of very well

called Sedgwick, I will show you what a charming place it is. We will walk along by the side of the stream it leads to a water wheel and a picturesque bridge.

The horse pulling the buggy trotted along and they began to relax, in no time at all they were in Sedgwick. At once Lilly knew what Annie had tried to describe to her, the cottages were made from large stone blocks riddled with age, quaint windows and wooden doors wrought iron knockers graced the front of the door this town was like a scene from a picture book. The horse and buggy transport was at the back of the town so as not to interfere with the quiet and casual appeal that was part of the image. Strolling along Lilly thanked Annie for bringing her on this trip, she was indeed enjoying it. The feeling of being carefree had been in little evidence these past few months. Coming to the old stone bridge they leaned over the arch and watched the water clear and crisp flow gently underneath it, the act was soothing and reassuring, this was a pleasure of the past, the water wheel just to the right was turning and there was no hurry or worry at all. The air that they breathed although a little sharp was pure with the scent of grass cutting in it Annie said

"We had better go to choose our silks Lilly, it will soon be teatime. With no hurry they retraced their footsteps arriving at the shops. "Not far to walk Lilly there is the shop over there" She pointed to a shop across the road on the right. Candles and lanterns were already lit but in Lilly's estimation these added to the allure of the scene. Annie spoke "If you look further up the road you will see a cake shop they do pots of tea we will go in there directly after we have chosen our silks."

"That would be lovely Annie I am already feeling a sit down would be more than welcome."

"Why didn't you say? Look there is a bench over there you can catch your breath before we go into the silk shop."

"The light will be failing very soon Annie I think we had better get our silks right now then go and have tea, there is hardly a glimmer of sunshine left."

"I suppose you are right that is the trouble with autumn sunshine it is fast to fall dark it is deceiving. Come on then silks it is." Excitement filled Lilly, Harry had kept her so close to home to see to his needs there had never been the opportunity to wander very far. Into the silk shop they went, as the door opened it gave a melodious' ting ting… and

there before them stood a world of opportunity, crafts of all kinds, canvasses of all sizes. The assistant was serving another customer so it gave Lilly chance to browse. "Oh look Annie that is the size canvass that I could imagine would look right on my bedroom wall." Annie looked and said "Are you sure you want a big one like that? What if you get fed up and can't finish it?" "I want one that I know I have done in prime position so that I don't have to squint to see it. I shall be very proud and have something of my very own to pass down to this little one." Lilly caressed her baby bump lovingly. It was their turn and the lady came forward to say

"What would you be wanting then my dearies?" Her casual manner put both Lilly and Annie at ease. They exchanged information about what their needs would entail and trays of the most beautiful silk skeins were placed on the counter before them. The pleasure this brought was unmistakable, Lilly touched the skeins with reverence wanting them all, for the choice had to be seen to be believed. The peacock blues ranging right down to sky blues, the burgundy reds through to the scarlet red and finishing in pink. The vivid purples and the

solid greens in all shades, their choice would not be easy. The lady said

"What sort of picture would you like to work on?" Transfers of all designs were brought out, now Lilly and Annie wanted totally different designs. Annie chose a sailing ship with full sails open and Lilly choosing a scene not unlike the bridge scene they had stood and looked upon earlier in the afternoon.

"I will always have the memory of this day when I look upon my work and I wanted a soft and delicate scene to showcase my colour choice. The picture can still be displayed in the nursery or even bring it out to the hall at a later date. A decision had been made. Now to the silk colours, Lilly of course chose a pallet of deep pinks, stone browns, white for the few clouds and sunset reds for the skies, just leaving the water flowing in pale blue. Annie had a stronger pallet choosing sea blues, white sails, black rigging and rugged brown for the body of the ship, these were brought together with a glow of candle light from the ships portholes so that red and amber had to be used. Annie and Lilly were transported into the world of the pictures each with its own allure. Carrying with great care their bundle of silks and canvasses they *headed for the tea shop.*

Arriving at the quaint little building that was the teashop Annie and Lilly peered into the window to see a lovely array of cakes Lilly said

"Are we going to have just a cake and a pot of tea or shall we have the proper set tea?"

"I am too excited at this moment to sit through a long tea I would like tea and a cake." Lilly was inclined to agree so in they went. Finding a table complete with a lit candle and at the windows edge it was good they could see other lights going on in shop windows, the candles flickered and danced and made a new scene to look out upon. Annie said

"Now Lilly what sort of cake would you like?"

"I had my eye on the jam and cream sandwich cake that is cut into portions Annie."

"Well that is a coincident I too liked the look of that, it is well endowed with cream and the jam looks as if it is raspberry so it will be tasty." The dainty maid came to take their order using her delicate charm to enhance the moment she said

"What would you be wanting then my dears?" Her casual manner was appreciated

by both Lilly and Annie, Lilly said
"We will have a pot of tea for two with milk
and sugar and I will come to the counter and
hand pick a plate of your delicious looking
cakes." The waitress replied
"That will be fine and our cakes don't just
look delicious they are a delight to eat."
Annie got up from the table saying
"You need not go Lilly I will go and choose,
you need to rest your legs for a while."
"Alright Annie but please be sure to choose a
good assortment, I have just decided I am
hungry it is the pungent aroma that is so
tempting, it won't hurt just for once to
indulge our senses will it?" Annie grinned
"Just this once then Lilly, you must have the
craving that comes along with your condition.
The baby will be born with a sweet tooth I'll
be bound. Sugar and spice and all things nice
ha ha I told you it will be a girl didn't I?"
The ladies exchanged knowing smiles and
Annie went for the cakes. A very homely
looking cake plate was filled and a variety of
sumptuous cakes delighted Lilly's eye. Pink
icing, cream buns, fruit slice, the jam and
cream portion that they both had chosen was
now on the table to be enjoyed. Annie said
"We were lucky to get the jam and cream
cake that we both wanted they were the last

ones to be had. They both laughed and it brought a light hearted atmosphere while they sat eating and having their cups of tea.

Arriving home legs aching and eyes sore but their hearts were satisfied and happy. Taking off hats and coats Lilly said "Well Annie it was a lovely afternoon of interest but I must confess it has worn me clean out."

"You put your feet up on the couch Lilly I will go and put the kettle on bet you wouldn't say no to yet another cup of tea? Will you want egg on toast later will that suffice our needs for today?"

" I should say so, the cakes have filled me to the brim nice though wasn't it?"

"Yes I thoroughly enjoyed the outing and we have our needlework to begin when we have the time, I am looking forward to that and I know you are too. The teashop do a nice set tea as well as cakes we could go and have our tea there on another occasion we need not do any shopping you will be too heavy with the baby to want to walk far, just go for tea as a break from routine eh?"

"Yes Annie that would be nice, it is early to bed for me tonight Annie I could sleep on a clothes line."

"Me too but first we will have the poached

egg I promised you, I will go and see to it right now."

"Just one egg for me and one slice of toast you are good to me Annie how will I ever repay you?"

"I don't want paying Lilly I am very content with our friendship Harry doesn't know what he is missing, he will find no good will come of his behaviour I don't mind if you never go back to him, you must choose for yourself though, when the time comes you will know what to do."

Chapter Twelve

Harry had spent the whole night being fondled and petted at Victoria's place finally finishing up in Lila's bed, she served him well but Harry was tired he was no longer the handsome stud he used to be, he couldn't understand this weakness although to others it was very apparent. He had aged ten years since Lilly left him, he never had realised just what Lilly did for him and even if in honesty he was not about to admit it to himself. At dawn he found himself stumbling home and was actually looking forward to getting into his own bed. At least he remembered the previous night, was it because the girls didn't entice him not in the same way Angel did? Yes he decided, a bit of fun he had with the girls, but nowhere near to the entire lure of Angel.

Harry went straight to bed when he got home he laid thinking not about the girls or Angel but about his own well being. Of late his ordered life had fallen into chaos. His pocket had been hit too. Not feeling well at all and ill at ease Harry fell into an exhausted sleep, his dreams haunted him, and he woke up with a startled expression glad to find the reality comforting. Nightmares were becoming frequent, Harry apart from body wear had dipped into the dangerous realms of mind, he was no longer in control and not the carefree man he once was. Lilly had played a large part in that design, Harry was only just realising this and as yet would not admit it. Getting up at three in the afternoon had become the normal, but was there anything left that was normal? His unwashed laundry lay on the floor and had gathered into the corner of the room. He kept turning it over to find a shirt that was less soiled than the others, but they had all been used several times and had the stale stench of body odour and alcohol. He had used his entire stock of fresh shirts underwear and socks not caring a jot about tomorrow. Now he must face the music and either wash or buy new replacements. He flung away the problem thinking... I will burn this lot on the fire and go to my Tailor, yes I will do that right now, he glanced at the clock remembering that the shops would be shutting, his late afternoon bedtime did not coordinate with the public at large. He plumped his pillow and tried again to sleep but sleep was a long way off, there was too much on his mind. Getting up and dressing in the best he could find Harry went downstairs and directly to the whiskey *decanter, pouring his drink which was to all intent and purpose his breakfast he sat down and gazed at the dead ash in the fire grate. Although the whiskey did its job and warmed his blood the air was cold and without comfort, blast Lilly she has made my life unbearable, his thoughts ran on, I hope she knows what she is putting me through Blast Blast Blast the woman! Self first self second and self last. Harry thought only of number one and that was Harry. Having almost drained the whiskey decanter there was a decision to make what to do this night, the whiskey had strengthened his moral and he felt like another night on the tiles. Having dressed in the best he could find he picked up his hat and his cane and went into the night. He didn't want to go to his club or yet to Victoria's place, he wanted new ground and he would find it out on the streets. He made his way to the seedy side of the town saying to himself… I will be choosey and find a wench worthy of my time he strolled and was accosted by several candidates for the job. He weighed there assets up as he went along feeling highly important. These women of the night were cheap and to Harry this was some sort of economy, what he wanted would not cost a fraction of the price he would have to pay much more at Victoria's place. Several girls accosted him, no he would see someone shortly that stood out above the others he was a hard task master, tonight feeling as though the world owed him and he was ready to take.*

"Ere ya ar Sir, freshly washed and ready to give you a good time. A nice clean girl I am."
Harry walked on

"Ow abart me kind Sir I'se a virgin I am and not long out of the cradle, just wot ya need eh?" Too young Harry thought no experience I want to be having known I have been laid, not a mere girl on the make. Harry walked on his own importance swelling as he did so. Now he liked the look of this one, her clothes were not as ragged as the others and she had a pretty face he approached her.

"Where do you play your trade wench? Is it out on the street or do you have a room we could go to?"

"I ave a small room and a single bed cum with me I will show ya." Harry found himself drawn towards this girl, a bit of grit he could get his teeth into, he followed her. The room in question was downstairs in an old terraced house, she said

"Cum in me laddo don't mind the litter I do clean up sometimes but of late I ave been very busy." Harry cast the state of the room to one

side, what did he care how she lived he only wanted satisfaction from her not a grand tour.

"Leave ya clothes behind me screen with mine I will serve ya well you'll see."

Harry went behind the screen and left off his top clothes including his trousers. The girl did the same saying

"Na wot do you want? I can give ya the full treatment for a small amount, or ya can ave a quicky for alf of that amount, ow say ya? I can give ya a small price option tonite cos I ave a cold blister on me lips, nowt to urt you know just a blip". Harry felt a warning in his mind but cold blisters were common so he cast away any slight doubt he had. Soon he was pawing all over this maids body, his lips finding exhilaration as he planted them on to her fanny he was allowed to do just as he wanted with this urchin of the night and he was making sure he had his money's worth and no mistake. The passion in him spent he rolled off her and lay on the bed. Immediately she got up and went behind the screen to dress, she was quick as she knew other men would be out in the streets and there would be other clients to charm. Harry paid the money, he had enjoyed the casual flippancy of this encounter, he felt his self esteem go high and *his confidences return. If he couldn't afford Victoria's place no matter, this street girl had done the job justice and cost very little. He had time too for going back home and to bed, next day he would see his Tailor as he would be awake in time to go to the shops. Yes all round a well spent evening he gave himself a pat on the back.*

Next day Harry felt well and ready to go and see Mr Lucas his tailor, he was met with a welcome Mr Lucas greeted him like an old friend saying

"Hello Mr. Baines haven't seen you about of late do sit down are you well Sir anything we can do for you today?"

"Yes Mr Lucas I am well, I want to see your shirt collection you will know what a fashionable man's vogue is, so show me a selection. I want the best, but you know that don't you?"

"Of course Sir it is a privilege to attend you."
This is more like it Harry thought now how many shirts shall I need? Mr Lucas could smell whiskey on Harry's breath and hoped Harry was in control. Mr Lucas although willing to take Harry's money would not be messed about, his reputation as a tailor and an outfitter depended on his polite manner. He decided to handle Harry with care and get

him out of the shop post haste. Mr Lucas placed five shirts on to the counter top, all was boxed. He opened the lids with reverence and showed them off to perfection asking Harry

"I am assuming the collar size hasn't changed Mr Baines?"

"Everything is the same measurement as when I came before I do not put weight on and can cut a dash with the rest I am happy to say." Mr Lucas had his own view on that subject but said nothing, he thought Mr Baines was a shadow of his former self and could do well to sit down for a good meal. He continued to show off the shirts. Harry bought one of each and several changes of underwear and socks. When it was all totted up Harry had to write a cheque as he hadn't enough cash to foot the bill. Again Lilly's shortcomings were brought to the fore, this was all her fault, this coming baby had already cost Harry a lot of money albeit indirectly. Harry needed to put an end to this state of affairs but hadn't a clue how to do it. He still didn't want a screaming brat about his home all he could hope for was that it would be born dead and save him the job of murdering the thing and this put a new idea into Harry's mind! An idea that could only

flourish in a mind that is out of control. He was Master, he would have things his way and his way was not by any stretch of the imagination the right way.

Chapter Thirteen

Lilly and Annie had no possible inclination of Harry's intentions, Lilly already loved the baby curled up inside her knowing that at her time of life this was such a blessing, at last after all this time she was going to have a baby. Her own and Harry's they had achieved it together how she wished Harry would acknowledge this fact, each week that passed she waited for his call but there was no such happening. Of course not wanting matters to affect the baby she had to dismiss it from her mind. Surely when the baby was born and Harry could see his own flesh and blood alongside Lilly he would repent and all would be well again, daily she longed for this to come to pass, patience and the key words… all would be well soon. Later on in the week Annie and Lilly sat looking where to start on their back stitch picture, they had made sure to get an embroidery needle each as the silk from the skein was bodied and to thread the needle difficult, they adjusted the canvass so as to make the stitch as easy as possible. Now they began and silence fell in the room while they each concentrated on their chosen piece. About half hour went by and Lilly wanted to talk to Annie she said

"There is something on my mind Annie could we talk as we sew?"

"Of course Lilly, now we have got a start the stitching is straight forward. What can I help you with?"

"Have you ever delivered a baby? Or watched a baby being born Annie?"

"Well yes, first of course there are my own children and I was there when my sister gave birth to my niece. Then there was my next door neighbour who begged for my help after her friend up the street let her down, between us the baby was delivered safely that is about all I know Lilly why do you ask?"

"Please Annie, I don't know a thing about bringing my child into this world, you have had hands on experience. Please I ask you when my time comes will you see me through?"

"I thought that is what you were leading to, now look Lilly all I can say is I will do my best but you must be on a Doctors panel. I would need someone to send for if things go awry. If the birth gets out of hand during labour you could lose the baby, my knowledge is very limited. I suppose sending for Harry will be out of the question?"

"No please don't send for Harry, seeing me

in such a compromising position during the birth is absolutely out of the question. I would never look Harry in the eye ever again. I know that seeing a baby born is not a pretty sight, and that there is pain and blood involved. Oh dear now I am getting upset myself." The two friends looked into each other's eyes and a silent pact was made. Lilly trusted Annie and she would secure a place on the Doctors list and live in hope she did not have to send for a Doctor. If he was involved it would cost a pretty penny. Lilly was left with her own private thoughts fear was creeping into her mind as time travelled on. Harry had kept her more or less under lock and key how very little she knew about the world and all its misfortunes. Her heart hung heavy. Harry had left her without support of any kind, it was the money her Father had left her that she now had to use. Harry had made it quite clear he didn't want her around and that the baby was nothing more than an inconvenience. Having no solid ground to build a future that included a baby bothered her mind night and day. Thank the dear Lord for Annie she kept things stable as well as she could. Annie's opinion of Harry was unspeakable. If Lilly tried to go back to him she would have no peace Harry was a bounder and no mistake. Again the room had fell into silence and their needlework commenced without further interruption. Soon …Lilly thought, it would be teatime and the lamps and candles would be lit, this always gave Lilly a sense of security, the fire would flicker it's flame to pattern the walls and glint on the polished brass in the hearth. The mantelpiece clock would chime five and the kettle would be drawn over the fire. Tonight this could not come quick enough for Lilly she was disturbed and needed to be calm. Many of Harry's shortcomings lay heavy like a weight on Lilly's chest. The more she tried to lay her worries to one side the deeper they seemed to get. Harry was Harry and there was the end to it. The clock began its chimes for tea at five.

The following week Lilly funnily enough felt a little better, in the garden sweeping autumn leaves alongside Annie the pressure lifted. Autumn sunshine trickled through the trees and the leaves to be swept were red and bright, soon they would all be down on the earth making a carpet. Annie said
"I like to get up the leaves a few at a time if I wait for them all to fall the job is too much, none of us are getting any younger you know."

"I am pleased I can help you Annie the sunshine has lifted my spirits and the leaves are so crisp they soon sweep up."

"Do you want to go anywhere this afternoon Lilly? Or would you rather get on with your picture?"

"I will tell you after lunch Annie, let's get this job done first, in fact go in and put the kettle on we will take a break eh? We have plenty of time."

"Alright Lilly but don't you get stretching or reaching while I am out of the way you have the little one to consider." Lilly heard a knock on the front door and called to Annie who she knew was in the kitchen to see who it was. Annie had a surprise on opening the door she said

"Well hello Liz what brings you to see me?"

"It is Lilly I really wanted Annie I have been told she is staying with you."

"Come right in me dear you have come to the right place but who told you of Lilly's whereabouts?"

"I went to Lilly's home first before I came here and Harry told me. They both went in to where Lilly was already sitting. Liz said hello to Lilly and continued your Harry looks dreadful Lilly have you seen him lately?"

"No and neither has Annie, do sit down Liz

Annie will put the kettle on we were about to have a cup of tea, you can join us I assume?"

"Thank you yes; a cup of tea would be very welcome." Lilly fidgeted in her chair covering her baby bump with a spare cushion as she didn't want Liz to see that she was with child. There was tension in the air as Liz and Lilly tried to make small talk. Annie came in with a tray of tea and biscuits. Placing it on the small table Annie spoke to Lilly.

"Why are you bundling the cushions around you Lilly you are not cold are you?"

"No Annie and you know very well why I am using the cushions"

"Lilly you can no longer hide what is going on; tell Liz about your predicament she has not come here to judge you, past times you were good friends and she has come out of her way to see you." Lilly knew she was cornered so spoke to Liz saying

"I am sorry Liz I didn't mean to be rude." Annie butted in

"We haven't seen each other for a decent while have we?" Liz said

"Lilly I promise I won't stay long." Lilly dropped the cushions saying

"Well you might as well know Liz, yes as you now see I am with child."

"How splendid for you Lilly I know you

thought children were out of the question this must have been quite a shock to you and Harry. Fancy Harry a proud Father I can hardly believe it. Wait until I tell Richard he will want to come and shake Harry by the hand the sly old fox, he has really pulled this one out of the bag!" Liz smiled and was full of enthusiasm. Lilly had to tell her of the rift the baby coming had caused. Liz continued "Why did you try to disguise the fact that you were carrying Lilly? Lilly patted her baby bump and said

"I have had to keep this little one a secret Liz"

"Whatever for? I should have thought you would be elated and ready to tell everyone, it is about your last chance isn't it Lilly?"

"I am proud Liz, well at least I was that is until I told Harry. He immediately told me to get rid of it he wanted no part in this child. I have tried to tell him this baby is ours not mine and he still won't hear of becoming a Father. That is why I am living with Annie she has been good enough to take an interest and see me through these past few months. I don't know what I would have done without her Annie said

"Panicked no doubt and maybe let Harry have his way." Lilly said

"I love this baby Liz it is soon to be born and I can't wait to hold the child in my arms."

"Doesn't Harry look after you at all Lilly?"

"Quite the opposite Liz, he has never been around to see me or ask how I am, I wouldn't comply with his wishes. I just don't understand his way of thinking."

"Oh neither do I you poor soul. That puts what I have come to say in a very different light, I wanted to ask why you have not replied to the wedding invite we sent you and Harry, but of course it was sent to your own home so you probably haven't received it. Our second Son Herbert is getting married and he would have liked you to attend the ceremony. You wouldn't know Herbert now Lilly he has made a fine young man tall and handsome, we are very proud of him."

"I am sure you are Liz but we won't be attending the wedding, you will have to forgive Harry and I. Wish Herbert well for us and leave it at that, my situation will take some resolving that is if it ever gets sorted out. Harry won't even pay for the babies' layette and he gives me absolutely nothing. He is ashamed of me Liz I have to ask Annie to take me to another village to do any shopping in case anyone of Harry's friends find out I am carrying." Tears began to

collect in Lilly's eyes, this was the first time she had admitted to anyone other than Annie about how Harry was mistreating her.

"You poor dear are you sure Harry doesn't want this baby? Men sometimes object thinking that when baby arrives you will be looking after the infant and leave no time for being together. Maybe it is just such a blip and all will be well when he sees the child. I must say he looks awful he is obviously missing you Lilly. Annie had to say something in her friend's defence she was well aware of Harry she said

"Missing Lilly oh! No, what you need to say is he is missing Lilly's service and pandering he is a man sorry for himself and doesn't give a damn about Lilly or her welfare. He certainly does not want this baby and would have been rid of it many times over by now if he was allowed to have his way. In my view he is a bounder and Lilly is better off without him. He won't bend an inch although Lilly has asked many times to reconsider and be a family again. I have told Lilly not to fret it is Harry that is out of order. I would do battle with Harry myself if I thought it would make a difference, he can be sharp tongued I have been on the receiving end and I certainly don't want to make matters worse, so I keep

my distance. Lilly is only doing what nature intended her to do she doesn't deserve how Harry belittles her." Lilly had a word to say "I would still forgive him if he would just ask but I wait and wait and still he doesn't come." Annie went to the kitchen to make fresh tea. Each one of them had said their piece and it hadn't made the slightest difference. Lilly's self pride was being shattered bit by bit, what would tomorrow hold? Lilly had no idea she was stuck in this mess and had no way of knowing how to get out. The more she struggled the deeper she sank. How a beautiful event could be turned into such a misery was unexplainable. Lilly was trying not to think too much about the actual birth and how it would distress her. Paling at the thought of pain, needing Harry more than ever before in their lives and he had snubbed her, didn't even want to talk to her.

The suffering that was Lilly's did not bother Harry as long as he was alright nothing else mattered, but was he alright?

Dear Reader.   No doubt at some point we will find out. Harry's attitude left much to be desired. Even Angel his favourite bed time girl was bored to tears with his mauling and pawing. "Get it over with and go you silly man, but before you do, leave my tip on the dresser."… together we will read on."

This is what Angel would have said out loud but she smiled and pretended to enjoy Harry and his fumbling attitude. Romance there was none, Angel didn't care, money was her foremost thought and she would take all that he was prepared to give and it would seem suggest he gave her more. Harry was not that simple he wanted his money's worth, he had the mind of a banker and he knew full well how to balance the books. Hearing of Lilly's plight Liz felt in the way, so lifted her handbag and said it was time for her to go, really it was out of politeness that she was leaving and because of the sadness in Lilly's eyes.

Chapter Fourteen

Harry was anything but alright He was soon bored and tired of playing games, the girls he was seeing were becoming matter of fact and losing their allure. Nevertheless Harry had to have women that side of his nature reminded him constantly that this was a fact of life, he was male and he was not ready to give up being male. He sort after a new attraction and the opportunity came quicker than he thought while at his club a new acquaintance was chatting to him he said

"I had a good day at the races, I won £100 pounds. Are you interested in the horses Harry?"

"I can't say I have been over enthusiastic Stuart. The race tracks are too far away and I have no-one to go with."

"Don't worry about that dear fellow you can accompany me I have a horse and buggy and I would take you with me."

"Oh I don't know about that Stuart, I am truly not accustomed to the betting game."

"Well I tell you last week I won and next week I intend to study form and win again. It is exciting Harry, a couple of whiskey's and a good lunch and it is the perfect day out. Pin

stripe suit, and a polished cane added to the Top hat and carnation in your button hole will fetch all the fillies flocking around, especially when you have had a win. I have known the time when a very attractive girl will take you home with her and we all know what that means eh? Come on Harry don't be a spoil sport, if you don't enjoy yourself you need not bother again but truly I think that will not be the case, look at the good times we could have Harry."

"I barely know you Stuart how do you know what I call a good time."

"Nudge nudge, wink wink, when talking to a man of the world I think we both have the measure of a good time, don't be frumpy let's get out and play the game together it will be twice the fun don't you think? Or have you a demanding wife at home Harry?"

"No I am footloose and fancy free, I am beginning to cotton on to your suggestion, when would we be likely to go?"

"I like Saturday at the races, there is always more going on and people a plenty, how would that suit you Harry?" So it was arranged Harry was off to the races and as Stuart had said it was exciting him in fact he was eagerly looking forward to this outing. Saturday came around and the day was fine

Harry was considering what amount of money he should take, it needn't be a massive amount he would have his cheque book if he needed more. The thought crossed his mind that the men he would put his bet with would not take cheques so he placed another £50 pounds into his inside pocket. Now to study form as Stuart had showed him. He lost his sense of time while bemusing at the horses names and in the first race he thought "Beginners luck" was worth a risk it was ten to one and would fetch a tidy sum into his pocket if it should romp home. Harry was made up, he now had something new in his life, he left home ready to be picked up by Stuart. The pair of them like children on a school holiday as the horse trotted along the cobblestones. At the race track Harry felt very important he had dressed the part and was in total control of the proceedings. Each of them went up to the bookie of his choice and placed a bet.

"What horse do you fancy Harry?"
"I think it is that filly over there." Harry pointed to a splendid looking horse with the jockey wearing red and white.
"What is it called?"
"Beginners luck" I thought it was appropriate. I must admit I know nothing

about horses, Have you made your choice
Stuart? "
Stuart pointed saying
"There a clear winner, she is called "Evening
Sky" What odds did you get Harry?"
"Ten to one I shall have made this trip worth
the while if she wins." Stuart pulled at
Harry's sleeve saying
"Come on let's go over to the rails they are
under starters orders." Harry allowed Stuart
to push him into the edge of the race track
even though there were already a crowd vying
for best position, pushing and trying to move
in to see the race clearly, Harry felt stifled.
"Their off" the crowd shouted the air was
electric and Harry had a job to hold his
balance against the milling crowd. He could
see his horse, the red and white of the jockey
stood out, and then suddenly Harry joined the
crowd and shouted with all his might,
"Come out of the middle girl! Come on, come
on." He felt his face colour with effort
waving his betting slip to encourage the horse
to be first at the post. Only it wasn't, it had
dropped back exhausted at the last push and
Harry's desire to win was squashed. His face
fell. He turned around to see Stuart almost
jumping for joy. "Evening Sky" had won and
he was jubilant Harry waited for his friend to

quieten down and then congratulated him asking

"What did you put on the horse as a bet Stuart?"

"Just five pounds Harry, I wish I had risked more now, it was five to one as the race took off so I still have a tidy sum to pick up. Sorry your horse didn't make you a shilling or two but that is the way it goes. I have been studying form for a long time now, not that I always get it right but just lately I have picked up a small fortune. I only hope my luck doesn't run out. It isn't a thing I can teach you Harry I know of several chaps that have been just downright unlucky. I have intuition when I bet and I am almost always right. What do you fancy in the next race? You have to speculate to accumulate Harry, let us look together and I will give you the benefit of my expertise." They studied the racing guide and Stuart said

"That is an unusual name, look he pointed to a horse called "Black Sam" shall we try our luck with that one?" Harry thought he would be on to a good thing if he followed Stuart and his intuition so he agreed and felt in his inside pocket for some money. He was so shocked there was no money in there. He sorted through his other pockets and it was *still missing Stuart said*

"What is the matter old chap can't you find your money?"

"No Stuart I had it in my wallet and in my inside pocket but it isn't there now."

"You have fallen victim of the race track runners, so called because they can pick a pocket to a very high degree and they run like mad when they have found what they want, how much was it Harry?"

"Fifty pounds, I brought it just in case so to speak now I have lost it and not even on a bet. Sorry Stuart but I do not call outings like this exciting if you win regular money good luck to you but it isn't my game."

"Don't be like that Harry, let us go and have a drink and perhaps pick up a girl or two, they have a nice bar here." They went to get a drink as they sat drinking Harry said

"I am sorry Stuart but even if I spotted a girl I wouldn't be able to pay for my pleasure, I have enough in my pocket to buy you a return drink and then I would like to go home, it is clearly not my day."

"I am truly sorry Harry, I hadn't planned it to turn out this way, if you want to go home we will go after we have had another drink, take your time there is no hurry. I have my winnings to collect so you can borrow money

if you would like to."

"I know I am not at all popular for saying this Stuart but I won't borrow it is not in my character to borrow it is one of the few good things about my personal effects, please don't take it as a snub it is good of you to offer."

"Not at all old Man, we all have our principles and I must say borrowing can turn ugly when it becomes time to pay the sum back. Home we go then Harry better luck next time eh?"

"I don't think there will be a next time for me Stuart I am not used to these crowds of people sorry if I disappoint you."

Getting home Harry went over the day's events in his mind, kicking himself for being so stupid to lose the money from his pocket. He had never encountered thieves such as these, didn't know they existed. He had been enclosed in the environment of a bank, being an accountant all his working life he knew about money and the importance of it but just of late it had slipped through his fingers. Harry sat in his favourite armchair ignoring that the fire wasn't lit and there was no food in the cupboard. He poured whiskey and took the first two straight down. He had tired his whole body while trying to have a good time he slumped in a much undignified fashion not caring that he had on best society clothes. Again he thought about Lilly and how the baby had caused this rift His mind began to work overtime thinking...If it wasn't for the brat Lilly would still be here looking after me. I will kill the damned thing after it is born. There is no benefit for me, I will not have it! He thumped the table with venom, the evil Harry had come to the fore again. Selfish and cruel and what he wanted was law. He fell asleep in the fashion of a drunk and when he woke he had spilled whiskey down on to his best pinstripe trousers. He was not best pleased, his head felt bloated and his mouth stale. No Harry was certainly not alright.

Chapter Fifteen

Lilly and Annie had returned from yet another shopping expedition. Sitting down together they began to unpack what they had purchased in the next town, this time they had gone the other way so as to keep things interesting. Out of Lilly's bag she pulled a parcel, in it was a cuddly Teddy Bear. Annie said

"You shouldn't have bought that really Lilly it is far too early to be buying toys."

"But Annie I love it and I know baby will love it too feel his soft fur and his loving eyes, perhaps I am silly but I fell in love with this Teddy as soon as I saw it. Annie sat it in the chair opposite to Lilly she was smiling like a Cheshire cat, the Teddy Bear comforted Lilly in a strange way, it was warm and yielded to the chair as though it had lived there for a long, long time. This gave a sense of security and she needed that very much. Annie joined Lilly picking up the Teddy saying

"You are not having my chair Teddy; you will have to sit on the floor." She carefully placed the Teddy to lean on the bottom of her chair.

"Be careful with that Annie I want it kept fresh and clean for baby there may be mites on the floor or even dirt, here give him to

me." Annie passed Lilly the Teddy Bear saying

"Goodness you can't half tell this is your first baby Lilly you will get sick of the sights of soft toys before very long."

"Don't be mean Annie I am playing my part to the full I shall be the doting soft Mother and my baby will have many such toys to play with and I don't care a bit what you think." Annie grinned to herself she liked Lilly in this mood they could have a bit of harmless banter she said

"Hark at you shouting your odds Milady what will you buy next I wonder? The shops are full of ideas all you need is the money."

"I have the money Annie not as much as I would like but enough to have a few frills and the like. What did you buy today? Yes I know a new frying pan, I say there was nothing wrong with the old one and the price of it tut tut they saw you coming."Annie replied
I will remember that my girl when I fry our bacon and eggs perhaps you won't want any is that the case?" They both laughed and the subject was dropped. Lilly said

"Mentioning food what are we going to have for tea today Annie? I am now feeling hungry."

"We will have a good basic meal Lilly I am

too tired to stand cooking for long, will boiled eggs and bread and butter suffice? I have fruit cake that I made the other day as a sweet I know you are fond of that." The fire licked flames high into the chimney as a sense of security enfolded around them, what price normality? Lilly loved the security that Annie had provided indeed where would she be without Annie?

A few days later the Butcher's boy called by to deliver Annie's order Lilly answered the door, the boy said
"You used to live with Harry didn't you?" He addressed Lilly, with an inquisitive look.
"Yes I did how clever of you to remember."
"I deliver to Harry now you know, he is a tight wad he never gives me a tip no matter what I have been asked to carry." Lilly replied
"Harry having meat delivered? Goodness I thought I would never live to see the day, yes I know he is tight with his money, may I ask just what you deliver?"
"Different things mainly sausage or bacon, I know he can't cook steak he was adamant that it was the butcher's fault because his steak was tough and he couldn't eat it. I should say he needs you misses he is hopeless on his own." This made Lilly titter, the picture that the boy had put before her

summed Harry up to a tee He was missing her then? Even if it was only through her cooking, the thought tickled her pink she had never thought about Harry doing any cooking it was his habit to go and buy at his club and eat there. Had he indeed got a money problem? He shouldn't have, Lilly understood he had plenty of money. Then again he had gone his own way and his delights were not cheap. Lilly despised him for going to the women in town and leaving their marriage bed as a fall back if his needs hadn't been satisfied. There were very little she could do so she suffered in silence. Lilly told Annie what the butcher boy had said and Annie got the same kick out of it as Lilly she said

"Well well well, Harry in a mess eh? Serves him right if he had done the proper thing he would have been much better off. You are not getting any sympathetic thoughts for him are you? He is just getting what he deserves; I wish I was a fly on the wall where I could see all his ham fisted attempts at housekeeping and cooking. What a show that would make." Lilly answered

"We are awful Annie laughing at Harry when he is in trouble." As she said these words she couldn't help but grin, without

doing a thing she had delivered her first blow back to Harry and secretly enjoyed the moment she thought...One up to me Harry I do believe? She carried on fondling the new Teddy Bear. Annie wouldn't leave this subject alone and said

"You know Lilly that isn't the first time I have been told Harry is not looking well. Is he always unwell?"

"Oh no Annie he prides himself on how fit he is, he thinks he is God's gift to women and often he rubbed it in about my few wrinkles appearing. I tried very hard to smooth the wrinkles out with applying night cream but just at that point my problems got larger and Doctor told me about baby, since then I haven't had the heart to bother about a few lines on my face."

"I have never noticed them Lilly, I think you have a lovely complexion for a Lady turned forty. Men can be downright rude when a Lady is ageing they can be very picky although they are ageing at the same rate. It is unfair men age and sometimes look better than they did before, a quiet sophistication and a beard usually this makes them more attractive in a different kind of way you do know what I mean don't you Lilly?"

"Yes I do but it doesn't really help I still can't

help getting wrinkles and carrying this baby has taken its toll."

"Lilly as soon as the baby is born you will begin to recover, you will walk along with such pride you won't recognise yourself. Harry has a bitter pill to swallow he must take a back seat for a while, don't worry I will look after you, together we will show Harry that it is not only him that exists. It will be your turn to hold the limelight when a beautiful Daughter is in the perambulator. Wonder how he will deal with that eh?" Lilly softly smiled at Annie knowing that her friend was trying to keep up her spirits. How Harry would react after the baby was born Lilly dreaded to think she would cross that bridge when she came to it.

Chapter Sixteen

It had given Harry something to think about having his money stolen, he was very upset, never in his life had he carried enough money to make a steal worthwhile, now just because Stuart had enticed him to go to the races he had left himself vulnerable enough to allow this to happen it had hurt his pride as well as his pocket. Study Racing form was not for him he was a ladies' man and no mistake. He thought he would give the girls another visit and that would stop him fretting about his losses. His bank had advised him of the sum he had in balance. He admitted to himself the spending lately had taken chunks out of the capitol. What did he care he was living the life that most appealed to him. There was no sense to it but this was Harry and Harry had what Harry wanted. If he ran out of money he had a few things he could sell and indeed would sell without a second thought. Still he thought…it may not come to that times change as fortune changes I may get lucky who knows?

Tomorrow he would go and see Angel she always made him feel special and gave of herself…well freely? Only it wasn't free was it? In fact it was the exact opposite she was expensive and knew how to please a man just as long as the tips were good. Angel would not discuss money it was beneath her, she expected the cash to be there without question. No money no love Harry knew that, but he still went to her like a moth to a flame.

"Silly Harry again I say to my reader what is it with men that they go so willingly to their demise. They have the power of decision and calculation and indeed business ways, yet they are so easily fooled by a pretty face or a voluptuous body... So be it I haven't the answer at this moment and I suppose I never will have the answer. We must read on and see if the story unfolds this "elusive" answer?"

Harry had his composure back and was ready to go and see Angel, he looked at the mirror and he liked what he saw, he had put on a brand new shirt, trimmed his sideburns, shined up his smile and polished his shoes. A handsome man indeed, but handsome is as handsome does and there are those amongst us that would not give Harry a second look, shallow and vain are the words that come readily to mind. Locking the front door he sallied forth into the night his anticipation giving him a glow. A street vendor was selling red carnations outside the Music Hall Harry pinned the flower into his lapel, gave himself a pat on the back and carried on. The nights were getting misty and murky damp air hung around the streets turning in some places to fog, the gas street lights were barely visible hardly a soul in sight. No matter he would soon be where all was style and grace among the ladies of ill repute. He could slap a few bottoms and run his hands up a few skirts and it would all be taken lightly. His step quickened in anticipation.

Once again he was standing talking to Victoria through the grill in the door saying, "Hello my sweet one, open the door to my pleasure I have time to spend as well as money." Victoria opened the door.
"Good to see you Harry and in fine form I see, go in to the girls they will be happy to see you, a man with charm is what they tell me when your name is mentioned." Harry preened himself and gladly went into the girls. Their faces lit up when they saw Harry and no wonder he was such an easy lay and he paid well. Again Harry only wanted fun with these girls his fervent ardour would come to the fore when he entered Angel's bedroom.

Angel sat at her dressing table when her door was tapped, it was Victoria she said "I thought you would like to know Harry is downstairs and has asked for you later on." Angel grimaced and said "I thought he had stopped bothering me, the truth is Victoria I can't stand the sight of him. He is so self opinionated he gives me the creeps." Victoria replied "Now now Angel you know his money is good and he readily pays up, you mustn't take a personal view it doesn't pay you to do that." "I know Victoria but he is such a slimy creature and he thinks I love him; he makes overtures and darlings me, precious? Well Harry thinks I am but he has another think coming, one of these days I will tell him what I really think of him and he will have the biggest shock of his life. Keep him occupied downstairs as long as you can let him use his spare energy's. Thank you for letting me know I can plan how to deal with him before he arrives up here." Victoria left none too pleased she needed her girls to be flexible they knew just what they were there for and too much pomp and soul seeking was not in the order of things. She would have reprimanded Angel in a definitely stricter way but Angel brought in wealthy clients so

Victoria had to hold her tongue.

Downstairs Harry was filling up with whiskey he smelt as if you could put a match to him and he would throw flame. The girls encouraged him and it was in Victoria's benefit too as the whisky cost double to that at the clubs or pubs. Let him get it down, Victoria could always throw him out if he became too much trouble. This is the state Angel strongly objected to nevertheless would have to deal with. His slobbering mouth his bloated red face, and hands that went everywhere. Harry would be out of control and everyone but he would know it, he presumed to be King of the Castle, when in reality he was worse than the Court Jester where on earth he had got the idea from that put him in such a superior position heaven only knows he tapped on Angel's door. Angel's grimace changed into a smile albeit false she called

"Come in." Harry boldly walked in saying "Here I am my darling Angel have you been waiting for me?"

"Of course I have Harry will you have a drink with me?"

"We will drink together, Angel fetched the glasses to the bedside continuing to say, I can fill them to overflowing with just you in

mind." Angel slid off the bed in a seductive manner and did as she intended. Together they sat up in the bed and sipped the wine. Harry by now was suitably inebriated and Angel just pretending to be sloshed. His hand went under her negligee, her skin was soft and warm, as Angel steeled her emotions. Pretending to feel as amorous as Harry she ran her hands over Harry's back, all she wanted was for Harry to be so delighted that it would bring on a surge of emotion and the rest she could finish off without undue fuss. Yes she was good at her trade she had no scruples the money was all that she wanted and Harry was like butter in her hands she fulfilled his every need and then rolled over away from his stinking breath praising her own tactics and knowing the only thing Harry wanted now was sleep silly Harry.

Walking or should I say wobbling home at dawn Harry wended his way home. He did remember his moments with Angel he was just cursing his own stupidity realising that it was his fault that the foreplay had been ended too soon. In part that was Angel's fault she enticed him in such a fashion it was difficult to resist those final moments. Soon he would be home again his bed was the first thing he would want he knew it. Stumbling up his own staircase he had to stop, his breath was coming in short gasps, he held the banister and lowered his body to sit on the stairs, trying to conquer the sinking feeling he had. Curses he flung out into the barren space "I need help" but he knew there was no one to hear him, why hadn't he stayed at Victoria's place for a while longer? This was not happening to him, these bouts of breathlessness were for other people not him. It was a full fifteen minutes before Harry dare to move and even then it was at snail's pace that he followed through into his bedroom and flopped on to the bed exhausted. Sleep that was the answer and Harry was never nearer the mark in thinking that. He never thought he would be his own critic. As long as the sleep did the trick he was not going to bother about seeing what was truly wrong with him. He didn't like Doctors at the best of times, he had seen one on the odd occasion and the Doctor would tell him to give up his drinking habit and cut down on his pipe tobacco. No Harry was not seeing a Doctor, another thing crossed his mind and that was cost, Doctors charged a pretty penny and never did him any good, they could clear off he would steer his own ship.

Dear reader, this may be a good idea when you are plain sailing but Harry wasn't in calm waters the turbulence got rougher each time he lowered his standards, he turned a blind eye and took another glass of whiskey. Lilly was well rid of this man don't you think? But was she rid of him? No doubt we will find out.

After getting up and managing to get downstairs Harry felt terrible he was shivering and every bone in his body ached. The fire of course was not lit who was there to light it? Harry hugged his own body for warmth and picked up a cover from the couch and put it over his knees saying his voice penetrating the empty air.
"Lilly if I could get hold of you now I would strangle you, and I would murder the baby what a state you have brought me to, it is all your fault, without this baby we could have jogged along as we were even though you got on my nerves and your performance in bed was without question staid, yes getting down to brass tacks my love life was being sadly destroyed by your minimal effort."
There Harry stopped his talking suddenly admitting he was talking to thin air and

would do himself no good. He went to his armchair and sat back, thinking …I must get warm this house is like a winter's day in the park. Brr brr. He again embraced his own body with his arms and thought fondly of his time the night before at Victoria's place. Even Harry knew he could not keep up the pace to frequent Victoria's any more than he was doing; there was more than one way to make your own self a laughing stock! Thinking…I can go to my club later but Stuart might be there I can't face him after the awful day at the races. I think I told him not to tell anyone, I don't want my failures blabbing about. I am a man of integrity No man looks down on me my choices are impeccable and my word is as good as law. While thinking deeply Harry nodded off to sleep again but his mind was actually in turmoil his self assurance was as thin as tissue paper. In the real world Lilly was his Anker, his situation now resembled the way he would be in quick sand, the more he struggled the deeper down he would go and he could feel his body sinking, if it wasn't for the numbing effect of all the whiskey he drank he would realise the peril he was in but of course the whiskey masked the truth and made him too blind to see.

Finally Harry stirred and managed to sit up. Still he was not feeling as well as he would like to. He wanted a warm drink but both the kitchen fire and the sitting room fire was sitting in a depth of grey ash, it would mean Harry lighting a new fire and for once he did just that, comfort that was the key word and a hot drink and a place by the fireside to sit was his best choice. He hardly recognised his own face in the mirror and quickly turned his face away. He had seen an old man, this is not me he told his own image and what is that sore place doing on my lips? I must be off colour, time to slow down and I think I must do both for the sake of my pocket and my health. I shall definitely not be going to my club until I have recovered, they would all be asking what was wrong with me. A couple of days indoors won't hurt, I will have the butcher deliver me some good meat and build my strength up again.

The fire had burned through and Harry felt so much better for that, the kettle was put on and he went into the kitchen to find the tea caddy he mumbled
"I hope there is sugar I don't mind drinking tea without milk but sugar is a must." A tray was fetched out and there was sugar in the sugar bowl. An unopened tin of biscuits sat

on the pantry shelf Harry eagerly brought them in with his tea. Sitting by the fire for once in many days he felt relaxed, there was nobody to please but himself, he opened the biscuit tin, in there were biscuits but they had gone off with the length of time they had been stood. Harry said loudly

"Damn and blast is there nothing in this house to eat again? Lilly has left no supplies that are edible I wonder if there is a grocery store that will deliver." Deciding to find out he sipped his warm tea, there was no bread otherwise he could have made toast, then again there was no butter. "Drat and blast he murmured under his breath I must get some wholesome food down, I must get myself well again."

That was the first sensible word Harry had said in many moons.

Chapter Seventeen

Annie poked the fire and put on some more coal saying,

"I must have a word with the coalman Lilly there is more slack than coal in the latest delivery. Don't know how they have the cheek to ask the price"

"That bad is it Annie? Trouble is the smoke it belches out, I am sure it makes the wallpaper dirty and it is not good for our throats and chests, I seem to perpetually have a cough it is not good for baby too."

"Don't worry I will get it put right, I pay my bills regularly and I will threaten the coalman as to my choice in having his firm deliver my coal, that will make him more diligent with the next lot. Five bags a fortnight he brings me and I pay for top quality not slack."

"It is starting to burn through now Annie, perhaps the coal is a bit damp as well, the fog has hung about just lately and that makes everything damp, the coal shed hasn't got a lot of protection has it?"

"I suppose it hasn't but it is still quite adequate for storing coal. The slack is there to see, I am not making it up you know Lilly. I will let the fire stop smoking then I will put

the kettle on, I can't abide smoked tea."
Annie's little moan was over and soon the
kettle had been put over the now stable fire
she said
"What would you like for tea Lilly?"
"Oh I don't mind Annie whatever is to hand
will be good enough for me."
"I have some of that nice ham I brought back
with me earlier in the week will sandwiches
do for you?"
"Yes, to tell you the truth I am going off
eating too much food these days, baby is
taking so much room and I get heartburn so
easily, as the time goes on I feel as though I
will burst. Has anyone actually burst with
sheer size Annie?"
"Don't be silly, nature has its own way of
making space, soon the baby will be born and
this ordeal will be over, bide your time Lilly
all will be well you'll see." Lilly managed one
sandwich and asked
"Is there any fruit cake left Annie?"
"Yes but you are naughty leaving your
second sandwich and asking for cake, I will
fetch it from the pantry." Annie brought in a
tin with the remainder of the cake inside.
"There is plenty in here for our needs I will
bake another one over the weekend it keeps
well and between us we see it off don't

*we?"Lilly nodded her approval and said
"I have been thinking about Christmas it
isn't far away now but Annie I will not be
able to attend Church with you, I can hardly
walk. I am sorry as I would have liked to have
heard the Carol Service it is such a lovely
little Church and with the tree lit up with
candles it looks really festive."*

*"Don't decide this minute Lilly you may
surprise yourself and accompany me, I will
hold your arm and keep you safe."*

*"Alright Annie you are so good to me and I
don't want to be a burden to you, what if I
start getting pains while I am in Church?"*

*"So what? In Church is a fine place to birth
your baby, but don't worry it is a very long
shot that baby will be coming by then,
January is the time and I think now you will
go full term Lilly." Lilly looked wide eyed at
Annie she was so educated in these sort of
things, how could she know Lilly's baby
would come to term? Annie said*

*"In a couple of weeks we will put a Christmas
tree up, I have a few baubles that I have kept
wrapped in tissue you can help me dress it
Lilly we can have a glass of sherry and enjoy
the moment, I might even make some mince
pies, would you like that Lilly?"*

"It sounds a treat Annie and I shall look

forward to it, my mind won't dwell entirely on baby, a distraction is just what I need right now I feel tons better than I did earlier on thank you Annie." The tea table was cleared and left a nice atmosphere in the room for Lilly to get out her stitching. The picture was beginning to show form and Lilly was happy with the way it was coming along. Choosing her next colour carefully she threaded her needle.

Pleasantly they had chatted all evening both absorbed in their needlework when Lilly said to Annie.

"Sometimes Annie I feel sorry for Harry."

"Sorry well I never, after all he has done to your mind and indeed to your body. If Harry had one shred of decency and paused for thought a moment you would not be in this mess."

"The truth is I am happy to be having a baby I do not look upon my situation as being a mess, tut, I know what you are going to say and I know Harry deserves the cold shoulder I am giving him but he must have his reasons."

"You are completely off your head if you think I can excuse Harry for his behaviour towards you and the child. Harry looks after number one and has no time for anyone that

136

will not toe the line. You are not thinking of going back to him are you Lilly?"

"I suppose it is because it is Christmas, goodwill and all that and I have heard now that Harry looks ill and I am not there to look after him. I keep wondering what his illness is, there are times he just won't get out of my mind, silly aren't I?"

"Silly is not a strong enough word, you are completely balmy to waste even a thought on Harry. You know what he is like with the ladies fancies his chance does Harry. It crosses my mind that he has not sent you a penny to live on or buy baby clothes. What sort of man does that eh? Change the subject Lilly or I will be saying things I ought not to say. It is about time we had a cup of cocoa with plenty of sugar in it to calm us down."

Annie having said her piece stuck her needle into the spot she had arrived at and stalked out into the kitchen. Lilly had certainly ruffled her feathers but she had not intended to, she had just spoken what was in her mind expecting Annie to put her point of view, yes Annie had spoken the truth but the truth sometimes hurts. Annie came back into the room with two steaming mugs saying

"Here you are Lilly and we will have a drop of Brandy in this it will be good for what ails

you, then it will be time for bed. Show me your embroidery turn it around so that I can see properly, ah yes the colours are blending very well, you have a very neat way of stitching Lilly you will be able to hand this picture down to your Daughter and tell her she was with you and not yet born when you stitched it."

"What a lovely thought Annie, I will keep that in mind whilst doing the rest of the tapestry, may I look at yours?"

"Mine isn't a patch on yours, I have always had a heavy hand when it comes to sewing, even mending I hate. It is a good job this has colour in it or else it would have been abandoned by now. I will stick at it though, I have started on the sails and the white is beginning to contrast the colours nicely do you see?"

"Why! you are doing a splendid job Annie don't put yourself down it is on a parallel with mine and I am sure they are both going to be displayed on the chosen wall very well."

Now putting away their sewing into tidy order Annie was pleased she had steered Lilly away from her caring for Harry he didn't deserve Lilly with her quiet thoughtful manner, in fact Annie still at times wanted to go round and see Harry and let him face a few home truths. Annie was quite convinced there was very little that was good about the man. As they went upstairs Annie felt for Lilly her struggle now to carry this baby was for all to see. Soon her time would come, Annie hoped she would be able to help Lilly with the birth but she had a few misgivings about that, she wasn't trained in such things and apprehension as the day drew nearer sometimes overpowered her resolve. Annie didn't want Harry at this late stage to come butting in she had a big enough job seeing to Lilly. So what if Harry was ill, it was probably his own fault. Too much overindulgence would make anyone ill."

Chapter eighteen.

Harry was still not well although he had administered his own remedy, he still had the cold sore on his lip and was still dealing with his problem as a bad cold. He had tried lemon balm but that hadn't done a thing. The Apothecary had made up a potion for him to take and that did no good. It is unfair to say that Harry wasn't feeling marginally better he even thought of going to his club. Tomorrow yes he would go tomorrow another day taking his self applied medicine would surely see results. He had pride in his own cooking now, although it was the simplest of meals he produced, he did know how to make beef tea Harry had spoken to one of his neighbours and she had told him how. It was simple but full of nourishing qualities, in fact he had been drinking the broth each day and he liked it.

Next day Harry went out and headed for his club. He still had a weakness about him but longed for company. Standing by the bar Harry ordered his whiskey, it would warm his body up and so do him good. In walks Stuart and straight to the bar he came complete with all the blasé he carried around with him. Slapping Harry on the back he nearly

knocked him over he said,
"Here you are Harry old man I wondered if
or when I would see you again, do I find you
well?" Harry played his illness down he
didn't want Stuart's opinion but Stuart had
noticed the cold sore on Harry's lip.
"I say old fellow that is a nasty cold sore you
have what have you tried to get rid of it?"
"I have been taking a lemon balm that the
Apothecary made up for me and I have
dabbed it dry hoping it would form a scab and
drop off but nothing has worked."
"Now I heard there is a new remedy being
tried it is in the very early stages of
administration how do you feel about trying it
Harry?" Harry looked doubtful and replied
I don't really like taking new medicines, what
is it called?"
The name of it is Aspirin; I am told it will
bring down a fever in no time."
"It is not the fever I am bothered about, it is
this great sore on my lip it is painful and I do
not show myself in a good light to the ladies."
"Ah now we know the crux of the matter eh?
It is the ladies you want to please be it?"
"I thought by now the damned thing would
be gone but see how you noticed it straight
away. Blast my sides I don't even know how I
picked it up, probably on a whiskey glass that

hadn't been clean when put back. Yes that must be it I will complain to the management my oath I will."

"Oh don't worry about it when we have had a whiskey or two you won't even know it is still there, drink up old fellow I will get the next round, I can see you need a bit of cosseting good job I happened to be along this way."

Harry didn't think it was a good thing he didn't like this man, he was always on top form and bragged about his conquests. It was like that day at the races when Harry had shown his weaker side losing all his money to a clever thief it had left a bad taste in Harry's mouth and he felt himself shrink as he stood in Stuart's company. Harry had never told a soul, Stuart was the only one that knew and it seemed to remind Harry just how foolish he had been. Harry fidgeted he was on the spot again and knew he must cut this conversation short. He wanted out of Stuart's company. Harry coughed and at the same time he said to Stuart

"I shall not be staying long, this cough is still bothering me I shouldn't have come out at all but I was getting downright morbid and needed the air. I must apologise and leave you to drink on your own Stuart."

"Don't worry about me old fellow you go and

get your rest I will soon find someone to talk to." Yes Harry thought, you will and I pity whoever you find perhaps there are some people who find you tolerable but that does not include me. Harry said his goodbye and left. This was not like Harry he was going home, not looking for a girl or going to Victoria's place, this illness was keeping him subdued. There were Christmas trees being put up in several places as he passed by but even the thought of Christmas didn't lift his spirit, usually he had plenty to drink and Lilly would provide as many cakes and pastry's as anyone would need, the fire would be lit in both kitchen and sitting room and on Christmas morning there would be a turkey in the oven roasting the aroma permeating the air. His thoughts of Lilly were still not good, it was her fault things had gone wrong and instead of looking after him she had chosen to have this baby, selfish that is what she was wanting her own way. In actual fact the reverse was the real truth.

Home again and Harry wanted to go straight to bed he ached all over; he found his medicinal compound and attended his sore lip. There was no fire to put the kettle on so he had a whiskey to drink. He sat thinking for a while… What the hell is the matter with me, I should be getting better from a cold by now but I am not, I am not going to have a Doctor he will make a long job of it and charge me a fortune. I would sooner have a night with Angel she would do me more good than any Doctor. My sweet precious Angel you must be missing me, I will come to you as soon as I have got rid of this inconvenience. My own special love my mind is calmed even when thinking of you, why didn't I marry such a girl as you perfect in every way? I was forced by families to marry Lilly a good match they had said, but not for me her performance in bed was pitiful and has never got any better, now a baby is coming Drat Lilly and Damn the baby. He now went to bed feeling almost defeated.

Next day getting up he still felt tired out, he lit the fire and sat and thought for a moment… I remember Lilly using "Friar's Balsam" when she went down with a cold there is a ceramic inhaler somewhere, I could go to the nearest Apothecary and get the Friars, If I inhale the balsam it will penetrate the lip area and help clear this evil cold sore. Now what else had she used to do…yes put Honey in her tea. Now what else is there I could try?
Lilly used to swear by "Chinn fang Mi" in

milk. I am going to try all those remedies they used to do Lilly good so why not me? Harry felt relieved because he had thought of something to try, he was a man on a mission. No he didn't have to seek a Doctor's advice he would get well soon enough without that. Settling down in home after his shopping at the Apothecary Harry felt better pleased he had readily got the medicinal compounds now he could try them. He made up the Friar's Balsam adding it to steamy hot water and into the inhaler, then just as he had seen Lilly do he put a towel over his head leaning forward to allow the vapour to rise within the confines of the towel. At first it made him cough, it was strong then he settled down and he felt the benefit of the warm vapours as they entered the nasal area and the mouth. Whether or not he was doing the right thing didn't occur to him, surely some good would come of it. He stayed in that position until the steam stopped rising then whipped off the now damp towel and shook his head to clear the fog that was causing his eyes to sting. A towel he had left over the fireguard quickly came into use it was warm and soft so it draped around his neck and was comforting. This small act had given his moral a boost as he relaxed in his chair, but not before he had looked into the mirror to see if the lip sore had shrunk. He wanted to believe it had but had it?

For the next three weeks Harry dosed himself up with everything available on the Apothecary's shelf, he was fed up of people saying try this or try that he believed he had tried it all but nothing was very evidently getting him well. As always his thoughts turned to Victoria's place and Angel. He vowed and declared…I am going to see my ladies yes this very night and I shall stay late and see my lovely Angel that will do me good I am sure of it.

It was dusk but as the light dropped it was only five o'clock. Being ready to go out he fidgeted, he did not want to seem too eager or Victoria might put the price up, ready cash was one thing he had to keep an eye on deciding not to leave such generous tips, now counting his coppers in a very realistic manner, he checked his wallet, he had a fair few notes in there surely that would be enough. It had to be enough.

Chapter Nineteen

Now Lilly would not leave the house, fact was the weight and pressure on her legs and feet was too much to carry. Even her stitching was hard to reach so knitting baby boots kept her mind off the confinement. It was the subject of the day Annie would lovingly say "Now what colour are you knitting? This baby will be very well endowed with bootees, I think you should choose the ones you like most and then send a few to charity, the Mothers who can't even afford to buy the wool would give a few half pennies for them, you would be doing a good deed whilst giving yourself a reason for knitting them."
"What a good idea Annie I would be happy to think they were all going to be used and I have plenty of wool. I haven't the concentration to knit bigger things and when I knit bootees there is no weight in the wool involved to bother me."
"Talking about wool I noticed at our local craft shop they are selling a few silks off all at one price, do you need any for your tapestry?"
"Depends on the colours Annie, I am getting short of green the cottage garden takes up the green, and maybe a pink a strong pink, I have

geraniums to do, Oh yes and a sky blue there is quite an expanse of sky to stitch. Not that I will have much time on my hands when baby is here but I shall finish my picture at some point merely because I want to."

"Of course you want to and I am here to take over the baby chores if you want to stitch, I don't intend leaving you all the baby work I am only too pleased to help."

"Thank you Annie you have been and are my lifeline it is always good to know you care, I only hope I have not taken you for granted I wouldn't have survived this ordeal without you and your wise words." Annie's eyes filled with tears she knew what Lilly meant and was humbled by the compliment.

Already it was Christmas Eve Annie had dressed a small pine tree with baubles that she had kept for many years. Lilly sitting by the roaring fire sipping a glass of Port wine, she was feeling pleased with the evening as she had contributed towards the Christmas fare by making mince pies. Not that she had done it easily she had to lean over her baby bump to reach the mixing bowl and to roll out the pastry. Both she and Annie had laughed about it, Lilly didn't mind Annie sharing her clumsy attitude she knew it was in good taste and not meant to hurt. The Port had gone to

Lilly's head and for once she felt free and less worried. The fire burned brightly, the candles were lit, the small chicken that was to be their Christmas dinner had been prepared to go into the oven in the morning all was well. Annie said

"Have you bought many Christmas presents Lilly?"

"No, you have been with me when I have been to the shops so you must know I haven't the cards I have sent are sparse as well."

"Sent one to Harry?"

"No I haven't he will only think I am trying to wheedle my way into his company again, this much I know, it is he that will have to sort me out, I don't want to talk about Harry tonight Annie, everything is so pretty around us why spoil the moment?"

"You are right Lilly, here let me give your glass a top up, it seems to be doing you a bit of good this Port." They talked and laughed until it was time for bed. Lilly said in fun

"Don't forget to hang up your stocking Annie you never know what you may have in it by morning."

"I do know what will be in my stocking Lilly…my foot, no-one is likely to have bought me anything it is a long time since I had a Christmas present."

"Doesn't your family buy you a gift Annie?"
"We done away with that idea many years ago Lilly, they have families of their own now to fend for, and for me to go all around my Grandchildren is not what I can do so it works both ways, it saves a lot of worrying."
"I hadn't thought about your extended family Annie, not having one of my own it didn't occur to me about the cost that this becomes."
"Yes as many things do it all boils down to money, my family are doing alright and that is all I care about seeing them grow to be healthy and useful young men and women."
"Yes it is a wonderful feeling you must have after spending all your time on having a family and bringing them up to be responsible people. I have never considered how big a job that is Annie, I looked after Harry and that was it, I just wish he had looked after me but now I know I was just a convenience for him. No I said I wouldn't speak of Harry tonight so I will go no further."
"Come on my friend let's go to bed, the air was very cold this morning I wonder shall we have a white Christmas?"
"It would be lovely to have a sprinkling of snow as long as it stays a sprinkling not six foot of it." Off they went to their separate

bedrooms each with thoughts about Christmas and the love that came quietly with it giving to all a blessing and a happy spirit.

"Happy Christmas" Annie said as Lilly joined her in the kitchen Annie holding out her arms to give Lilly a hug."
"The same to you Annie, just toast for breakfast or I will never be able to eat my Christmas dinner."
"I agree with that we have Christmas pudding as well I am just preparing the custard so that later on it will only have to be boiled up, here Lilly take the weight off your feet and have a cup of tea, do you want anything in your tea Lilly like a spot of Brandy?"
"Ooha! It is a long time since I had Brandy in my tea, go on then just a drop." As they sat drinking tea Lilly produced a little package out of her pinafore pocket saying
"This is for you Annie." Annie said
"I haven't got anything for you Lilly, you shouldn't have."
"Open it Annie and I should think you have given me quite enough caring for me as you do." Annie opened her gift, it was a Cameo brooch with the cameo set into a figured silver back."
"That is lovely Lilly how did you manage to

get it without me knowing?"

"I have to tell you the truth, it is one of my own bought for me by my Mother many years ago, but I thought, Cameo's don't go out of fashion and it is a good one I give it to you with my deepest regard Annie."

"I shall treasure it Lilly it is a beautiful brooch and I shall wear it with pride thank you so much. I said I hadn't anything for you Lilly well it is not for you it is for your baby, she passed a small bag for Lilly to open."

"Oh! Look at that isn't it pretty, thank you very much Annie did you knit it?" Lilly was looking at a pink bonnet and tiny mittens to match for her baby and considered that a lovely thought

"Come on then don't let us become too sentimental there is kitchen work to do, Annie bustled around saying

"You do the Brussels sprouts and I will peel the potatoes, when we have finished this veritable feast we will play cards this afternoon, got any farthings in your purse?"

"I have no idea we will have to play for halfpenny's if I haven't, will they do?"

"Of course they will, bet I beat you Lilly, are you good at cards?"

"Absolutely not I can't remember the last time I played at cards. It will make a change

and you never know I might win." In pleasant humour their banter went on until they sat down to dinner. A table cloth white as snow, red candles and green holly with berries set the mood. The holly fresh from the garden centred the table and in the centre of the holly a single red candle held in a candle stick matching the holly berries, the best cutlery and table napkins finished the table off to be inviting and pretty.

"Well Lilly will you look at that." Lilly turned to look and found Annie was telling her to look at the snow it was coming down fast and furious she said

"Well I never! We have a white Christmas after all, oh how delicate it is and it is settling, the first fall this year and right on Christmas day it looks like a picture post card doesn't it? The trees take on such a delightful sight and the remainder of the autumn leaves all get a clean new look as if they are frozen in time" Annie said

"No more gazing out of the window we still have our Christmas pudding to eat, I will fetch it in." The pudding had been laced with brandy and a match was put to it on arriving at the table, it flared beautifully much to their delight. A very comfortable and loving atmosphere surrounded Annie and Lilly.

They hadn't very much but wanted for nothing. Sitting in the afternoon playing cards and chatting Annie said

"There was a small brass band playing in the market centre, real Christmassy it sounded I put a few coppers in the tin. The Salvation Army do help those in real need. Did you know there is a Brass Band Festival going on at The Crystal Palace in London I overheard a lady speaking of it saying her Son was there."

" That's interesting Annie I wonder which group will win the prize, what is the prize?"

"I don't know but I think it would be money. I bet there are some posh people attending. I like brass bands, well that is if they don't go on forever, and of course they can play the instrument well. Changing the subject Lilly are we going to have just a mince pie and a cup of tea later? I am still very full of Christmas pudding I can't eat much more. I have a box of chocolates for this evening, a little indulgence I have, I treat myself, I like those with Turkish delight in them, what is your favourite?"

"Without a doubt the nut chocolate is my choice."

"That's good I am glad we don't both like the same ones we can share can't we?"

The fire had settled in its burning, the whole range sent out heat, the room was warm and Lilly found herself dosing the cards in her hands dropping to the floor. Annie didn't disturb her, smiling she put a pillow under Lilly's head and a hand knitted rug over her knees. It wouldn't hurt anything if Lilly had forty winks and Annie felt much the same.

Chapter Twenty

Harry had decided early or not he just couldn't wait any longer. Pulling the front door shut for a moment he felt good. It was short lived, strolling down the hill he thought the keen wind would blow him right off his feet. He had lost weight and the strong wind was enough to blow him over. He pulled his coat closer and lifted his collar up, he was shivering and for once Victoria's place seemed a long way to go, he plodded on picking his way around icy patches on the cobblestones. There was a café on the corner so he paused and went in the young waitress came over to him saying
"What can I get for you Sir?"
Just a pot of tea please Harry thought... is this really me ordering tea? The tea came and Harry laced it from a whiskey flask taking care that no-one saw him, as his eyes looked around the tea room he spotted one of Lilly's friends there was no way he wanted to talk to her but she had spotted him and came over saying
"Hello Harry are you well? I never seem to see Lilly these days she doesn't frequent the shopping area in the town centre I always used to bump into her there is nothing wrong

is there? I mean she isn't in the hospital or ill is she?" Harry didn't quite know how to answer but played safe and said

"Lilly is well enough and of late I think her friend Annie has been taking her to other villages to shop."

"Just as long as she is alright, I can't stay to chat I have an appointment to keep so I have to be brief, nice to see you Harry Happy New Year my dear." She was gone and Harry thanked the powers that be for her appointment, he considered he had a narrow escape. Quietly he sipped his tea, trying to make his mind up where to go next. Yes he wanted to go and see Angel but he had to admit he was not feeling top notch, but neither did Harry want to go home, the fire would be out and the place without pleasure. He was sick of bed and of medicine that was doing him no good at all. I will go to Victoria's place the atmosphere is inviting and she always finds a spot for me, it will be warm while the ladies cosset me I could do with a bit of cosseting without a doubt. He stepped out of the café to find the icy cold wind had got up its strength and a light fall of snow hit his face like pellets, he pulled his coat closely around him and held his hat on. It wasn't far to Victoria's place now he would *be glad to be inside again once more he felt the chill it made him shiver.*

Standing outside of Victoria's he tapped the door with his cane, the grid was opened and Victoria greeted him saying
"Step inside Harry out of the wind, it is a fierce night and no mistake." Harry went in and Victoria took his coat. The light was dim as Harry had stepped from outside, it was kept that way so that privacy was observed. Through the heavy curtain Harry could hear the girls, Victoria smiled up at him but her smile was momentary she said,
"Are you ill Harry?"
"No, he lied I have had a bit of a cold that is all."
"What is that on your lip my dear?"
"Just a cold sore it is clearing up now."
"How long have you been suffering that Harry?"
"A couple of weeks I suppose I haven't paid much attention to it." Harry told another lie.
"Let me look at you in the light my dear."
Harry thought Victoria was feeling sorry for him so he stepped into the light of the oil lamp Victoria said
"I am sorry Harry but I can't allow you in to see the girls this night, come back when you have no cold sore, they are nasty and you

could pass on the unsightly thing." She proceeded to get Harry his coat trying to soften the blow because Harry paid well. Harry was aghast! Victoria was sending him away, what could he say in his own defence? "That is a bit harsh isn't it Victoria? Sending me away just because there is a cold on my lip?"

"I am indeed sorry Harry but look at it like this would you go to Angel if she had a sore on her lips? You would certainly think twice and then decide no. I have to take care of my ladies it is too big a risk I have my livelihood to consider." Harry thought Victoria was over reacting and tried again saying

"Come on Victoria don't be a spoil sport this sore will be gone in no time at all, I have bought a whole roll of notes with me." With that Harry went into his inside pocket and drew out a fat wedge of notes, he rolled a couple of notes off and tried to give them to Victoria she wasn't interested, she merely said

"Put your money away Harry, you spend it on seeing a Doctor he will give you a remedy for your lip and then all will be well again" Victoria ushered Harry to the door in an insistent manner holding his elbow as they went. The door was unlocked and Harry

found he was out in the street again and yes he was flabbergasted. Feeling sorry for himself his thoughts ran on… No need to treat me like a leper just because of a mere cold blister. Doctor indeed I do not want a Doctor. He indignantly forced to walk away but really Victoria's words had shattered him. Now there was no place to go but home, he had been rejected he was shame faced he would show Victoria hers was not the only place to take his money. He walked along under the gas street lights and came to the same corner he had seen the voluptuous street girl he suddenly remembered she at the time had a sore on her lip, so that is where it came from his mind was working fast, well where is she I will give her a piece of my mind. There was no-one on the street corner, blast everything to bloody hell what is happening to me thought Harry.

It had started to rain mixed with the snow so Harry quickened his step he didn't want to aggravate this cold he had been nursing, it could turn into pneumonia, well what a sell where to go now? The debonair blasé middle aged show off, the man with the cane and top hat was coming to grief and Harry didn't recognise the fact. He was sorry for only one person and that was himself, he hadn't a *single thought for Lilly. Harry didn't want to go home there was little enough to go home for, so he decided to go to his club for a while to break the monotony. He arrived and immediately found the most comfortable chair, ordering whiskey and picking up a financial newspaper. No-one would like to disturb him if they thought he was engrossed in financial matters. He gazed at the newspaper but all was blurred all he wanted to do was bury his head and forget the grip that this continuing illness had presented him with. What else can I do to get better? His mind ran on going over what should have been a simple ailment. Harry asked himself why isn't this unsightly nuisance on my lip getting better he didn't have a clue. Lilly would have known what to do to heal it. Damn and blast Lilly, he was not going to give way, he still didn't want the baby and as sure as he could be Lilly was coming up to the birth date there was no way he was getting involved in that fiasco. Women thought they knew it all Harry decided not to ask Lilly for advice. He sat where he was until he was ready to leave, stubborn and wilful to his own best avenue of interest. He had to keep faith with his own self, he must not lose heart and he must not tell a soul how his situation was affecting his life, this must be his own secret there was no-one to be sympathetic to his cause, he had been blanked off every time he had looked for support. He now stood a bewildered and lonely man without anyone to turn to. These thoughts ruffled his mind and left him in a bewildered state poor Harry!*

Arriving home at last he decided to start afresh and dose himself up with the medicine he had now in full supply on the pantry shelf. Energy that was the thing, nothing seemed worth the effort, all he wanted to do was sleep.

He slipped a couple of aspirin down alongside his whiskey and went to bed.

Chapter Twenty one

*The New Year celebrations left behind
Lilly was looking forward to the birth of her
baby, it was now 6th of January 1905 Annie
was keeping Lilly cheerful and taking any
weight off her mind. The tapestry they were
both doing was a real help Lilly got quite
absorbed and this took baby worries away,
she had to dismiss the fact that she "waddled
like a duck" when she walked, her own
description was very near the truth she said it
was like having a tray laden with food on her
waist front and she was expected to carry it
all the time. Annie pacified her knowing this
was a crucial time to get through. Annie also
had apprehension she wanted to deliver the
baby for Lilly a very responsible task she
must keep calm for Lilly's sake, the days went
on with both friends waiting for the day of the
birth.*

*Annie had gone out shopping leaving Lilly
to rest. Lilly for no reason at all felt restless
and wanted Annie to hurry back, full of
apprehension and fear Lilly knew that the
birth of baby was getting near. Not ever
seeing a baby born she had very little
knowledge of how it all started, what to
expect. How would she recognise when*

labour began? It was all an ongoing mystery to her. She had tried to be active all morning to take her mind off her imminent position but nothing she seemed to do had the desired effect. Breathing a sigh of relief when she heard Annie's key in the lock Lilly called to her

"Annie I am so glad you are back I have been so fidgety all morning, should this happen? Does it happen to all new Mothers?"

"There is nothing to be alarmed about Lilly. Go in by the fire and I will put the kettle on. I tried to hurry but as you know more haste less speed, it is bitter cold out there this morning I too am very glad to be home."

Annie put the kettle on and quietly appraised Lilly's face seeing her pinched look Annie realised Lilly was really suffering, she said "Are you in pain Lilly? I need to know, I have to keep my eye on your progress you must tell me as soon as anything out of order occurs."

"Oh I will Annie but as I don't know when this all will begin I am not sure of anything."

Annie pacified Lilly and felt sorry that her lump of a husband was not here to console her anxiety, where was he indeed? In some other women's bed Annie guessed, she had no kind words for Harry. In fact she never *could stand the man. Turning her thought once more to her dear friend Lilly Annie said "What is it you would most like to do this evening Lilly? Shall we play cards or have you something in mind that you particularly want to do?"*

"I hadn't got as far as thinking about this evening Annie, this afternoon I think we should take down the Christmas decoration it is about time isn't it? Preparation for baby is foremost in my thoughts so we need to be organised don't we?"

"Good thinking Lilly that's the spirit keep your chin up and cheer up, yes we will do that job between us and chat as we go." The small items that had been put into the room for decoration soon were dusted and packed away in a box ready to use again next year. A new Calendar was hung in the kitchen, they both felt as though progress had been made, and Lilly seemed more relaxed. Evening came and the cards were being shuffled when Lilly said.

"Annie I won't be able to play cards for long."

"Why not? You are not yet that tired are you?"

"Not tired so much but the ache in my back is troubling me, I don't have the power to reach

to the table to play, sorry."

"That's alright Lilly, where is this back pain?" Lilly signified by putting the back of her hand across her hips saying

"It has been coming and going all day really but tonight it is strong and won't be ignored." Annie's eyes went up she said

"Dear Lilly I think you may be in early labour, now don't get alarmed the birth won't happen suddenly, the pain will increase and become regular that is when I will need you to climb the stairs and get into your bed, all is well don't worry, come on let us have a couple of hands of cards it will keep you relaxed."

"No Annie I just couldn't my mind is full to overflowing I just need to sit quietly. Do you really think this is it and that my baby will be born very soon?"

"I don't know about very soon, babies take their own time to come but the thing is you have started the process. How about a good hot drink eh? That never did any new Mother any harm. Annie went to the kitchen and came back with two steaming mugs saying

"Here you are Lilly I have bought the biscuits too must keep up your strength you know." Lilly smiled her thanks she was too busy concentrating on her pain to engage in small

talk. How bad did this get she was wondering? The pain was almost unbearable now, not wanting to be a cry baby all she could do was to keep her back cushioned against the chair and wait for more results. Time went by and to Lilly Annie seemed to be in a never ending conversation with her, this was silly Annie knew Lilly would not be able to answer her, in fact Lilly's head was swirling with the pain. In the background she heard Annie say

"Come on now Lilly it is time we went upstairs, your progress is good we will have this baby born in no time at all between us." Annie helped Lilly negotiate the climb upstairs, having to stop on two occasions while the pain passed.

"Sit on the bed Lilly I will prepare you for the birth, let's have these clothes off for a start." Annie pulled Lilly's dress off over her head and loosened her undergarments, these all came off and Lilly put on a lose nightdress. The beads of sweat stood out on Lilly's forehead her whole being was encased in agony, nothing that Annie said registered. Lilly was in a world entirely of her own and she had a job to do.

Hours went by reducing Lilly into a ferment of sheer pain, there was no separating the pain it had been every two minutes and coming strong, now pain was the only thing real to Lilly, trembling and feeling sick and a deep desire to have this baby in her arms pushed her forward she heard Annie say

"Now Lilly push, push with all the strength you have, I am here I will deliver you, trust in me Lilly." Vaguely Lilly heard her words and started to push, the pain was unbearable, a mass of uninterrupted misery that she was locked in, nearer to death she had never been, it seemed an impossible task to bring this baby out into the world, sweat run down her forehead and tears run down her cheeks. Coming now a desire so great to be out of this suffering and free, loosing conscious thought almost passing out at each new effort only Annie's voice calming instruction kept Lilly alive. Annie's voice came through to Lilly once more saying

"Stay with me Lilly keep going push, push, I see baby's head, come on push more and more." Lilly felt as though her legs were being pulled to either side of the room and her vagina was ripping open, Lilly screamed as Annie using her hands gripped the baby's head telling Lilly once more to push Annie pulled and Baby's head was born, the

shoulders at the next push and baby lay
between Lilly's legs. Lilly totally exhausted
lay back while black clouds swamped her.
Annie wrapped the baby into a towel and
turned her attention to Lilly saying,
"Don't give up on me now Lilly your baby is
here." Carefully Annie patted Lilly's face and
saw her dear friend being swallowed up and
slowly drifting away, saying with stress
"Lilly don't give way now come back to your
beautiful baby, not now, not now, please
come back to us Lilly baby needs you." Annie
rubbed Lilly's hands trying to instil life into
the bedraggled and worn form. Tears now
run down Annie's face she had spent all her
energy on Lilly and the baby, she too was
worn and she was faced with an unconscious
Lilly and a new now crying baby. The cord
had to be cut and the condition of Lilly's
vagina had to be seen to, she was still losing
blood. Annie pulled herself together although
she barely knew how and prayed for help.

Lilly stirred and began to ramble, Annie
said
"That's it Lilly open your eyes and see your
lovely Daughter." Annie turned around and
picked up the baby girl laying her on her
Mother's breast Lilly with all the strength she
had left lifted her head and looked on her

Daughter for the very first time, she smiled but was too weak to say anything. Having got Lilly back into the land of the living Annie turned her attention towards baby. She cut the cord and bound the wound wrapped baby tightly into a soft blanket and decided it was time to get a Doctor to come and look at the state of affairs. Lilly needed stitches as baby came she had torn the wall of her vagina, this must be stopped and Annie with her limited knowledge didn't know how to apply stitches, it would mean leaving the house but she had no choice. Quickly pulling on her coat as she went she took the keys and banged the door behind her. Annie ran as fast as her legs would carry her. The Doctor was the first one she came to, she didn't know his name or anything about him Annie must throw herself on to his regard to save life and implore him to see Lilly. No doubt he would reprimand Lilly and herself for trying to do a homespun job and bring baby into the world without a Doctor but Annie was past caring and told the Doctor

"Please Doctor I implore you come and save my friend's life, your fee will be met with in due time, this minute is of paramount importance for you to come right now. The Doctor could tell the importance of Annie's

plea, he picked up his black bag and followed Annie to her home. Annie was so relieved to see that the baby and Lilly were none the worse for being left and let the Doctor take over. Doctor quickly checked the baby to see all was well then turned his attention to Lilly who by now was looking very pale. He spoke to Annie

"Your friend is at the moment in dire straits I will administer the stitching and hope it will stop the bleed, the baby is comfortable and will come to no harm while I see to the Mother." He continued to do the job, Lilly just conscious screamed out as the stitches were pulled together, a very painful procedure indeed. Now a gentle calm took over, the Doctor satisfied he had done all he could to help left saying

"All should be well now it is just a matter of time and nature's way of healing, I advise you to keep your friend in bed for at least ten days and if you do encounter more upset to let me know and I will visit. I will take out the stitches in due cause, the flesh was jagged and ripped so the stitches will take a bit of time to knit together as I said all in good time, I will say goodbye to you now, tend the Lady with care. My fee will be sent in the post." Annie struggled with her own feelings she

*also was worn out and she had now a baby
and a sick friend to take care of. She leaned
over to whisper to Lilly*

*"All is done now Lilly I want you to get well
and strong then you will be able to love this
baby girl and alleviate me of many problems.
For the moment sleep will do you a world of
good, I will try to feed baby with a breast feed
substitute I will do the best I can until you
can feed her yourself as I know you are
longing to do." Lilly fluttered her eyelashes
in recognition that she had heard just what
Annie had said then settled and slept. Annie
made a pot of tea and left everything even the
baby who was now cuddled and safe while
she tried to revive and look at the situation in
a positive fashion. It would all wait until
tomorrow the hell that had been torture for
her and Lilly was over and she thanked God
for that. Annie had drank her tea and was
looking all around the room, it was still in
disarray from the birth. Lilly was in a deep
sleep Doctor had administered a potion that
had quickly put her in this position. The baby
too was quiet Annie did not know where to
start as she began to tidy up, her eyes went
fondly to the cane bedroom chair, she sat
down very wearily. The ordeal had taken the
best part out of her. Her legs were weak and*

her eyes were tired, the cane chair which now she occupied felt good no sooner had she sat down for the intended five minutes her chin dropped on to her chest her eyes fluttered and sleep claimed her.

Annie woke up with a start and her wide eyes gazed at the still untidy scene that lay before her. It was the baby's cry that had brought her out of her short sleep. Knowing what to do Annie hurriedly put on the kettle to boil some water, the fire was very low so the kettle was filled only with the cup of water that she knew she needed. Annie went over to the crib to see that baby was alright and a quick glance at Lilly who was still in a deep sleep all seemed well. The kettle had boiled so Annie went over to the wicker basket to find a baby feeding bottle, all that the basket contained was for baby so the bottle came to hand quickly. Quietly she went over to the crib baby was again passive Annie looked down on this tiny scrap of humanity and said "Rose yes that is the name your Mother has chosen for you, you are indeed sweet as a Rose. Your lips are exactly like a Rosebud so shapely and well formed, well Rosie I must give you your first feed. I think a little condensed milk and boiled water for now, very soon your Mother will feed you and all will be well." Annie picked the tiny form from the crib into her arms kissing baby's forehead as she did so. Annie was glad the Doctor had bound the cord Rosie was now in safe hands and indeed had made her first conquest Annie already loved her.

First things first Annie fed and changed baby Rose put her back in the crib and started again to clear the room so as it would be desirable when Lilly woke up. The sheets Lilly lay in would have to be left until Lilly woke up. Meanwhile Annie methodically made the room as cosy as possible. A fire had been lit to warm the room before baby had arrived, it was now grey ash and embers it had been difficult to boil the kettle an hour ago. Annie pulled the embers together and set some small cobbles of coal on top, the grey ash at the bottom of the fire grate she poked out and drew the ash tin out ready to empty. The dry coal was soon burning now that the ash tin had been removed. Annie felt a bit better after her short sleep and was determined to bring a happy atmosphere into the bedroom, she must drive away all the pain and suffering that Lilly had endured. It was over and Rosie was here. Lilly would be so proud and Annie after her work that had tidied everything up couldn't wait for Lilly to

*join her and look upon her Daughter Rosie
for the first time.*

*Annie felt Lilly move rather than see her
open her eyes but yes her eyes were opening
and as Lilly scanned the room and called for
Annie dear Annie was immediately by her
side. Lilly said*

*"Annie I am awake is everything alright
where is my baby?"*

*"Decided to return to the land of the living
have you Lilly yes everything is alright."*

*"Annie I really have no idea what has gone
on I remember the baby coming and the
awful ordeal of being stitched from then until
now is a blank." Lilly's eyes scanned the
room and settled finally on the crib. Annie in
a soft tone said*

*"Yes Lilly your baby has survived and a more
beautiful baby I have yet to see. You have a
daughter Lilly and she is waiting to be with
her Mother." Annie went over to the crib and
picked up Rosie placing her in her Mother's
arms. Lilly was in a semi sitting position and
held her arms open wide saying*

*"Oh Annie how I have longed for this
moment." A tear fell down as Lilly tried to
control her emotion. Annie also felt this
emotion this moment in time had been
brought about by the solid friendship between*

Annie and Lilly Annie said
"This is the moment you will never forget
Lilly, Rosie so new in your arms and the pain
gone. You will mend from the parts that had
to be stitched all in good time. Yes Lilly you
have a precious little girl there are many that
will envy you, you are so lucky."
"Look at her rosebud lips Annie and when
she opens her eyes I could swear she is
looking at me."
"She senses she is in her Mother's arms Lilly
she won't focus properly for a few weeks yet.
I know what you mean though it is as if she is
appraising her surroundings in an intelligent
manner and who are we to say she is not?
Doctor's don't know everything you know!"

Chapter Twenty Two

Christmas for Harry had been tolerated more than enjoyed mostly his time was spent at his club. He had booked in advance for his Christmas dinner but was very aware of his solitary position. It all seemed so silly walking around with party hats on and singing carols it was not on Harry's agenda. There was one bright spark the cold sore on his lip was at last healing. He eagerly looked forward to seeing Angel again, why Victoria had been so strict about a mere cold sore was beyond him. To feel better would be a treat and to himself he had to admit as yet he didn't feel a hundred per cent well. Winter weather and dark nights he was sure was to blame, what he needed was a bit of sunshine and some regular good food. That was another admission he still was not eating in the proper manner and that was Lilly's fault leaving him in the lurch to go off and have the baby, it was obvious who had the bigger claim on Lilly, he was disgusted… Lilly should be by my side here and now this blasted baby has thrown my life into chaos his thoughts ran on and on always putting Lilly as the one who had offended him and leaving the baby out of the equation. Half a chance and he would strangle the baby and have an end to that, for now he decided to try Victoria's place once more. He had a lengthy look in the mirror and grimaced at what he saw, bags under his eyes wrinkles down under his chin and his teeth yellow for some reason. Knowing he had to pull himself together was not an easy thought, he consulted his wardrobe, hmm no change there then! His one trump card was a brand new shirt which without a doubt would be worn today. He began to get excited his own darling Angel would be in his arms very soon. Harry went to the bathroom and started with shaving deciding the stubble on his chin was not doing him any favours. Now washed and cleaned he felt better. The shirt was carefully put on and he felt his confidence returning. No, Harry was not going to be put down for long.

He arrived at Victoria's place after a brisk walk and smartly tapped the door. The grid was opened and Victoria said
"Oh it is you Harry haven't seen you for weeks, have you got rid of your sore lip?"
"Yes Victoria at last it has gone and I want to visit Angel may I come in?"
"Yes come in Harry but there is something I must tell you." The door was unbolted and

Harry was allowed in he said

"That's better I feel at home now, when can I go up to Angel?"

"I am sorry Harry but Angel has made clear to me that she will not receive you."

"Not receive me." Harry blurted out

"She knows she and I have the fondest of understandings. Why does she not want to see me?"

"It occurred when you had your sore lip, you see Harry I give my girls chance to have their own opinion about whom they see, I am only interested in the money they earn me and if Angel doesn't want to see you that is that."

Harry was floored he couldn't imagine Angel rejecting him he felt as though the rug had been pulled from under his feet, devastated is the word like a lost soul. Victoria studied his disappointed face and said,

"Wouldn't it be better Harry if you went in and had a bit of fun with the other girls, they have missed you, a couple of drinks and a warm welcome would do you no end of good, don't be downhearted perhaps Angel will change her mind when she knows you are in much better health."

"Yes I suppose you are right but I must say I am feeling my heart strings pulled, I must see Angel as soon as I can, I leave it up to you to *tell her of my lonely heart."*

"Yes Harry I surely will, come on my dear let's get your coat off and tell the girls they have a visitor, you will feel as right as nine pence very shortly you'll see." Harry followed Victoria into the smoke laden den of pretty girls. He didn't waste his time he let the girls devour him.

Going home in the early hours of the morning was to say the least depressing, his money was spent, he had a feeling of doom and gloom and he ached all over. Now he had to face a world without Angel, that is unless she had a change of mind, how could she have rejected him her Harry? His feeling of nothing being worthwhile saturated his entire being, he paid good money, he always left good tips and in his own fashion he loved Angel, hadn't she said many times that she loved him too? Where had he gone so wrong?

Girls or no girls including Angel the truth was he was glad to be back and in his own bed, why did he feel so low, the sore throat and the swollen glands still persisted alongside the ache in his entire body ,once again a Doctor came into the equation and once again Harry would not submit. Lilly should be here to tend him. He looked around the dishevelled bedroom nothing was in its right place the dressing table was loaded with male lotions and potions, socks and underwear littered the floor, empty mugs and cups not washed and collecting fluff. The bottles on the dressing table all had a sticky trail of liquid running down the outsides, mainly cough mixture bottles, to finally sit in its own pool on the dressing table top. Yuk! I believe is the appropriate word. Harry didn't care it was not his job to clean it was Lilly's job and why wasn't she here to do it? Sleep claimed the chaotic thoughts. Harry was his own jailer he needed to accept Lilly with the baby but would he? He would not.

Upon waking Harry collected his bedraggled mess of a man and put on his dressing gown, glowering at the same untidy mess he had noticed when he went to bed. The moment he got downstairs a thought came that might help…if Lilly wasn't here to clean up then he would find a housekeeper. Ah! He smiled to himself I don't pay Lilly any money so I think some lady would take over her cleaning jobs for next to nothing. I am not going to clean, perish the thought! Where can I put in an advertisement for a cleaner? Perhaps the local shop has an advert board.

This gave Harry purpose so he got dressed

and made out a card as to where to apply for the cleaning job. It had bucked him up thinking he had a solution. At the shop he asked about leaving his advert, they said yes they could oblige him and took Harry's card. Harry watched as it was pinned securely on the board. Saying his thanks he left.

It wasn't long before his door was tapped and the job applied for. He interviewed a middle aged lady and said,
"I am sure you would do a good job for me but I must see the other lady's before I make my decision you understand? It wouldn't be fair otherwise. Good day. Before the day was out he had seen five ladies and thought the younger lady suited him best. Her name was Alice she would be nippy on her feet although maybe her cooking skills would not be as good as the elder ladies. Oh yes Harry was going to get his money's worth no doubt about it.

Alice was in her early thirty's she had problems of her own and needed the money Harry would pay her, not that she was too keen on tidying up Harry's grotty mess. It was a means to an end, she had three children and her husband had lost his job. Not that she told Harry that, the least he knew about her private life the better. They

*agreed that she would start the following
Monday. On that day it was pouring with rain
and cold, Alice had been given a key to let
herself in. She opened the front door Brr the
cold of the house hit her it, was like an
icebox. Leaving her coat on she proceeded to
go into the kitchen where the pots were piled
up all needing washing in the sink. Where to
begin she looked around getting her bearings.
Yes for a fact the fire needed lighting when
the kitchen was warm the jobs in there could
be tackled easier. My goodness she thought
look at the state of the ovens, before she
could light a fire the black burnt on food
must be scraped off the oven door and floor.
Taking her coat off she shivered but her
sleeves needed to be rolled up to get this dirty
task done. Scrubbing and rubbing and
scraping the foul residue into a sheet of paper
was a thankless task but it had to be done.
There were no proper scouring tools to help
so a knife from the kitchen drawer had to be
used.
Again I say Yuk! Poor Alice she would surely
earn her money. At last the job was done just
as she heard Harry stepping downstairs. He
came straight into the kitchen again
scowling,
"No fire yet, I thought that was the first thing*

you would attend to." It was a statement but Alice felt as though she had been told off. "I was going to light the fire Sir then I noticed the ovens where in such a mess and would burn on more if the fire was lit. I can light the fire now as I have seen to the ovens."

"Well be quick about it, a colder morning than this I cannot remember snow is in the air I am sure. You get that fire going so the kettle can be boiled for tea and I will have a bowl of warming porridge so a saucepan of milk needs heating. Come on girl come on what do you think I am paying you for? Alice frowned he wasn't giving her chance to reply she wasn't feeling in her element, cleaning other peoples mess up after it had stood for days was not the thing she enjoyed doing. She went out for coal. Returning and asking where the kindling wood was kept she shuddered both at the task in hand and the coldness of the kitchen. A lively fire would do both Alice and Harry good. What a start to Alice's new job. Harry never ventured to give Alice a helping hand, physical work was not his scene. Soon enough Alice had sorted out the fire and it was merrily sending large flames up the chimney that is until a large fall of soot fell down the chimney and practically smothered the fire. Harry found fault again.

"You have drawn that up too fast girl, now look what you have done."

"I haven't done anything sir it is the chimney that needs sweeping."

"Another expense is there no end to your needs; get the fire rake and remove the soot woman, don't tell me you are as useless as you are." Alice resented his accusations, her own home although very small was spick and span a regime of set plans every day kept all in tidy order. Here in this kitchen was weeks or even months of neglect, nothing could be well done until it all was set right and order restored. She said nothing Harry had too much to say without her joining his patter of discontent. Alice had been pleased to get the job but now she was not too sure. Harry was not the kind of man she had taken him for. His house was nothing short of dirty and for her work Alice had to restore it to order, this was not going to be easy.

The time passed and day by day Alice did her utmost to restore Harry's home, he never gave her a word of praise or encouragement, Alice found him to be a cold man set in his own ways, when payday came he reluctantly gave her the sum due but his attitude told

Alice he was loathe to part with the money. Asking for new dishcloths or scouring powder sent Harry into a rage saying there was no need for new stock and to use the ones she had, these were falling into ribbons with more holes than cloth, and the scouring powder had been used so very much the quantity was sadly depleted. Alice needed these things to get the place liveable again her hands were sore because of all the water they had been in, what is more her patience was beginning to run out one of these days she would give Harry a surprise and place the mop and bucket into his hands along with the shredded floor cloths and the mean bit of carbolic soap that was used on the well worn scrubbing brush. A skivvy that is what she felt, her husband wanted to put the scales right and was trying hard to find a job, his lack of education made it difficult jobs were scarce so Alice had to hold her peace or there would be no money going into her house at all and three children had to be fed without counting her husband and herself. Times were certainly hard Alice tried to make the best of it. If only Harry could be more pleasant and tell her she was doing a good job was that too much to ask of this man? The only thing she could say for him was he didn't trouble her with sexual advances or cheekily slap her bottom, he must have known just what Alice would do if he had tried it on, yes left post haste without a second thought. Alice's life was clean and her marriage stable and that is the way it would always be. It crossed Alice's mind as to where be this man's wife? She knew he had a wife perhaps she had died but Alice didn't really think she was dead. There were remains of a lady's wardrobe upstairs, and underwear in drawers that were definitely female. Small size shoes in the cupboard but Harry never ever mentioned this absent lady. Alice decided to let sleeping dogs lie and not ask about these things that puzzled her, best way it wasn't anything to do with her anyway. Secretly Harry was well pleased with the house and how it looked mind you he paid a good wage so he expected things to be done right, he wasn't going to give praise to Alice she might ask for more money and that would never do he was reluctant to give her the money she earned now, but he must admit she was useful, the house felt more like a home and the fires were regularly lit keeping damp and condensation from seeping in. Now that his cold sore had gone he felt a bit more like himself, but it was a feeling of being under the weather all the time, that annoyed him most, his bones ached and his glands intermittently kept swelling giving him a sore throat, at times he felt nauseous and just plain dead tired. No he didn't want a Doctor they cost money he would be fully well again soon of that he had no doubt. Still he wanted Angel and still Angel didn't want him. It was one of the reasons he wanted to get fully better, he would show her just what she was missing then she would fall into his arms and all would be well.

Chapter Twenty three

Lilly was up and running about like a lady with a purpose but of course she was a lady with a purpose. Now that she had Rosie her world was more complete than it had been for a long time. Both Lilly and Annie loved having Rosie to look after she had given them a new lease of life they even felt younger. Nothing was too much trouble and Rosie thrived on this gift of their love a picture to behold. Now her eyes did really follow them around the room and she gleefully laughed and played with both Lilly and Annie. Lilly had no jealous thought about Rosie taking to Annie in such a way they were all in their element and life was sweet. Lilly had stopped going into different villages to shop she strolled around as though she owned the place and so proud of her Daughter. There were a few very surprised people who stopped by to see Lilly's new Daughter, exclaiming how much she looked like Lilly and Lilly was glad about that, there was no way she wanted Harry's features to be resembled in her baby. Lilly wasn't too sure about never seeing Harry again, the way he had treated her did not endear his memory. What did cross Lilly's mind was how happy Harry would have been if he had accepted this beautiful baby, their marriage would have been complete. Silly Harry! He had shot himself in the foot as the saying goes, now he had to reap what he had sown and these were seeds of hate and denial. Lilly had heard a few comments about Harry's failing heath but chose to ignore them, he only had himself to look after Lilly lived on the money her Father had left her she was comfortable as long as she kept her eye on the purse strings. As far as general living she was happy with Annie by her side. Harry had given her the run around most of the time seeing to his wants and needs, never being satisfied, grumbling at the least thing wrong oh yes she could gladly dismiss Harry. Looking after the baby was nothing compared to looking after Harry he had been a dead weight to Lilly and she was glad to be free. It didn't matter a bit that Harry had not been to see or acknowledge Rosie in any way, Lilly wanted a clean cut and to leave her past behind her she had very nearly hit rock bottom while she carried Rosie and almost lost her life in the birthing of baby. No she would not look back she and sweet Rosie was happy and she didn't want that to change.

The weeks went by and Harry had not

contacted Lilly as she thought he might when the baby was born, in her innermost self Lilly was not sorry Harry had kept away it would be too much of a gesture for Harry to be concerned about her. Speaking to Annie on the subject Lilly said

"Did you think Harry might come around to call after the baby was born Annie?"

"It crossed my mind Lilly but knowing Harry as we do, we neither of us expected a visit. It is perhaps just as well. He would be thinking of his own self even if he had bothered to visit."

"Sometimes Annie I get an overwhelming desire to show my beautiful Rosie to Harry he is her Father after all."

"Some Father he is and that's for sure, Rosie is better off without his approval if you ask me. What she has never had she won't miss."

"I understand what you are saying Annie but how is Rosie going to react when she is old enough to realise her Father didn't want her?"

"Cross that bridge when and if you come to it Lilly, if Harry ever acknowledges Rosie it will be when she is growing up and looking pretty maybe then he will step in and want the flattery of conceiving such a Daughter. I don't trust Harry and never did, I wouldn't

put anything past him, he has a devious mind and things have to be right for him as he puts himself first second and last."

"Perhaps he will mellow as he gets older Annie, at some point we have to meet because I want our joint "Will" to leave the house to Rosie, I will leave any money I may have at the time to Rosie and Harry will have to please himself about his own bank account. The house you see is in both our names, half belongs to me by Law so Harry can't do very much without consulting me, which I must say I am glad of considering the circumstances."

"I didn't realise Lilly that half of the house was yours how did that come about?"

"It was when my Father left me my inheritance, Harry was the one that suggested it he wanted more cash in his bank balance so he actually sold half the house to me. I never thought anything would be wrong between us and I gladly agreed because if anything happened to Harry the house would automatically be my own and so secured my future. Rosie was well out of the picture at that time and it seemed the best thing to suit us both."

"Well that is a turn up for the books Lilly counting the money that is held in bricks and

mortar you are a Lady of considerable wealth. I'll be bold over, I have never thought of you in that way, a dark horse and no mistake!" Annie giggled to herself in appreciation of the fact that had been disclosed saying

"So we haven't done with Mr. Harry have we Lilly, he has a rude awakening coming his way, I wonder if he has thought about the situation?"

"Actually Annie I don't think he would have he always treated the house as his own. Many a time I would try to put the fact forward that half the house was mine but he would talk all around the subject he was like that, never wanted any other opinion than his own. I let him have his own say because at that time it made no difference to me and life was quieter, which was worth a lot."

"Then it will be quite a shock when you want to change your "Will" won't it? My goodness I would like to be a fly on the wall when he is given the facts of this matter, he will be livid."

"Annie go and put the kettle on there's a dear, I feel worn out just talking on the subject. I shall make no move as yet but one foot out of place and I shall insist on a better understanding as regards leaving Rosie her due money. It is Rosie's inheritance and I

must make sure she will get it." Annie left the
room to go and make tea, but she could see
Lilly meant just as she said, at last she was
standing her ground and Annie was glad of
it. Harry had held the whip hand too long.
Now Lilly had Rosie and the event had
instilled Lilly to count what was her own to
leave Rosie, a very proper thought.

Funnily enough their talk had cleared the
air and Annie knew better where Lilly stood
bringing in the tea she said
"You know Lilly you have really surprised me
I never would have thought Harry would let
you buy half of the house."
"It was for Harry's own benefit Annie and I
had enough money left to me to pay for the
house and keep a tidy sum in my bank and
look how handy my inheritance has become.
All the baby costs have been dealt with and I
still have enough money to live on without
asking Harry for a penny, my Father would
have approved I am glad to say.

Chapter Twenty four

Having Alice in to cook and clean had not changed Harry's outlook and it should have done, all around there were signs of a woman's hand, it had taken some weeks for Alice to make this improvement, everything she touched wanted cleaning and the sticky dust in the bedroom sickened her, she picked up the bottles of this and that mixture and had a bowl of warm water to take off the spillage that had run down to the dressing table top. Moving the offending bottles another sticky mess was uncovered as the mixture had made a pool that ran under the cotton lace doyley that had been put there to be admired. It all had to come off for washing Alice had to just get on with it and grit her teeth. There was no encouraging words spoken or yet even a thank you, no sign from this man other than to grumble when things were not done that he expected to be done. Again Harry was Harry wanting his own way. When he felt ill he took it out on anyone that was near enough to listen, poor Alice at the start of this job she had been pleased to be chosen, she and her husband needed the money as paying rent had become too much for her husband to do on his own. Alice expected to be talked to in a civil fashion but Harry just couldn't be bothered and Alice couldn't wait for her hours to be finished. Harry was a pain and to be quite blunt Harry was literally in pain it was one of those pains that never seemed to leave him for long and depressed him completely. He ached all over and felt nausea, his appetite was poor his love life almost none existent. Angel would still not see him and it was her to his way of thinking that was causing his weariness. He wanted to feel alive again and Angel made him feel alive and needed. Why did the women in his life treat him so badly? Lilly had left his house... but that was good riddance, now Angel was acting awkward. His mind turned to Alice his housekeeper, what could she do for him in bed? Was it worth a try? She was young and pretty in her own way might just fit the bill.

As an added extra she was readily available Harry thought he was so very clever Alice could cook and clean for him and see to his bedtime needs with no extra salary, he would give it a try and his eyes shone at the prospect. He lay on his bed and planned how he could bring this about, casual that was the way he would show her attention and try to endear him to her, it was only a few days

*after when Harry tried to put his plan into
action*

*Harry could hear Alice in the kitchen
what was she doing he wondered? He had
been sitting before the fire and felt relaxed so
he strolled into the kitchen. Alice was on her
knees an opportunity that Harry had waited
for. Casually walking to the table he had to
pass Alice so he gave her a suggestive slap on
her bottom then dug his fingers in to pinch
the flesh. Alice was startled she at once
turned her head and gave Harry a scornful
look but said nothing. Harry had made
contact so he let things be for the moment he
would stalk her and find each moment as
they presented. Devious and sly he knew what
he was doing. He went back to his fireside
chair so as not to cause Alice any suspicious
thoughts that may have passed her mind, he
would have her, and why not? He paid for
her services didn't he? He still considered
himself in his prime and any girl should be
honoured by his attention. How Harry had
got it so wrong we will never know but he still
had an appetite for the ladies.*

*Alice was very glad when the time came
for home, should she tell her husband of this
intrusion of her privacy? Deciding it would
only anger and put doubt in his mind Alice*

decided to put the incident out of her mind. Her family needed the money she was earning and in all honesty Harry had only made a pass at her, she knew from past experience men liked to be thought of as sexy and did a number of decidedly silly things to prove their manhood. Now Alice would be aware, Harry would be kept at arm's length in future, not that Alice had enticed him he had approached her from the rear and took her completely by surprise. Silly Harry yet again! As Harry was not feeling too bright he didn't approach Alice any further. His thoughts were in chaos his libido almost none existent, in fact he actually kept out of Alice's sight he did not want her to see this weak side, he just couldn't understand, why the weakness? He was eating fairly well and getting his sleep, where was his old pizzas he could charm the ladies with no effort at all knowing just what to say and of course what to do. Dissatisfied with this daily routine of existing and not as he called it… living, this life was no good to Harry, he had to shine, the brightest button in the box, but it was not coming naturally.

Surely he wasn't going to land up at the Doctors whom he despised. Paying for his advice would not be an option he would get right soon despite Lilly and her offspring. In his calculating mind it was all Lilly's fault, he wanted to make her pay but how? He would find a way he was sure. He calculated the months that had gone by and was sure Lilly would have delivered her baby of course he would be the last to know, in any case he didn't want to know, fancy a brat running around his house and eating his food, he shuddered at the thought. What could he stop that Lilly had of his owning? He went through all the possibilities and had to admit there was very little he could consider. Something would come to mind he was not going to be beat.

All the time feeling low Harry had never given Alice another thought and Alice was very pleased about that. Harry was hells bent on getting his own back, yet it was he that was doing the wrong, never in any way did Harry ever think things that had gone so badly wrong was due to his lack of consideration his conscience never told him to look again, he was completely without blame in his own eyes. He didn't long for Angel, he didn't want the girls fussing around him or pick up a stray on the night streets, this floored Harry, he began not to attend his club, but he did drink more whiskey in the drowning of his sorrows. A middle aged sorrowful man with thinning hair and bald patches, his teeth were troubling him and his body ached. Was there no justice in the world? Harry wallowed in self pity, he had degraded his own self with his appetite for sex and all that went with it. His head in his hands he almost wept. What was happening to him? Age, he wouldn't admit it! Lack of understanding didn't help. Soon a Doctor would have to be consulted, this feeling had to be checked before he was no more his mind went in the search for a good Consultant.

Harry fought the urge to stay in bed, dragging his body over to the wash stand getting washed and shaved was quite an ordeal. Nevertheless he managed it, he wanted to go and see his colleagues' at the club feeling sure they would have the address of a good physician.

On arrival he headed for the chair in the corner not wanting to be noticed, he would pick out the companion he wanted to speak to, he didn't really want to converse at all, but he badly needed advice. Now his eyes moved around the room searching.

He spotted a very earthy looking fellow and recognised potential, Harry was sure he had been ill and was now getting better again so he would know who to contact. How to catch this fellow's eye? He couldn't just walk up to him and ask about his physician no he must be delicate about his enquiry. There was a vacant chair close to where this fellow was sitting so Harry sidled up and asked if he could sit beside him.

"Are you keeping this chair for someone Sir?"

"No it is vacant please sit down if you want to." Harry started a quiet conversation about the weather of late. Half hour later he was able to talk about what he wanted to know.

"I believe you have been ill are you quite better now?"

"Yes thank you, it is good to be out and about again...Harry, you did say your name was Harry didn't you?"

"Yes and you are Bill if I am not mistaken?"

"I haven't seen you in the club before Harry but perhaps I have not attended for some time due to illness anyway I am glad to make your acquaintance."

"Have you been seeing a physician Bill?"

"Yes a good man I put my trust in him and here I am almost all well again, I must say I

thought his costs were steep but without health the world becomes unobtainable so it is money well spent."

"Do you think you could give me this Doctor's name and address it is always as well to consult a Doctor whom someone has had success with and you never know when you might need professional information."

"Of course, but I hope you never need to use a Doctor." Smiles were exchanged and the name and address wrote on a piece of scrap paper.

"Very good of you, as you say I hope I never have to contact this Doctor, at the moment I am as fit as a fiddle." Harry told this barefaced lie knowing if he said he was ill other members of the club would hear of it and he wanted to save face.

"Sorry I haven't the time to carry on our pleasant conversation Bill I am pleased to have met you and will look for you in the club at a future date, time flies doesn't it." Harry said his goodbyes and had achieved what he had set out to do.

Chapter Twenty five

Lilly and Annie now knew all there was to know about each other, Lilly found it most therapeutically an advantage to have Annie and to be able to tell her just anything. Discussing the matter in hand often found a solution in many dilemmas. Annie was steadfast and strong giving Lilly the support she badly needed. Baby Rose was a delight for them both and had their full attention. Now there seemed a lot less time to sit and brood over Harry, he became yesterday's news. Now and again Lilly would think what Harry would have made of the baby, surely on seeing this lovely little mite it would have softened his heart? These thoughts had been turning over in Lilly's mind while sitting with Annie, turning to her friend Lilly said "Annie I still have to see Harry."
"What on earth for?"
" I told you some time ago, for the sake of Rosie and her inheritance. Our present Will states when I die Harry will get my share of the house I do not want Harry to have the house I want to provide Rosie with an inheritance of her own my Father's money that he willed to me has become of paramount importance. I want to be sure

Rosie will have her own money to fall back on when I am no longer here to share her life."

"Yes I see what you mean Lilly, Harry is not going to like that though is he?"

"No I expect he will be livid, that is why I keep putting off the evil day, but I must do this deed for my peace of mind."

"I will go with you if you want me to Lilly."

"No Annie I would rather you stayed and looked after Rosie, I must face Harry on my own. He has not done one thing to recognise Rosie as his Daughter and in my view he has forfeited the right to be named as Father. I despise the man I am at last seeing him in his true colours."

"Don't you think you will soften when you confront him?"

"I will not, he will probably flaunt his freedom in front of my face, I almost expect it. I shall stand my ground, he will wonder about the woman I have become. It will shock him to see me in a demanding role but I will not back down, not this time he has hurt me in so many ways. I think the sooner the better but I do want to be in control when I do this deed so I must get all the facts together and go well armed so to speak. He will think he can tie me into knots with his knowledge so I *must be well advised so that Harry can't hoodwink me with fancy words."*

"I certainly don't envy you Lilly, he never did like me and I know how lethal his mood can be and his cutting words."

"It is obvious the first move I make will be to visit a good Solicitor he will tell me how to phrase the subject and be objective in my approach. Oh yes he is not getting away from this one my Rosie's future is at stake and she means the entire world to me."

"I agree Lilly it is a good job all those years ago you purchased half of the house although at the time I suppose it had a lot less importance. Houses have increased in value quite considerably, it is the battle you will have in getting this legalised that bothers me. Let's shelve it for this moment and I will go and make a pot of tea, this serious talk has dried my mouth but I am with you every step of the way Lilly." Annie left Lilly who was still deep in thought. Returning with a tray with tea and biscuits Annie sat down saying "I don't want to be nosey but I feel I must ask is there a mortgage on your house?"

"No thank goodness it is a straight forward split and I can't see any way Harry can keep out Rosie's name as my choice to leave my half to." Annie poured the tea saying

"Do you realise Lilly unless Harry has the capitol to give to Rosie at the time of inheritance he would be forced into selling the house to pay Rosie your half?"

"He didn't care where I was to go when I came to live with you so he would have to buy a smaller property and sell as you said. Annie I most adamantly want Rosie to inherit not Harry, it is my money from my Father that went into the buying half, it was at Harry's request, now he would have to give Rosie her due demands and as you are here Annie I will ask you to be executor to make perfectly sure that this wish is carried through."

"Yes I will do that for you, that is if I live beyond your years, as an alternative I think you would have to ask the chosen Solicitor to carry out that task for you, it will probably cost you but it will be well worth the effort and all will be signed sealed and eventually delivered with little or no bother, it also will give you peace of mind cos you know how Harry can manoeuvre his position for his own good."

"Only too well Annie, I am glad we have talked on this subject soon I will be able to put the wheels in motion, I just want to feel a bit stronger and ready to face the ordeal, because I know it will be not something I can

*do lightly. Is there any more tea in the pot
Annie I could drink another cup."*

*"I will go and make a fresh one Lilly this has
stood and will be too strong, won't be a
minute dear." Lilly said*

*"Harry will not like this move in any way he
always kept this fact of joint ownership as a
secret, he wanted to have the upper hand and
led his friends to think the house had been
paid for by himself alone, he showed off that
fact well the time has come for the truth I
shall stand by my word until all is settled."*

*"Yes I can tell you mean business Lilly,
Harry as always portrayed himself as the big
"I am" your move will bring him down to size
and long overdue if you ask me."*

*Lilly didn't know really where to begin
Harry had always dealt with money matters
night and day it was on her mind. Taking
Rosie out in her perambulator and reading
the brass plaque's that told of the particular
Solicitor that held his business on the
premises. Two names she chose to write down
these two being, "Mr. Strong" and the second
"Mr. Penny" she would make her choice
later and then make an appointment. Lilly did
her shopping and then took a steady walk
home. Annie greeted her saying*

"Did you find what you were looking for

Lilly?"

"I haven't been into any office but I have a couple of names that attracted me." Lilly told Annie her choices Annie said

"I should go for "Mr Penny" it is a money problem you have to sort out and his name is very apt you obviously thought so yourself, you don't know any of the Solicitors so stick with "Mr Penny"

"Yes I will Annie next time I go out I will make an appointment and see the fellow, I may see him in person before I see him for the job in hand, I will ask at the reception if I may be introduced if I catch them in a quiet moment he may oblige me." Annie could tell how Lilly felt and she wished she could help more but it was such a private thing that Lilly was dealing with and Annie knew Lilly would have to sort this one out for her own self esteem. She needed to know the facts.

Chapter Twenty six

As soon as Harry was home doubts began to fester in his mind he had the name of a decent Doctor but he was very reluctant to follow up on the advice he had been given. Bill had said the Doctors fees were not cheap that had given Harry cause for thought. Maybe he didn't need a Doctor, he had been feeling a bit better of late, he hesitated then dismissed the conversation all together thinking... I will get a good elixir from the apothecary I have been taking stuff for a cold and maybe this isn't a cold, I am not paying a Doctor if I can possibly do without one, they tell you anything to get money out of you. Here was silly Harry fighting shy of spending on Doctor's fees no wonder he was suffering. He didn't even know the illness that had befallen him lest know how to cure it. He was gauging by his sex drive just how well or unwell he was. Still eying Alice up of course at a safe distance, he was planning to make his move as soon as he was able to carry out the deed in question. He had a picture now of Alice in his mind and because he was not able to perform he made lurid pictures of her complying with his needs, a fantasy world with no substance but it gave him his pleasure and Harry only thought of Harry full stop. If Lilly was around he could have played around enough to satisfy his male ego never thinking of how it served Lilly that didn't matter. What did matter was Harry's cunning way with the ladies, always he must be top dog, the only person that he had considered was Angel but he was far too weak in body to tempt Angel to lie with him. In fact the thought depressed Harry but he thrust it to one side and carried on in his own sweet way thinking of himself as still debonair and youthful, it was this dragging ache he had all over, there must be a cure without spending, he would find it and when he was well he would paint the town red everyone would know Harry was still a kid on the block, he would show them, he would push away Victoria and go to his beloved Angel then she would fall into his arms with no hesitation. The day was longed for but was very slow in coming. What have I done to deserve such a reckoning? Harry asked! He was never at fault not this time, in fact not any time. He went to lie on his bed still with Alice in mind, planning how to captivate her attention. She was a nice little thing a good deal younger than Harry. Harry liked young girls they had vim and vigour to please his whims, perhaps in a few moments he would call Alice and ask for tea to be brought up, now how could he advance his position and find out if Alice would accommodate his desire. At this moment he didn't want full sex, just to play around a bit and see where her thoughts lay as regards his own desire. Harry rang the service bell and called Alice. "Did you call Sir?"

"Yes would you please bring me a pot of tea up, I was hoping you would join me and tell me something about yourself, if you prefer you can bring up the whisky and take a glass or two of that with me."

"Indeed not Sir, I will gladly bring your tea but I have nothing I want to talk about, my life has to be apart from my work, my husband would be very annoyed with me if I furthered our acquaintance." Harry sized her up and saw he was not going to get what he wanted, not this time anyway. He said "I did not wish to offend you Alice, just to get a little better acquainted, for many hours we live in close proximity I always like to get to know any staff that work for me." For once Harry was at a loss as regards what to say. He edged in,

"What is your husband's name Alice?"
"I don't think it is necessary to discus that

with you, I do my work to your satisfaction don't I?"

"Oh yes Alice indeed I would be lost without you, please don't take offence I want you to relax with me more, I would like to be friends not solely your employer." Alice adjusted her apron and brought herself up to full height saying

"No Sir, it is better we kept the position we are in, you have my respect and I think I have yours I wish to leave it that way."

"A pity Alice, I must say I could teach you a thing or two but if you are not willing to learn so be it. Close the door as you go out I shall not want the tea I am going to rest." Harry had lost this round but he was not one to give up at the first hurdle, at least he had broached the subject of companionship who knows Alice might soften if he wasn't too pushy.

" In the distance he heard the front doorbell ring who could it be? He wasn't expecting anyone, thinking that Alice would answer the door he let it ring, but Alice did not answer she must be in the garden Harry thought so he got up and put on his dressing gown in order to answer the door...confounded nuisance whoever it was. Arriving at the door Harry opened it, he said

"Oh it is you." His tone was nothing if not stern saying

"What do you want?" Abrupt, so this lady answered him in the same manner.

"I have business to discuss with you Harry."

"You are not getting any money out of me so you can decidedly turn yourself around and go back the way you came." Lilly steeled herself

"No I am here and I want to discuss our Will."

"Our Will! that was settled many moons ago I might have known it would come down to money, that is unless you were begging for your place here beside me and I can tell you here and now both requests are negative. Where have you left the brat you gave birth to? Not here with you I see. Quite conclusively I do not want to see or hear from either of you ever so be off." Lilly summoned all her will power to keep her tone within sanity level saying

"Yes I know all that you want Harry but this time you cannot have it, half this house belongs to me and I want to step inside to discuss that fact. That is unless you want the whole street to know your business for I will have it out with you whether you like it or not." Harry had never seen Lilly in this

commanding role she had changed so very much it astounded him. Having no choice he asked her in, Lilly went straight through to the sitting room uninvited, underneath her façade her legs were like jelly there was no way she would let Harry know this, so carried on showing only confidence and pride. Out of her handbag she drew a paper a copy of their Will. Harry was informed. Quite honestly Harry was bewildered what did Lilly actually want? He knew she had a fair way of getting it with her positive attitude, now he was worried he said

"Just what is it you are after Lilly? I don't want to play guessing games a few facts if you please." Lilly was jubilant she had Harry now, he would have to listen to her he had realised the importance of her demands, this was no game Lilly was playing. Bluffing her way forward she stated her case and Harry listened.

"You do see don't you Harry When I die I will certainly want to leave my Daughter a lump sum to help her should she see hard times. Of course you will be able to live as you always have in this house until such times as you die. I would hope you would want our Daughter to inherit my share and alongside of it your share. If you object to

this then it will be my own share that my Daughter inherits. I need you to see a Solicitor with me and get the new Will drawn up. I shall not be bothering you for any more money for myself I have an adequate supply from my Father's Will for me to live on and bring up dear Rosie, yes that is her name Harry and she is as pretty as any rose you may see." Lilly could see venom developing in Harry's face he said

"You have been nothing but trouble since the first day you knew you were pregnant. This brat has stolen my life, instead of doing your duty and looking after me you chose to give birth…and to a girl indeed. Now you say she will have half of this house, is there no ending to this farce?"

"This is not a farce Harry as you put it, common sense leads me to this solution and I will have my way. Arrange a meeting with our Solicitor and get this done. Now is the time, you won't be any the worse off yourself and I shall be satisfied." Lilly had him and he knew it, he said a few chosen words and then asked Lilly to leave. Lilly had done what she required herself to do and was more settled she had confronted Harry and won she had no doubt he would look for loopholes but the initial and most important request was going

forward. Now she was ready to leave, the house gave her the creeps Harry was welcome to live his remaining years in solitude, it need not have been that way but he was a man that would not bend so the consequences were all of his own making. As Lilly left, Harry went back to his bed to lay down…what next? He thought all my women are against me. He opened a drawer and from that he took out a whiskey bottle, drinking deeply straight from the bottle he obliterated his encounter with Lilly.

Chapter Twenty seven

Lilly hurried home, it had taken more out of her than she realised standing up to Harry was still a major job. She whisked by people and shops taking care only of her footing as ice still remained here and there. Getting home to Annie she went straight in and said "I am so glad to be home Annie, put the kettle on my mouth is so dry, I had a job to finish speaking to Harry. He never knew though I played my part very well." Lilly sat down in an easy chair Annie asked

"What did he say Lilly and more to the point what did you say?"

"Me? I kept straight to the point Annie, at first he didn't want to know not until I said I would state my case right there on his doorstep for the next door to hear if he did not ask me in and listen. To tell you the truth Annie I was just as aware of his wrath as I used to be but I wasn't going to let him know that of course. Do you know Annie I had a moment when I almost felt sorry for him, he is not at all well and a shadow of his old self to say the least. I didn't ask after his health I just wanted to get out of the house as soon as I possibly could, I think he has a housekeeper as things were in tidy order... just as long as

it isn't me running around after him he is welcome to a maid. I don't know why I should feel sorry for him at all, I suppose I remembered the better days...that is if there were any."

"Sorry for Harry? Oh no Lilly you mustn't think about feeling sorry, look how he has treated you and Rosie he had no sorrow for you did he in your hour of great need. I can't stand the man. Did he ask to see Rosie?"

"No on the contrary he still had the birth as a thing I conjured up to spite him and he thinks a girl is an insult and can't possibly be his own child. I could have stopped all day just talking about the subject but it would not have made the slightest difference. He will not commit to Rosie and it has made my case stronger, Rosie ...will...have her inheritance I have completely made up my mind and with no strings attached such as Harry contesting the Will after my death."

"He wouldn't do that surely Lilly."

"Oh yes he would, Harry and his money are never going to be parted, he was an accountant you remember? This time I shall tie the strings tightly and leave no if's and butt's Rosie will inherit."

"No wonder you need a cup of tea, sorry I have to put the kettle on to boil it won't be

long, settle yourself down Lilly." Annie and Lilly quietly sat together; Rosie was asleep a good time for them to talk things over.

"You say you didn't enquire about Harry's health Lilly?"

"No I certainly did not but it was clear to see, he has lost a lot of weight and had that grey look about his face, his walk was stooped and everything about him denoted illness. I mustn't forget either Harry is getting on in years now his debonair character is bound to be fading time stands still for no-one, perhaps it is just aging that I noticed but I really think there is another underlying reason."

"I might meet any of his friends Lilly, I will try to get to know what it is ailing Harry."

"As Harry and I are safely in the past I won't let it worry me Annie, I don't want to know really, it is not now my affair and I thank goodness for that. He was a trial to live with when he was younger and healthy so I pity anyone who has to take the sharp end of his tongue now. I wonder who his housekeeper is. An unfortunate person that's for sure."

Rosie began to wake so Lilly went to her, picking the precious little mite up she cradled her in her arms thinking…this is one thing Harry can't undo if he doesn't want you my precious I certainly do. Lilly's whole

*countenance altered as she tended her baby
the love overflowed and she was whole again.
Annie was happy to see this kind of love it
made all else seem futile, the depth of feeling
a Mother has is beyond any other and the tie
was binding.*

*Mr Wright was the name of the Solicitor
that Lilly finally had chosen to deal with the
legality of the pending Will. He was a man
Lilly could talk to and well recommended.
Patiently he listened to Lilly while she told of
her intention, he nodded his head once or
twice agreeing with the plan Lilly had in
mind. When Lilly had said her piece he said
"I fully understand my dear and all is going
to be dealt with in a straight forward manner.
There is no need for you to worry I will keep
you informed as to the position I arrive at as
it happens. Do you think your husband Harry
will contest anything you have said?"
"I expect this Will to be drawn up without
any input from Harry, my request will only
affect Harry upon my death and I do own
half of the property. It was Harry's idea when
he retired he wanted more money to spend so
talked me into giving him a tidy sum for his
own use. I had the money and didn't see any
harm in doing as he asked. If Rosie hadn't
been born the Will would have never again*

been mentioned, now Rosie is here I want to safeguard her future, quite a natural thing to do in my view."

"Indeed yes, you may leave all the correspondence to me I will only let you know if I have come to any stumbling blocks. Then of course for your signature and Harry's then the Document will be duplicated so that you both have a copy and all will be done."

"That will be a happy day for me Mr Wright I will leave all in your good hands." Lilly got up and extended her hand for Mr. Wright to shake then departed settled in mind that she had done the right thing.

Although she had said she was not going to worry about Harry and his failing health Lilly found Harry's image in her mind time and time again, and although she had said she did not want to know what was ailing him her mind was unsettled, Harry was after all the Father to Rosie although he did deny this fact. Lilly knew the truth of the matter. No other man had ever touched Lilly she had been entirely faithful to Harry and there was an end to his argument. It was beyond belief that Harry should think Rosie was not his own in Lilly's view it was just a way of not having responsibility for her, well Rosie could do without Harry the same as Lilly intended *to, at least Lilly owed Harry nothing and was content in that situation.*

Settled in Annie's house and money in the bank made Lilly independent she prided herself in the fact. Annie delighted in her friend living with her and she adored baby Rosie so everything was stable and nothing left to be desired, in fact when Lilly did mention Harry feeling pity for him Annie was quick to jump in and remind Lilly of Harry's curt dismissal and all that went with it. Lilly would not be hurt a second time if Annie had anything to do with it.

Chapter Twenty eight

Harry was feeling very sorry… for himself that is! His health continued to determinate his state of mind which was never free from worry he drank more to hide away the truth avoiding the realistic point of view. He knew he had to now find a Doctor. When the Solicitor contacted him about the change in the Will he laughed out loud saying "Why bother me with this trivial endeavour?"…
Lilly it is your fault I am in this terrible mess and now you give me more worries. New solicitors to contend with! All to get your own way what a farce, you should be here to consider me and me alone but no you abandoned your position and left me to fend for myself, the fault lies directly upon your head and it is I who suffer".
Harry had given up all but his drink, and the truth be known it was entirely the other way around it was the lady's he so frequently visited that had given Harry up not wanting his heavy laden company. Quick to see there was something entirely wrong with Harry and wanting no part of it. They had robbed him of a small fortune, he had little or nothing to show for it in fact he was in a mess.
Rummaging through the drawers in the

bedroom he tried to find the piece of paper that his friend had given him with a Doctor's name and business address written on it, where had he put it? Harry was indeed anxious to find it as he had another lesion on his back very similar to the first one that had manifested upon his lip, blistery and sore and indeed he could not get at it, the sore was only identifiable when using a mirror to reflect his naked back, it hurt and that is what had told Harry that there was something more there annoying him. Lilly's hand mirror revealed the truth when reflecting in the long mirror. At bedtime he could hardly move in his bed it was so painful. He had fought shy of seeing a Doctor but now the time had come to ask advice. Harry couldn't find the address he was looking for so decided to go a scout round where the Doctor's premises were mainly situated.

Managing to get dressed he went out but it was not a comfortable outing as his clothes especially his heavy coat rubbed on the sore spot. Confounding everything he came in contact with Harry decided to go into the very next Doctor he came to. This was not a good idea but he was quite desperate. He advanced up the drive, the brass plaque said simply… "Mr Mortiver. Physician" Harry hesitated

*then rang the bell when the door was
answered Harry stumblingly said
"Is Mr Mortiver the Physician in please?"
"He is Sir but will only see you with an
appointment. Please step inside and I will
give you the times that Doctor has free"
"I want to see a Doctor right now it is
important."
"Then I can't help you Sir." with that the
door was closed and left Harry standing
disgruntled and miserable.
Blast, yes damn and blast! Confounded
Doctors! His mood had changed Harry was
cold and shivering he decided he could do
better at the Apothecary. This Apothecary by
now knew Harry and so was greeted as soon
as he went through the door.
"What can I do for you today Sir? Is it cough
mixture you want?" Harry found himself
relating his predicament to the Apothecary
who replied
"Ah it will be Calamine lotion you will be
wanting." He turned around and reached a
bottle of pink content from the shelf saying
"Just dab the wound three times a day and
your sore should heal quite well." Harry was
delighted he had side stepped the Doctor once
more and the Calamine lotion was cheap so
he was well pleased, the only thing is he*

reminded himself he could not reach the position that this sore was in, would Alice do it for him? Surely this was not too much to ask.

Harry arrived home and was pleased to see Alice was still doing her duties he said pleasantly
"Alice I have a job for you to do that is not strictly in your line of duty. I would be obliged if you would come up into my bedroom."
"Now Sir I have already told you my place is not in your bedroom, we discussed this only the other day."
"No Alice you have got it wrong, I have a spot on my back that I cannot reach and it has to be dressed with Calamine lotion, I am hoping you could just dab the lotion on it for me." Alice looked suspicious a funny request and no mistake!
"Are you sure that is all I have to do Sir?"
"Yes I promise it is I would be so grateful if you would help me I will give you an extra shilling for your trouble." Alice was still not convinced so Harry told her the pain this spot was causing him while wearing his shirt.
"I am not sleeping at night Alice and I know I shouldn't trouble you with my ailments but I have no-one else to ask, please help me will

you?"

"Alright then but as soon as any funny business occurs I shall be off like a shot so don't get any daft ideas."

"Thank you Alice, there will be no funny business as you call it and I will be most grateful, can you do it right now?"

"What is it you have to dab on the spot Sir?"

"Calamine lotion, you will need a clean piece of linen to tip some on to then just put it on the sore place." Alice followed Harry upstairs when in the bedroom she kept a very safe distance between them and left the door wide open Harry took off his shirt. Shaking the Calamine lotion to mix the content Alice gingerly put some on Harry's open sore saying

"My oh my Sir, this is more than a spot it is an open festering sore, you need a Doctor I don't know if I am doing the right thing in helping you."

"You are doing the right thing Alice the Apothecary has sold me this preparation for the sole purpose of treating this sore I would not have bothered you at all but I can't reach all around my back."

"Well on your own head it is Sir I don't think this is right at all." Alice quickly did as she was asked and left the room immediately.

Alice wasn't too sure of what she was doing, the lesions looked angry although Harry said they were not sore that is unless aggravated by a shirt or vest rubbing on the spot. After doing as Harry had asked she immediately went to wash her hands thoroughly feeling revulsion at the pit of her stomach. Harry should see a Doctor not an Apothecary and Alice were of a mind to tell him so if this condition carried on for much longer. Thinking about her family at home and all the diseases she just might carry to them was making her miserable and rightly so. Time passed and Harry told Alice the lesion had healed up and was disappearing altogether. In fact he was well pleased, Alice and the Calamine had done a good job, for a while he almost felt like his old self, even thinking of going to Victoria's place and being treated in a very pleasing way, why not he was only human after all. The girls would be glad to see him after this time lapse. He thought…I will see how I feel tomorrow, for tonight I will eat a good homely dinner and pick up my strength. I am going to be alright.

Chapter Twenty nine

"Annie please don't carry on with those jobs I need to talk to you. Lilly was flustered and Annie wondered why so she dried her hands smoothed down her apron and went in to where Lilly was sitting
"What is it Lilly are you not well?"
"I am alright Annie but I can't get Harry's image out of my head, it is festering in my mind, what could I do to help him?"
"Stay away that is what you can do Lilly are you mad? Even if you could help Harry he would shun you and for goodness sake we do not know what is wrong with him, it may be contagious and you could bring this ailment back to Rosie or me, perish the thought! We lead good healthy and clean lives we eat well and sleep well what more can we ask. In my own opinion from the bits you have told me Harry needs more than a wife he needs a nurse and even then a nurse that knows what Harry is up against. Don't rush in blindly Lilly I beg you. We both know how you got the sharp end of his tongue when he knew you were carrying I really don't know how you can even give him the time of day or how you can allow Harry to even enter your head he just isn't worth it Lilly."

"It is because of Rosie, Harry is her Father it is a fact no matter how I try to dispel it. My mind gets into such turmoil sometimes I come close to tears. It is one thing to forget him and quite another to dispel him as Rosie's Father. Why must he be so adamant? It is plain for all to see the life he lives now is doing him no good at all. I feel I might be able to talk him round and in doing that could give him a better life."

"You are senseless Lilly, why are you giving yourself this burden to carry? Harry cares nothing for you. My biggest worry is that you will go back to him and I tell you there is no doubt in my mind of how he would treat you and Rosie. Pull yourself together Lilly and let things be, life could be a lot different with Harry but certainly not in a good way." Lilly tried to speak again but Annie firmly said "I am going back into the kitchen Lilly, I am washing the net curtains in the sink they were going quite yellow but now I think I have saved them to give us another wear. Yes the same as I saved you to live another life think on Lilly and leave that particular burden in the gutter where it belongs. Annie's words were strong. Annie herself was strong and she knew just what she was talking about. A few moments later Lilly followed Annie to the *kitchen saying*

"I am sorry Annie you have tolerated me very well and I am grateful, it is just the blood tie that Rosie has with Harry, sometimes I think I should do my duty and at least try to bring them together. Please forgive me in my heart I know you are right but blood ties are strong and cannot be denied. When Rosie is old enough to know do you think she will resent my secret? It does have to be a secret because I don't want her to think of a Father that has denied her and doesn't want any part of her do you understand me Annie?"

"Yes of course I do, but Rosie may have to bear more than a secret if Harry becomes involved with her, now do you understand me Lilly?" The two lady's fell silent each right in their own way there would never be a simple solution. Life and time would tell.

The next morning the day was brilliant sun was shining and it had that first power to feel it's rays as warm Annie said

"Beautiful day Lilly let us go out for a walk with Rosie it will do her good after being in so long"

"It would indeed, a stroll with Rosie in her perambulator how lovely is that? We could go as far as the cake shop and have cream cakes for tea ooh! I like the ones filled with cream

and although I know a cake fork should be used I like to bite into mine so that the cream sticks all over my lips…now don't laugh Annie we all have our little ways that are our favourites. I shall dress Lilly in pink and put the pink knitted cover over her legs to keep her warm. How I have waited for this day to arrive Annie I am truly excited." Annie could see the flush of pink that had brought Lilly's face to life, joy in what she was doing for Rosie and happiness in her heart. This is all that Annie wanted for Lilly and was very glad the talk the previous afternoon had completely gone from Lilly's mind. Annie thought…it is when Lilly has time to brood that she gets worried over Harry I must find her more work to do it may be the answer. Soon they were strolling along chatting and stopping every now and again for acquaintances to peer inside the hood of the perambulator and see Rosie for the first time. Lilly was so proud and the truth be known so was Annie. This was a good clean healthy life that would stand Rosie in good stead if adversity ever came her way. Annie prayed that adversity wouldn't attend Rosie. The little mite was loved by Lilly and Annie, both cried at the time of her birth, strong ties and memories of gold. They approached the cake

*shop and there in the window sat Lilly's
cream cake filled to overflowing her eyes
gleamed and she said to Annie*

*"You chose your favourite Annie and then we
will have them placed in a box so they will be
pristine when we get home, I am going to ask
for that one in the centre of the window my
mouth waters at the delight it will give me."*

*"You are a one Lilly for your cream cakes we
will be able to roll you down the hill shortly
with your rotund figure." They both laughed
it didn't matter one jot. Simple pleasures
suited them both Annie said*

*"You were just the same Lilly when we went
to the next village, remember? You still made
a bee line for the cake shop and what's more
we both enjoyed that outing and the cream
cakes. I am glad now that we can stay on our
own ground, you will get to know more
people and feel part of the area it was one
thing I didn't like about Harry he never let
you go anywhere, didn't you feel yourself
stifled by his commanding presence all the
time?"*

*"I lived that way for so long Annie it was
quite normal to me. There were times I was
glad that Harry had gone to his club then I
could do just as I pleased for an hour or so it
never occurred to me to go out by myself*

where would I go indeed?"

"It wouldn't have done for me Lilly I would be bursting at the seams if my outings were only to get provisions with no other interests. I would look around the shops at least. Didn't you want to go to the Emporium? The many delights entailed in a look around that place were delightful, always something to find and new stalls opening to catch the eye, I couldn't keep away."

"You see Annie, Harry only gave me a set amount of money enough to pay for groceries in fact, and a set amount of time. He would always be waiting for me looking out of the window anxious for my return, in the early days I thought it was because he was inclined to be jealous but he never did change. My place beside Harry was taken entirely for granted; it became our way of life you see."

"Well now you can see just what you have been missing Lilly, no-one can be cooped up like that it isn't natural." They walked and talked until it was time to go home.

Chapter Thirty

Harry turned up at Victoria's place feeling less like going in than he had done an hour ago. It had taken all his time to get decently dressed, if he turned up to speak to Victoria looking worse for wear she simply would not let him in. Victoria looked after her girls the best way she could, they earned her a good living a fact that Victoria never let slip her mind. They deserved her care and always gave good value for money. Harry attentively tapped the door close to the grid and waited.
"Hello Harry my dear, Victoria greeted her client, giving yourself a little treat dearie? Do come in. You look better than when I saw you last time Harry, all well again now?"
Harry bluffed his way around the subject he did not want to discuss health.
"Fit as a fiddle Victoria, is Angel in can I see her?"
"Sorry Harry I have to say no she is still sulking, about what I do not know, did you two have cross words when you last you saw her?"
"I was a little worse for drink as I remember it, I will apologise if that will help."
"I will carry your goodwill to Angel but tonight it is out of the question she has to

rest. Of late there has been something bothering Angel she won't tell me what it is, I would feel better if I knew. I have to adhere to her wishes and gladly do so probably it is something to do with lady's ailments and fools rush in if you take my meaning Harry."

"I am sorry to hear that Victoria, you know how dear she is to me."

"Be patient Harry all will be well just a little time is all she wants and I must see that she gets it. You do understand don't you?"

"Then I will do as I did last time and have a frolic around with the dear lady's in the pink room will that be alright?"

"But of course Harry they will be delighted to see you, have you got rid of all those lumps and bumps that bothered you dear?" Victoria was very aware of illnesses that befell the loose living and tried to keep her girls clean she felt it was part of her duty to do that. Their nether regions had to be clean Victoria had a duty towards her male visitors to see that this was so. A jug full of soapy water would have to be stooped over and private parts washed every day, a full bath once a week, and hair washed once a month. This was the general rule. Then it was up to Victoria to look over the person who requested entrance to lie with the girls and judge on the spot if this male was healthy. It was a difficult judgment for her but she seemed instinctively to know whether a man was clean or not. Harry was a long standing visitor the sort Victoria liked as she believed she had come to know him through and through. Her girls liked him too and no-one could deny his tips were extra special. Victoria trusted Harry, although Harry was chuckling behind her back. On the other hand Harry had got rid of his lip sore and the lesion on his back was indeed much better. Victoria held back the red beaded curtain for Harry to enter. Harry cast his eye around the female company finding nothing had changed except there was a new face, his eyes settled upon this pretty girl. He turned to Victoria and said pointing to the girl

"Is she new Victoria? I don't recall having seen her the last time I came."

"Not entirely new Harry but you could have missed her as she only comes to me if things are unbearable at home. She has a family and a husband that drinks. It is partly for his alcohol money that brings her to me, he is totally unbearable when he hasn't got the money to drink. When she has enough money to get food for her kids and get booze for her husband she vacates her position. Sometimes *it is weeks on end before I see her again. Now and again she comes to me with bruises, not that I mind just so long as they are not on her face. My girls have to be pretty as you well know Harry." The explanation of this girl's life interested Harry, her name was Bess, he would make a beeline for her as soon as he went forward into the room. Harry never thought of himself as needing drink, that was because he always had enough money to buy good Brandy or Whiskey when one bottle emptied another would be bought to take its' place, these bottles were always at arm's length away and Harry drank his fill. To suggest he was dependent upon them would have gained much argument from Harry's point of view, but the truth be known he depended on this drink more and more each day and was in a very unenviable position. He sustained his image of youth and virility only when he drank enough to fool himself. These ideas were far from the truth. A little self deception was applied to keep Harry happy turning to Victoria he said*

"I shall go and acquaint myself with Bess."
"Do you want me to introduce you Harry?"
"Indeed not, far too formal I have the words at hand that I shall say to her, she is I assume available to anyone interested?"

"But of course Harry help yourself." Harry sauntered over to where Bess was reclining on a scarlet elongated seat, he smiled saying "Well my beauty I don't think we have met before." He picked up her face in his hand to see more clearly her features.

"Indeed for a fact I know I haven't met you because I would have remembered your lovely smile, may I sit beside you my petal? I am Harry all the girls know me, Victoria tells me you don't attend all of the time is that so?"

"Yes Sir, and yes please do sit beside me I am happy to make your acquaintance." Harry sat down his eye catching Victoria's meaningful nod as she returned through the beaded curtains, Harry continued

"I shall have my usual whiskey to drink will you join me my dear?"

"Yes thank you, I too like the odd whiskey." Harry's eyes glinted, this was just playing into his hands, how far would Bess allow him to go his interest now deepened. Harry knew full well the downstairs girls were there for exciting foreplay and not the real thing they enticed their men and made them ready should they want to go upstairs. Encouragement to spend too, Victoria benefitted from this and done stage by stage it

got more money into her pot. The girls had a set amount of money plus any tips she could wring from the gentleman who had chosen her, the main fee for the real thing went to Victoria. The downstairs girls knew their part well, they had to pleasure the men interested in them and be prepared for a lot of groping around under their volumes' skirts. These skirts and pantaloons were made especially for this very job. There were layers upon layers of silk frills and fancies often purple or red; these were designed to make the gentleman search for his desire. The final layer stocking top would be left as a bare piece of flesh between corset and leg, the suspender belt always excited and the touch of bare flesh. Finally stroking and finding the slit that was in the pantaloons made for the purpose, it was open to the vagina for easy access and many a gentleman wanted just that, to feel touch and grope until the vagina released the natural scent of the female which was a goal to be achieved, his hands and fingers would arouse the genital juices and bring forth the scent of his desire. This was like nectar and the gentleman's mind running a riot as the thrill ran through him. This would be enough for Harry, just at this time his libido was low and lacked verb and thrust, He was surely fooling himself whilst thinking he was fooling the chosen girl. It didn't matter Harry wanted casual satisfaction and the girl wanted nothing but his money, she knew very well how to play her part and get it. Their liaison continued for about an hour all in full view of the other room occupants, some with men, some just sitting smoking and waiting. The atmosphere was dense, the room low lit and the cigarette smoke filling the room in swirls. There were to be had, at a price, cigarettes which were called "pure delight" but these were expensive and the smoke from them intoxicated the whole den of iniquity. This intoxication along with the whiskey soon had Harry's mind captured, he for this moment in time was in paradise. Money could buy this? For some it could, they were the sorry men that had let true desire go astray a sad state of affairs to be sure, it was surely love that had to come first and then meaningful devotion that led to the right place to join in a sexual union. There were men who would never know the meaning of faith and devoted love searching their whole life through and finding only the dirt in the streets to satisfy their sexual need. Harry now had his head underneath the volumes' skirts of this promised hussy. His nose nuzzled her pubic hair whilst his hand caressed her fanny, hoping this sensuous scent he so desired would sufficed his need. Harry dipped his tongue into the well of moisture and scent which overpowered his senses. He realised by now he should be ready for the natural penetration, but no, his manly parts were placid and uninterested. He had suddenly gone very tired he pulled himself away from Bess without a word disgusted by his own performance. Straightening his clothes he pulled a note out of his inside pocket and gave it to Bess she said

"Are you alright Harry? You look so pale, did I not please you?"

"Your tip should tell you Bess."

"I will look for you again Harry, next time I will treat you better, anytime Harry." Harry said nothing, he turned and walked away as if Bess did not exist. He had taken his pleasure albeit he had pleasured Bess more than he had pleasured himself and had left a good tip. He needed another drink but it could wait till he got home, Victoria's whiskey was expensive suddenly he was counting his money. Stepping on to the cobblestone pavement the night closed around him, it was pouring with rain Harry pulled up his coat

collar and quickened his step. It was late spring but it could have been January the way the wind was driving hard and hitting Harry's face, he grimaced thinking he ought to have stayed a bit longer in the warm. No it was home he wanted to be, he planned to light a fire and sit down close by it a glass of whiskey in his hand. This feeling had come across him just before leaving Victoria's place. This was getting a regular occurrence, a sinking feeling with his mind set on warmth and comfort. Unsafe reality stared him straight in the face, his body ached all over and his throat was sore. He trotted along as fast as he could thinking... what is the matter with me? Nothing pleases me or lifts me from this pit of despair. He turned into the road which was his home address and thanked God for letting him put one foot before the other in order to get there.

Once home he immediately took off all his wet garments laying them over the backs of chairs to dry out. It was sheer delight to put on his night attire and a cosy dressing gown. He was astonished at his own thought pattern in regard to this. Wasn't this the defeat that came with old age? Harry shuddered shivers went from head to foot making his body hair stand on end and bristle. He said to himself *quietly...don't be silly a couple of hours ago I was at Victoria's place taking my pleasure from Bess, but there it is again my private parts did not get aroused I should have gone on and done the final deed as a full blooded man, could it be my lack of stamina is it so apparent? I am afraid.*

"The fire was throwing long licking flames up the chimney Harry was drawn in by its splendour and with whiskey in hand and glasses of it filled several times his head nodded and he fell into a deep sleep. Yes whiskey was his best friend that is until it would become his master, Would Harry who knew best about everything fall into that dreadful trap? The thought never crossed his mind, he had heard of this illness but it was just a myth that people made up, he was his own master dictating to his own flesh. Harry was a survivor in natures design and perfect in every way. His mind turned to Lilly.

Lilly was far too fussy why she did the good deeds for others he had never understood. Lilly and Annie were a pair Harry always thought they were trying to do him an injustice. He had to admit though it wasn't Annie that had made Lilly pregnant, but it wasn't him either, Lilly the slut had to have another lover the brat was not his responsibility and never would be. All these thoughts travelled through Harry's dreams while in a drunken sleep. Vengeance he stated as he woke up, Lilly must pay for her infidelity. It was entirely down to Lilly leaving him like this; it had given the space that his present illness needed to take hold. Time yes time would see to bringing a reckoning, he would see to it that she had her true justice. Harry's mind was in a state of utter confusion and he totally believed his convictions deeming himself as the victim in all this present secret living. Harry's twisted mind conjured up a truth that was not a reality in practical circumstances. Lilly had always been and to this day was an utterly devoted wife never had another man touched her or yet even kissed her. Harry's picture was all in Harry's warped mind, his womanising and drink orientated mind was of his own making. He used Lilly's image to have a bad side, someone to take the blame for his present position the faults all laid at Lilly's feet a prolonged state of affairs to say the least. Harry needed Lilly back to look after him, but NO he still would not allow her in his presence with the child whom he always referred to as "the brat". As if he could possibly be the Father to a girl! When she grew up she would be another addition for Victoria's place.

Harry's mind was never at ease as time went by he felt more and more persecuted and hard done by. His ill favoured humour on waking up after sleeping crunched up in his chair made his body ache all the more. He had when falling asleep a lively fire to sit by but now he sat beside a sunken pile of grey ash. He looked around for someone to blame but he was alone and only had himself to reproach. Again he staggered up the stairway cursing and blaspheming at every step, now into the bedroom flinging his tired withering body on to the bed. He suddenly knew there was something different about him, he sensed it rather than saw it. With a puzzled brow he scanned his open shirt looking at his chest in so doing he saw two more lesions. Quickly he pulled off his shirt and looked all over the area, trying to see his back through the dressing table mirror. He breathed a sigh of relief there was just the two, now he questioned how had these two become apparent? Every time he thought he had treated and cured these accursed things more would come and take their place. Harry was not a well man. His life in general had taken an all new down turn, he lay looking at the ceiling searching for an answer. His thoughts were varied and unexplained he could come to no sensible conclusion. Then he asked himself… could this malady come from his mind? Was his mind using his body to manifest the fragile state it was in? There were Doctors who dealt only with the mind should Harry see what they thought and could they cure him? It was worth a try, but in all truth Harry was so inclined to be wary, he had paid out to so many advisers, who said they knew the answer, cost none effective. Lotions Potions creams medical compounds anti bacterial washes, balms and oils all had failed. Tomorrow he would go and put his case before a Doctor that dealt with the mind and the "subconscious mind over matter" approach. He climbed the stairs with effort this thought had calmed him so getting into bed he pulled up the sheets around him and closed his mind to worry. It was the oblivion of sleep he sort after, but he tossed and turned sleep denying him. He reached over to the drawer and brought out yet more whiskey. Harry was in a state all of his own making, like a fly caught in a web of secrecy and disillusion. When all came to all he was no better than any other man and made the same mistakes as any other man. He was self opinionated and thoughts deemed him to be a fine figure one that could do nothing wrong, well he could fool himself but others that stood by and looked on saw Harry slipping into his own private hell. Friends they were said to be, but Harry were fast losing all the friends he ever had. Whispering behind his back and sneaking long unwanted views as to how many glasses were empty on the table that Harry sat. Harry blissfully unaware of their interest drank his fill. All looking on wondered how Harry ever got to his feet, but he did and walked the distance home seemingly reasonable sober. He knew how to punctuate and reasoned that when at home he could open another bottle, poor Harry. His way of thinking was out of control, there were demons that interrupted his sleep and his answer to that was another glass of whiskey, this only sending him into a hallucinating terror.

Chapter Thirty one

Lilly could not shake off the image of Harry. How did he become to look so ill? Indeed what was the matter with him? Annie said

"Oh no not again don't tell me you are thinking about Harry? I know that look in your eye. You are such a fool Lilly he cares nothing for you or dear little Rosie." Lilly felt the indignant pang that Annie reflected, it cut through her she replied

"You don't know how I feel Annie I am still Harry's wife and he is still the Father of my Daughter. My aim is to settle the peace between us so that in future years Rosie grows up to know her Father and Harry recognises Rosie as his own Daughter. Surely that is not too much to ask?"

"Lilly we are talking about Harry here, Harry who cares for no-one but himself. He has no conscious feelings for either of you. It would be a miracle if Harry ever did what you are asking. Even in future years in fact I don't think you will ever change him at all, he is adamant and stuck fast in his own ways, how many time have we gone over this ground Lilly?" Lilly felt the cold tang in Annie's voice so tried to change the subject

"Sorry Annie I know you are right but I have to keep trying for Rosie's sake don't I?
"I still don't see why after the cold shoulder he has turned to you this past time. You have been a slave to his every whim while living with him, he used you Lilly. How you didn't repel against his iron rod rules I will never know, he had you trapped and now low and behold you are considering his welfare. It is beyond my comprehension to say the least."
Annie abruptly stood up shook her skirts level and said with a definite dismissal of Harry
"The fire needs building up I must get some coal in from the yard. Then we will boil the kettle for tea and Rosie's bottle, she has slept well bless her I don't know what she would make of the situation I am sure." Off went Annie to the coal shed importantly swishing her long skirts in defiance. No she would not give Harry the benefit of the doubt he had shunned her right from way back when. Annie visiting Lilly would curb her visit to Lilly as soon as she heard the key turn in the lock bringing Harry home, she knew what Harry thought of her yes very much below the status he held for his own importance. He looked down upon Annie and he never wanted Lilly to treat her as a friend in fact he did his utmost to sever the tie that Lilly and

Annie had made over the years but despite all odds Annie and Lilly had made a solid connection that couldn't be broken easily. Lilly went over to the cot that held Rosie and looked lovingly down on Rosie's sweet face indeed it was hard to believe Harry had any part of this delightful little child but as her Father he was bound to be in there somewhere and it was that fact that held the drive in Lilly's mind. Reconciliation, even in a set apart manner, Lilly wanted peace for them all would Harry allow this peace to settle upon them was it too much to aim for? Lilly was nursing Rosie when Annie came in with a scuttle full of coal. As Annie leaned forward to build up the fire Lilly couldn't help but notice how broad in the hip Annie had become. Lilly wasn't going to hurt her friend by passing a comment and so attacked her own weight saying

"Annie that will be a splendid fire when it has burned through, are we having a pot of tea or do we have to wait for the fire to burn up to boil the kettle? Annie replied

"We don't have to wait the kitchen fire in the range is all aglow, in fact I thought about baking a fruit cake while the oven is good and hot with even temperature. Would you like me to do that Lilly?" An ideal situation

for Lilly to say

"Well you know how I like fruit cake but I have been thinking of late how tight my clothes are becoming. First I blamed having Rosie for the weight gain, I realise I could do with losing a pound or two. Now your offer of freshly made fruit cake is too much to resist. What I need is a good corset to squeeze my middle in and remind me not to indulge in cake and the like."

"Now then Lilly if I make cake it has got to be for the two of us, it isn't half as nice to eat it on my own."

"Perhaps then Annie you need a corset as well as me? We could go and get measured next week. I know just what I need and the assistant would advice you as to your requirements"

"I know full well what my needs are Lilly and you will never get me into one of those tight waist monstrosities. They are made for torture they are, boned and laced. I don't know how you could contemplate wearing such an item. I truly believe they could cause internal damage. When I see ladies that are tight laced I do not envy them to the contrary I pity them. I know I shall probably finish up as round as an apple but my life style doesn't dictate that this is not a suitable weight for

me, my Mother was just as I am now and it never did her any harm, she had a happy and long life and I don't recall her ever mentioning a corset. It is only a fashion fad you know Lilly, and you with your liking for the creamiest cake in the bakery window well not for you not any more, your diet would have to change drastically and no mistake. Why can't you be satisfied the way you are? Now then Lilly shall I go and get a fruit cake into the oven or not?"

"Yes please do Annie. The delightful aroma while the cake is baking will make us both change our mind about dieting." Dear Annie Lilly thought, it isn't for me that needs to diet, I was thinking more for you. You are quite right if it is as round as an apple you want to be please bake the cake, I will certainly help you eat it. Lilly said

"Yes Annie you are quite right middle age and a rotund figure go hand in hand and what occasion do either of us have to show off a wasp waist?" The atmosphere slackened as the flame in the fire burst into action and once again all was well in their world. The fruit cake was now in the oven baking, there was fresh tea in the pot. Rosie was in Lilly's arms, peace and contentment now in their minds and hearts. Corsets abandoned forever,

very soon the table cloth would go on for teatime the cake taking centre stage and only just cool enough to eat, the Demerara sugar sprinkled top made it glisten in the candle light, a delight to the eye as well as it tasting so good. Boiled eggs newly laid, toast soldiers with plenty of butter there was very little to spoil their world that is until Harry emerged again into Lilly's mind. If only Lilly knew just what Harry was thinking about her and Rosie she would not have given him another moment's thought but Lilly had a forgiving nature and wanted to reconcile as much for Rosie's sake as her own.

Chapter Thirty two

Harry had made his appointment and was getting ready to go and see the Doctor who knew about "mind over matter" Where had all his clean shirts gone? He selected one from the pile on the floor cursing Alice at the same time! What did he pay this girl for? Harry would have to reprimand her when he returned, he dare not say too much because Alice was dressing the lesions on his back that he could not reach himself and they were improving, his eyes wandered down to where the most recent two had settled on his chest, yes they were still as obnoxious as before ugh! How he hated the things. Perhaps the Doctor today would have the answer? This thought spurred him on to finish getting ready. Stupid life why do illnesses occur? It was enough to just keep up with everyday living, now he had this menace to contend with. Why me? He had not seen or heard of anyone else with this affliction, he felt put upon and sorry for himself, his spirits were low and unless he had whiskey the world was a dark place to live in. He stood before the dressing mirror and weighed up his image deciding it was the worry of this illness that had made him look so pinched and pale.

Come on Harry he said to himself time to get a few answers.

Harry dressed as smartly as he could and walked to the appointment previously made. Arriving at the wrought iron gate he stepped up to the door. He noticed a brass plaque on the right side of the wall it had on it "Doctor Ross and Son treating malady's of the mind." Harry felt as though he was in the right place so lifted the brass door knocker and gave it three loud bangs. A lady came and said

"Good afternoon Sir. Can I help you?"

"I have an appointment with Doctor Ross My name is Harry Baines"

"Ah yes the Doctor is expecting you do come in." Harry was shown into a smartly furnished room with green upholstery, his eyes scanned the décor and the content. There were head shapes made in a yellow and white hard substance with markings all over them to signify the brain and it's various functions. Harry was quite intrigued and walked around to see first one then the other. He heard a voice and turned around to see Doctor Ross, he looked a capable man strong in his stature and tall. This put Harry at ease, they shook hands and Harry noticed the Doctor had on surgical gloves. Harry was

shown to a reclining couch and asked to lay back on it. Various questions were asked, how long have you had these symptoms? Harry answered as near to the truth as he was able. Strings of questions that took Harry back to his childhood, then Doctor asked Harry

"You say you keep getting lesions on your face and body, please show me these." Harry said

"Only one on my face and that was like a cold sore that wouldn't go away, the two on my back and the most recent two on my chest. Now today I find my Penis is attacked. I am full of fear Doctor.

"Hmm, show me please." Harry undid his shirt and showed the front ones on his chest and the ones on his penis saying

"The back ones have almost disappeared, I have had them treated with calamine lotion."

"Hmm and are you treating the front ones in the same manner?" Harry looked down at these front lesions and said

"To tell you the truth Doctor I have only just noticed these come up and I don't know what to do hence my visit to your good self."

"Well Harry the mind can do extraordinary things do you have worries that you can't deal with?"

"Yes Doctor I feel this is my entire wife's Lilly's fault." Then at great length Harry streamed out the story of Lilly and of how she had left him and of how he had suffered the humiliation and the lack of thought that had made him so ill." By now the Doctor had a picture of Harry and what is more he knew what the disease was that Harry was suffering from but he didn't say a word to signify that fact, instead he smiled and replied

"Harry my good fellow you will need more counselling than I at first thought, your way of thinking needs a lot to be desired and until your mind is clear your body will keep reacting in the manner you see it now. It may take some time to personalise your treatment and it will cost you without a doubt. How say you Sir?"

"Will I be cured Doctor? Will these lesions stop coming and what is even more will I get back my libido? My whole body is affected headaches, vomiting, and times when I am only fit for bed and sleep, if you can relieve all these ailments I will certainly stay with you and I am willing to pay your price. I know no peace."

"Ah you see Harry I know you will know no peace, I will treat you urgently. You do *understand though I can't guarantee you a cure, if you had come to me earlier I would be more optimistic but you have let this state of affairs go on too long. It is up to you if you want me to proceed how do you say?"*

"Please Doctor Ross I have had every treatment other than this one and nothing seems to work, if you can help me I would be so grateful."

"I can't do any more today Harry we have gone over a lot of ground and I have to think this out as to how to follow for the best results, it will not be easy. Please make another appointment within the next week and I will give your history a good think over. Then we will start to provide you with a cure." Doctor Ross's eyes twinkled he would make a pretty penny out of this client before he told him the real truth of the matter. Doctor Ross had examined Harry mainly by putting his gloved hands on Harry's head. He then asked to see the lesions on Harry's chest just once more; again he did not touch them. Harry found this very strange but as this was a Doctor of the mind he dismissed the thought. Doctor Ross now having examined Harry for a second time seemed satisfied. from his bent position he stood up saying "I will have my work cut out and how long it

will take I really don't know, you see part of the cure has to come naturally from yourself mind over matter you see Mr Baines. I think I can help you. We can fit you in this coming week as you feel this urgency. Harry smiled at this Doctor believing a cure was to be sort after and he was in good hands, he was ready to comply to any suggestion put forward he said

"Will the same time next week be alright?"

"That would be fine Harry, now do you want me to address you as Harry or Mr Baines, I hope I haven't offended you by using Harry when I have spoken. We try to keep a cordial atmosphere and use Christian names."

"No I don't mind you calling me Harry it is far less formal than Mr Baines."

"Yes quite so, there is just one more thing, do you wish to pay the fee weekly as your treatment commences or would you like a bill at the end when the treatment is over?"

Harry dropped himself in the right spot for Doctor Ross by saying

"I will pay each time I attend I will know how my finances stand that way. Do you really think a cure is at hand Sir?"

"I will do my very best and more than that I cannot promise." Doctor Ross went to the door with Harry both men happy about the *arrangement but for very different reasons. On the way home Harry thought about all the things he would be able to do when this cure took place. His mind wandered over to the good things he had previously enjoyed thinking…Angel yes he would see Angel and the girls at Victoria's place, he wouldn't get so tired as he did now, his libido would return and he wouldn't have the need to ask Alice or Lilly to tend his sore body! I think it is fair to say that at this moment Harry was a happy man. He also questioned his own reasoning, why didn't I go to Doctor Ross earlier I would have been cured by now ah well! I at least have an appointment with him next week and he assures me all will be well. Harry had rose coloured glasses on, as there was an element of doubt in his statement. Doctor Ross as he told Harry couldn't promise anything, he was only willing to try, the one thing he could promise is that he would take the fee from Harry. Even he had to touch Harry with great caution, he knew this disease was highly contagious, and yes he knew what this the disease was called, but first things first he could take a tidy sum from Harry before he told him the name of the illness and that this disease was incurable. What difference would it make? Harry in fact was slowly dying and wouldn't need money where he was destined to go. Doctor Ross was already calculating the time that he could be involved in Harry's cure one month two months or more? He would calculate satisfaction levels in Harry's mind and go on as long as he had his fee from Harry paid. Really there was nothing he could do except keep Harry reassured, surely that was worth something?*

Chapter Thirty three

Bright sun was shining and summer had arrived with its splendour Lilly called to Annie

"Annie it is a lovely day should we take Rosie a walk around the park."

"Can't think of anything to stop us Lilly, get Rosie ready and I will go and change my dress, I won't be long." This prompted Lilly to look at her own attire and she decided to change into a pretty dress.

"What colour are you wearing Annie?"

"Pale blue it goes with my bonnet."

"Then I shall wear pink and a pink bonnet." Now Rosie can sit up in her reigns she will have pink on and look oh so pretty." Going out of the front door they all looked well turned out, the perambulator had a frilled parasol to keep the strong sunlight off Rosie and Rosie was full of smiles. Walking along the park railings in order to get to the gate Lilly said

"Can you hear Annie the brass band is playing must have known we were coming." The nearer they approached the louder the sound and the clash of the symbols resounded through the park, there were chairs around the bandstand and a few people had already

chosen their seats. Annie said
"A proper sunny afternoon this is, band and all. A treat no less for us weary housewives."
Lilly smiled she too was enjoying the band and Rosie had her rattle shaking it as if she was beating time to the music. Lilly said
"We will go around the outer perimeter of the Park then we can hear the music without it being too loud." They strolled along, coming towards them walking in the opposite direction were two men, their paths collided with them and one man said
"Well hello there! Haven't seen you or Harry for ages he turned to his friend saying, you know Harry don't you Oswald?"
"Yes I do but it has been so long since I saw him."
"Well Oswald this is Harry's wife Lilly."
"Well of course it is, how are you Lilly?"
"I am well thank you, have I met you before?"
"Yes but it was briefly many years ago"
Ernest was taking all in; he liked the look of Lilly. He played safe and asked
"Where is Harry these days we could perhaps meet up with him and talk over old times. Is this beautiful child your Granddaughter?"
Lilly felt embarrassed, but picked up her chin and said

"This Ernest is my Daughter Rosie."
"Sorry Lilly I thought you were too late in life to have a baby Daughter, so Harry is a dark horse is he how did the old man Father such a delightful baby girl?"
"A long story Ernest, I live with Annie my friend now, my life with Harry has come to a close but in law we are still married." Ernest found he had stepped upon a hornet's nest and shouldn't go into detail at this time. Meanwhile Oswald was talking to Annie and they had found a topic that they could share chatting away as though they had been lifelong friends. Lilly felt this conversation had gone far enough and said
"Nice to have met you Ernest and you Oswald but we must be getting along it will very soon be teatime."
"Perhaps our paths will cross again sometime Lilly we live in this area now. I have enjoyed seeing you and as Oswald is getting on so well with Annie maybe we could take tea together, I would look forward to that immensely, how say you?"Lilly turned to Annie and repeated what Ernest had suggested, Annie said
"Maybe some time when we get better acquainted and we would always bring Rosie along. We live happily together and Lilly

would have to agree upon anything that was suggested."

"But of course Annie, we will leave it for now, when we cross paths again I will see what you think, thank you Annie and you Lilly it has been a most pleasurable encounter." They touched their hats in a salute as they left and Lilly with Annie wondering just how that had happened. Neither of them said a word as they resumed their walk, but they each had thoughts of their own and they were both thinking along the same lines. Were these two men sincere? Or did they want to get their feet under the table? Talk was abandoned between them as both had been flattered and it was not very often this happened, their lives didn't include men, it was so strange, inviting and that was it there was a big but. Lilly was still sick at the thought of the one man in her life Harry, he had proved a cad and if there was the slightest implication such as talking to this man in the park he would pounce upon it, as if Lilly had been seeing this man regularly. Another man! Harry would swear that Rosie was not his own child, Lilly didn't want to give Harry any cause at all to suggest this so as soon as Ernest and Oswald had gone out of sight Lilly was closing this page, it had

been just a pleasurable encounter Lilly knew Annie would tell her what she thought later on this evening in fact it would give them something to talk about. Never had either of them thought of other interest from men, at least it was a feather in their caps to know they were still a desirable entity. Rosie oblivious to it all enjoyed the afternoon the most, her brand new small white teeth gleamed as she smiled up at Lilly.

Lilly knew Rosie was all that mattered to her, men well they were out for the pleasure that a lady friend might indeed bestow upon them. Not this lady Lilly thought, but even Lilly's head could be turned. It was natural and no one was invincible it was a very long time since any man paid Lilly a compliment. Lilly quickened her step on the way home the ladies had their tea and Lilly put Rosie down in her cot, she picked up her needle work and joined Annie downstairs.

"A nice peaceful evening Annie isn't it? I must say our encounter with Oswald and Ernest did me no good at all. I felt myself tremble when Harry's name was mentioned. I couldn't get away quick enough how did you feel Annie?"

"I let the chance meeting go over my head and as far as meeting to take tea I will have

my own tea from my own teapot thank you very much."

"So you feel the same as I do Annie?"

"Yes Lilly we have enough of Harry's pathetic way of living. Men think they can do as they please and it is up to us women to show them we do not succumb to their flattery and the like. I think we did the right thing. Notice their wives were never mentioned and you can bet on it there will be wives back at home! The cheek of it eh?"

Lilly smiled and said

"Now I can sit and do my canvass picture relaxed, I was worried that you might have taken a shine to Oswald and would want to meet up again as they suggested. It is quite a relief for me Annie really it is."

"Is that why you were so quiet while having our tea Lilly?" Lilly didn't answer she just looked down and turned the subject saying "Now show me how far you are on your picture." Annie swivelled the canvas around saying

"Some of the stitching is easily done but there are parts that seem to take ages the stitches are so small, it is coming along nicely though" Lilly looked at Annie's picture.

"Your stitching is very neat Annie and you are further advanced than me. A nice frame

and it will be worthy of any wall you decide to display it on. I have to keep stopping on mine to see to Rosie, but it is taking shape isn't it?" Lilly showed Annie who said

"Lovely Lilly the colour in the cottage garden jumps it to life, and the way you have taken a great deal of patience with the thatched roof there is potential there, yours will be better than mine when we have finished. You are going to frame yours aren't you?"

"I will see what I think when it is complete, I am doing my best but this is the first picture I have attempted. I must say they take a great deal longer to stitch than I thought but it is a labour of love so it doesn't matter does it?"

There is no reason to hurry. It would be good if the pictures were framed at the same time we would both be happy having produced them in our quieter moments sitting together. Quiet an achievement I would say eh? So you will have to slow down on your work and I will have to pick up speed on mine."

"Slow down for me and get on for you eh? Well in that case I will go and make us a nice hot drink, what sort of biscuits would you like?"

"It doesn't seem long since we had tea Annie, so just a couple of plain biscuits please."

Annie went to the kitchen, the cups rattled on

the tray and Lilly heard the kettle bubble and steam as it boiled, what a dear friend Annie was. Putting the tray down on the coffee table Annie said

"I have been meaning to ask you Lilly when you go to the Solicitor to get the Will changed will Harry have to go at the same time?"

"Oh I don't know he has sent no word at all typical of Harry, he doesn't want to change the Will it won't benefit him to do so he is hanging on hoping I will change my mind. I am not going to Annie I want Rosie to have money that she can rely on as her own, Harry has made our lives completely out of coordination has anyone got a good word for him these days?"

" No that is what I hear anyway, I still don't know about his illness so even if it is that he is getting better I am completely in the dark."

" Do you know Annie I know now I have lived my life beside Harry always in the dark? Life has opened up for me since we have had Rosie I mean you and me, not Harry and me! I wouldn't trust Harry as far as I could throw him he is cunning and devious and wants all his own way how I ever lived the years I did with him is beyond me."

Chapter thirty four

Harry couldn't think about anything else other than getting better. Solicitor's appointments were not on his list, in a dreadful insecurity of ideas, first he had thought Doctor Ross was compiling a cure, certain lesions would go without a scar but then others came in different places. It was now six months since the treatment was first introduced and Harry's pocket and Harry's patience was being stretched to the limit. There wasn't a part of him that didn't hurt and the vomiting had got worse. What is more he had got rid of Alice so the house was getting into a state and he had no-one to see to his sores. Eating had become a thing of the past and the only time he washed was when he went to see Doctor Ross. This was Lilly's fault and Lilly could come and clear this mess up, if it wasn't for that brat she would still be living alongside of him, how he hated that child, if Lilly thought she could bring the child back to Harry's house she had another think coming. Adoption was the only answer, perhaps she had seen the error of her ways by now and would be only too glad to come back and resume their married life, how could he approach her to start her mind bending towards reconciliation? Harry was not good at begging he liked to be boss but this time it might win him a solution. How could he begin to get Lilly to change her mind? He flopped on his bed of tumultuous bed linen and put his whole mind into action. Starting with the ...I told you so...idea, could he win her with his attention? Flowers all seemed futile she would think he was dying, but unbeknown to Harry he was in fact dying. He reached for the whiskey bottle which was always at hand and drank from it not bothering with a glass. This stupefied his mind until his reasoning was beyond help he fell into a drunken stupor oblivious to everything. There he would stay until the effect of the whiskey wore off and pray goodness helps anyone around when he woke.

Inevitably he did wake and found his way to the closet to be very sick. His vomit smelled vile and all this was his own fault clearly it wasn't Lilly who had wished this upon him but he reckoned it was, he never gave an inch of space to make him think otherwise, the woman was evil. Harry's mind was beginning to take a road of no return, he had his own demons and it was almost impossible to decide which reality was and which was of his own making. Clearly he did not have a balance where a decision could be made. He clung on to Doctor Ross counting on him to have all the answers but soon Harry would be too ill to attend his appointments with Doctor Ross. Now and then a window in Harry's mind would steer him to his Doctor. It was at that time that Doctor Ross decided enough was enough, he had made a tidy sum from Harry and it was time Harry knew the truth before Doctor Ross became blamed for Harry's demise. Yes this ruthless man had no compassion for Harry he had treated him and took his fee end of story, what happened next was none of his affair. Doctor Ross just thought Harry would be getting his just rewards for living the way he had. Everything has a price and Harry would pay the price before it was all over. Poor Harry!

Harry's next appointment day had dawned and Harry decided to give Doctor Ross a piece of his mind. He put a coat on with a high collar and a scarf to cover his face because now he deemed himself not fit to be seen, privacy and secrecy had become the name of the game, there was no way he could explain his illness so he avoided the public and drew a veil of secrecy around his person and until things got better he knew he must

*keep away from the public at large. Harry
entered Doctor's waiting room and observed
he was the only patient waiting*

*"Ah come in Harry you are prompt today."
Harry followed the Doctor into his
examination room and immediately attacked
with words saying*

*"My illness is getting worse Doctor not better,
I don't know which way to turn, your medical
applications and your pills are doing me no
good at all. You told me you would get rid of
this illness at least get it under control and I
see no sign of that happening. Please explain
to me why I am not getting better." Doctor
Ross was at a loss for words he had planned
to tell Harry the truth but having this
confrontation had upset his well devised
speech. He must defend this onslaught of
Harry's, he collected his dignity and said
"Well Harry I said I would do my best, to
bring about a cure and I have, you can
hardly blame me for your discomfort I didn't
cause you to be ill that was your own doing. I
am not the responsible one; in this case you
must look to yourself and your past life for
the answer. Matter of fact I was going to ask
you to discontinue your visits to my surgery
because even I couldn't see any improvement
in you. A Doctor can only do so much then it*

is up to the individual to find a cure or go for a second opinion from another Doctor. I hope I am making myself clear Harry. Do not make any other appointments with me I have done all I can for you, I am sorry my method has not worked not all people find a cure with the first Doctor they attend. Good day to you Sir." Harry was devastated he had not expected this, he couldn't leave his chair to stalk out in disgust he felt so ill and now the Doctor he had relied upon had dismissed him. He was alone now in the room and wanted to leave but it was impossible his body felt a dead weight and he couldn't rise to his feet. After a little while he tried again but it was useless, he reached out and found he could touch the bell that was on the desk, he stretched a little further and tipped the bell on to its side, it rolled towards him and he clutched his hand around it, he shook the bell several times and after a while a Nurse came to see what the commotion was all about, she went straight to Harry's side and Harry told of his predicament she said

"Be still Mr Baines I will fetch Doctor Ross." Returning she had the Doctor with her he said

"Come now Harry what is all the fuss about?" The nurse said

"This man is very ill and couldn't stand up without my assistance but I find him a dead weight. Doctor Ross became immediately concerned the last thing he wanted was for Harry to collapse in his surgery, he must place him into the nearest Hospital to be assessed and looked after. Doctor Ross looked after the mind more than dealing with the body so Harry was placed into a straight jacket and taken to the nearest Asylum with very little fight left in him, things had come to a pretty pass! It had become years not months or days that Harry had been suffering in fact some portion of his bad behaviour could be attributed to the onset of this disease, he was now in its grip. At the Asylum he was quickly dealt with given an injection to calm him down and put into a room which had padded walls. He was still fully dressed. It wasn't long before two strong men appeared. Harry closed himself off into a corner and pulled his knees up to his chin not wanting to be touched. These men said very little and certainly nothing comforting. They made Harry's protesting body undress, Harry fought with all his might part understanding where he had been admitted. They would have no nonsense so a straight jacket was again applied and Harry was trapped as firm

as any other animal in the wild. Now he could writhe all he wanted to and his language came forth with no holds barred. Harry's thoughts were disconnected but even so Doctor Ross had his place within the abuse. Lilly, Lilly he wanted Lilly, he needed Lilly but she had no idea what had happened and at this moment in time was oblivious to Harry's unhappy state. Harry had to calm down he just hadn't the energy to keep up this pace of abuse, it was to be hours before any other Doctor came to see him. When the Doctor finally came Harry tried to tell him

"I am Harry Baines this treatment is totally wrong, I am Doctor Ross's patient bring him to me." There was hysteria in his voice and tears in his eyes as he pleaded his case but this Doctor had seen it all before and got his syringe out to give Harry an injection, This had the desired effect and put Harry into oblivion. Now the Doctor with the help of the two men took off the straight jacket and examined Harry

"My God, this man is suffering." The Doctor had surgical gloves on and he told the men to put theirs on as they were looking at a very advanced stage of "Syphilis" Harry's body was covered in chancres with an ulceration of

the skin all over him, his hands covered in dark patches back and front. His genital organs didn't look like anything normal as they had reached a state of no return. Doctor said

"Now we know what we are dealing with, this patient's dementia is part of the "Syphilis" disorder he is too far gone to ever benefit from the application of treatment, we must find his next of kin and inform his recent Doctor, how this disease has got to this stage we will never know, this is happening all over the country, people hide themselves away, it is beyond the boundaries of decency. You can bet he has been to many Doctors and they have no cure or words of consolation this is a crippling or fatal disease. We must find out if he has a wife because she surely will have this disease passed from her husband. We can do very little other than make his last few months tolerable, yes it is as bad as all that. I feel sorry for this man in his ultimate misery. An isolated bedroom was found for Harry with an adult cot complete with barred sides all Harry kept repeating is

"Bring Lilly to me" Lilly had to be found and informed of Harry's dilemma. The men in attendance to Harry picked up Harry's clothes and searched in the pockets to find

his wife's whereabouts. They found an address so they would check with Doctor Ross to see if this was correct.

"I have asked Doctor Ross to come into the hospital to identify this patient, ah! This may be him. Doctor Ross said the address was correct but added

"I don't think his wife lives with Harry, they separated some time ago an argument they couldn't agree on you know."

"Where do you think his wife is living?" Doctor Ross hadn't a clue all he had been interested in was the fee he had from Harry at the end of each month. There were times Harry would pay weekly but it was always brought up to date monthly, this way seemed to suit them both. Doctor Ross said

"I think you had better go to the Police Station and let them find Lilly, yes Lilly is her name Lilly Baines." The Hospital Doctor came back into the room saying

"You say you have been Harry's Doctor for a while? Did you give this man a diagnosis?"

"Harry didn't want to know all he wanted was support and a cure, I began to have my doubts about a cure and was just going to tell Harry the unpleasant truth when he fell ill in my waiting room. You know the rest I do not have to give you chapter and verse." Doctor

Ross was trying desperately to cover himself, all along he had known the conclusion to Harry's story, it had suited his pocket to string Harry along with vague promises. Now he must be careful of any statement he made there was more than Harry to convince. All at once he wished he had never set eyes on Harry, what a court would do to him if this truth became known? Yes he was guilty of taking money under false pretentions. Was Harry too far gone to relate how he had gone to Doctor Ross each week and had Harry saved all the receipts from his visits? Doctor Ross was a worried man. He must hold his peace and plan a story that would make any accusation of Harry's nonsense. It wouldn't be hard to do Harry now was in an Asylum his word could not be taken as gospel. What about Harry's wife had she known what had been going on? For the first time in his life Doctor Ross felt insecure.

Chapter Thirty five

*Very soon Rosie would be one year old
the nights were drawing in and cold winds
made outings almost impossible. Lilly and
Annie had a second Christmas and all was
well. Now they planned for Rosie's birthday.
Annie would make the cake and Lilly was to
buy a wooden horse for Rosie to push along.
Annie had a soft toy a white bunny rabbit for
Rosie. The lady's were more thrilled than
Rosie herself, but of course Rosie didn't
know what a Birthday was, she being well
and happy dealt with each day as it came.
Which is I do declare is what we should all be
doing! As January rolled on the nearer
Rosie's Birthday became. Annie and Lilly got
more excited but also a little concerned as
Rosie was not very well. Lilly had stated that
if Rosie did not get any better she would have
to call in a Doctor. Annie said
"Children have all sorts of different miner
illnesses Lilly I think you are being worried
for nothing."
"I am not that sure Annie I don't recognise
the rash that is on Rosie's back, it is like
nothing I have seen before and it is making
her so uncomfortable."
"Give it a chance to go Lilly many children's*

ailments do without any help and go away as quickly as they came. We don't want to cause Rosie any alarm by letting a Doctor get his hands on her do we?"

"Well no but there again I don't want to cause her any harm by turning a blind eye."

"Give it one more week then Lilly and we will go to the Doctor, I will go with you I would like to hear what he will have to say."

"Thank you Annie, you know how I worry. At the same time I shall ask him about the repeated cold sores I keep getting. I must need a tonic for I do declare I am not a hundred percent well myself

"Oh it is just the winter blues I get the odd cold sore and a chesty cough but I pay little attention to it especially when half the community at large has the same symptoms' sore throats, headaches, swollen glands, you name it, the germs are all out there ready to pounce at the first opportunity. We can hardly place ourselves under lock and key as a prevention I do get annoyed though if I am on the horse drawn bus and someone sneezes all over me no consideration some people eh? Don't be gloomy Lilly all will be well when the sun begins to shine again. Now what about a nice hot cup of tea and stoke the fire up ready for making toast for tea." Lilly

grinned Annie always knew the way to dig her out of her melancholy moments she was a cure for all ailments with her ready smile and Lilly never knew how she would do without her.

Annie shuffled around the kitchen spreading the checked table cloth and making places for her and Lilly to enjoy their tea. The butter dish and bread that Annie had already sliced, Lilly called them doorsteps, but the butter would melt right into the depth of bread and run down the sides. Its smell was delicious and there were no wonder that a second helping would be offered and taken. Toasting only one slice at a time, the toast tasted mouth watering. The fruit cake in the tin would be the sweet to the meal and every mouthful enjoyed. Even Rosie had a toasted crust and as long as Lilly kept her eye open seeing as she didn't choke she gurgled with delight.

At that moment a tap came on the front door. Lilly went to answer the caller she opened the door and to her dismay found a Policeman waiting. He addressed Lilly in a very matter of fact way saying
"I have come to speak to Mrs Lillian Baines, is this right address?
"Yes I am Lillian Baines what is it you want

me for? Is there something wrong?"
"May I ask, are you the Lillian Baines who is married to Mr Harry Baines?"
"Yes I am."
"Will you verify his address for me please?"
Lilly gave him Harry's address wondering what all the fuss was about she said
"Please tell me what is wrong, you are upsetting me."
"Your husband Harry Baines has been admitted into the Asylum situated on the outskirts of this village. It is up to you whether or not you want to see him. He is asking for you. Sorry to be the bearer of bad news Mrs Baines but we have a job to do. I will leave you now to digest this information I wish you good afternoon madam." With that the Policeman left knowing he had left a bomb shell in Mrs Baines lap. Annie had joined Lilly wondering what was taking her so long. Annie had overheard the latter part of the information now realising something was very wrong. As the front door shut Lilly almost fainted, Annie broke her fall saying
"Come on now Lilly pull yourself together."
Annie held on to Lilly steering her into the living room where a warm fire was burning she sat Lilly down saying
"Stay as calm as you are able Lilly, I am

going to make a pot of strong tea, it is a good job Rosie is sleeping because I don't think either of us could cope with her right now."
She placed a cushion on Lilly's lap something to hold on to. Lilly sat in a stupefied daze considering the news. Tears began to trickle down her cheeks. What would have to happen next? She had no idea. Annie brought in the tea with a bowl of sugar saying

"Here we are Lilly put plenty of sugar in the cup it will help you sustain the shock. I am not expecting you to talk it over not yet anyway there will be time enough for that when you are feeling better." Lilly was in a withdrawn state. Knowing the bitter truth but not wanting to accept it, she felt sooooo weary and completely out of control, the unbelievable truth had hit her hard and she knew inevitably she would have to deal with it. Never in a million years would she have believed that Harry had broken down to this level. He was the one that knew how to live and enjoy life. Lilly was absolutely distraught Harry had dealt her his last blow and she was reeling from its impact. Recently Lilly had been planning reconciliation, and happier times but now that would be impossible. The future looked bleak would she have to look

after Harry? Lilly wouldn't know for sure until she had seen Harry. Must she see Harry? Her peace of mind would not let her do otherwise. So that much she had decided upon but it would take a great deal of courage to face Harry in a hospital for the insane.

Annie asked Lilly if she would like a bite to eat. Lilly declined saying "I couldn't eat anything Annie I keep feeling sick, if you would look after Rosie when she wakes up I would like to go to bed. I feel so insecure when I stand up. Annie helped Lilly up the stairs all the while Lilly was talking about Harry's dilemma but none of it made sense ....Trust Annie thought, I am thinking about Harry and a Harry that has hit rock bottom he is selfish and cares for no one, he will not drag Lilly and Rosie down I will see to that.

Lilly sobbed into her pillow wanting only the darkness of the night, she fell asleep exhausted. Annie took care of Rosie and until another day dawned a veil had been put up separating and pushing away the news about Harry. Of course it had to be faced but Lilly wasn't well. It seemed that both Lilly and Rosie would need a Doctor, Lilly had said as much in the previous weeks. There was ground work to be done.

Next morning Annie left Lilly until 9.30am in bed then took her tea and biscuits. Annie knew she must tread carefully, Lilly would be volatile but she must talk to someone, where to begin? Tapping the bedroom door saying

"May I come in Lilly? There was a pause before Lilly called

"Yes come in Annie." The tea was put down on the table and Annie asked

"Feeling any better Lilly?" Lilly's face was grey and sunken it portrayed disappointment and disbelief she said

"Harry has robbed me blind Annie I don't know where to start or what to do next." Annie poured the tea trying to assess the situation without it offending Lilly.

"I don't want biscuits Annie thank you." Annie sat down on a high backed cane chair she said

"About what you must do first Lilly, I think it is time to put yourself first, I think Rosie and you should see a Doctor. Yes you will have to tell him about Harry but at least you will know how you stand."

"How can I Annie? I don't really know as yet what the cause is that has reduced Harry to this state, has he just gone mental with

pressure and age or is there a serious underlying problem? Harry never told me anything but even I had my suspicions about his health, I thought he looked very ill when I last saw him, he was still out and about but he had lost his upright important figure, his head was bent and he couldn't look you in the eye. I think I have to go to the Hospital first before I see a Doctor they will tell me what is wrong and I will be able to assess what is the right thing to do. I need to know before I can judge him. I also need to know the state of Harry's mind and if there is any chance of him getting well again. Do you know Annie it is going to take all my will power to see Harry, I really don't want to ever set eyes on him again what good will it do?"

Annie let Lilly rant on for a while before replying

"Quite honestly Lilly I think you have to see Harry it is to do with the Law and you being his next of kin" Lilly answered

"Well if you put it like that Annie and you are usually right I shall want to get it over with as fast as I can. It is beyond belief what Harry has put me through these past few years. I wish he was in his right mind, then I could give him a piece of my mind and I would

deliver blow after blow in return for the blows he has dealt me. Yes Annie this is a side of me you don't see very often and don't recognise it is because I am truly furious."
Annie knew it was best to leave Lilly and let this venom out of her system, it would be better for her in the long run she said
"There is nothing that you have said Lilly that I don't agree with, you won't shock me. My only query is how you put up with Harry for so long I have never liked him. The quicker out of his way the better if you ask me." Lilly said
"Do I have to go to the Hospital today Annie?"
"The sooner the better Lilly then you will be able to assess Harry for yourself. You only know what a third personal opinion is as yet. Now you are going to ask…will I go with you. Yes of course I will but what about Rosie her welfare has to be considered. I can't think an early impression of an Asylum will do her much good do you?"
"Of course you are right Annie but who can we ask to look after her while we are away?"
"Now let us think who do we know that we can trust? We don't have many friends do we? You and I are usually sufficient enough to meet most disasters and get through them.

I can only think of the lady in the embroidery shop you know where we buy our silks from. She is always ready to chat and is a solid character. We could take Rosie in her perambulator and see if she would keep an eye on her. A couple of hours would be sufficient to get there and back. We need not give any information out, just that we have to go to the Hospital. Somehow the title Asylum is daunting to most people."

"Seems like a plan Annie and as I have no further suggestion we will try to do as you say."

It was two in the afternoon before they were ready to face this ordeal. The lady in the embroidery shop (now they knew was called Hettie.) had willingly fallen in with their plan. Rosie was such a lovely child she said it would be a privilege to have her for a couple of hours.

Chapter Thirty six

*Now Lilly and Annie had to find the way
to the Asylum, they were able to hire a horse
drawn buggy and were very glad of the cabbie
knowing the way; he knew exactly where to
take them to the front of the building. It was
ominous, a daunting grey building with very
high walls and very small exits. They paid the
cabbie and approached the building. A man
at the main gate tall and sturdy asked for
their names, he looked down upon a list and
was satisfied enough to allow them through.
Walking on to a cobblestone driveway they
approached a high heavy wooden door. This
had a huge knocker and Lilly banged upon
the door with it. After a few minutes a sturdy
looking lady answered, her voice was brusque
and hard she said
"Who is it you wish to see?" She glowered
down on them Lilly replied
"Mr Harry Baines, I am Mrs Lilly Baines
and I have my friend accompanying me."The
matronly lady said
"I must have her name she wrote down
Annie's name and said
"Follow me." There were many doors to go
through each one with a different key. They
were unlocked and then locked again after*

the company had passed through. It was cold
but Lilly found her whole body was
perspiring she shivered. Annie took her arm
and squeezed it to let Lilly know she was right
beside her. This was a place of torture in
Lilly's mind; it was alive with shouts and
screams that echoed along the white washed
corridors. Surely Harry was not in one of
these rooms that they were walking by. A
dreaded fear filled Lilly no-one surely
deserved this kind of treatment? Looking
upon things from the inside of these
miserable walls was a unique experience and
one that Lilly and Annie could well do
without.

The air was cold and hung with the
overpowering smell of antiseptic. They
walked yet further into the corridors, the light
became dim Lilly wanted to turn around and
get out into the daylight. There was no day or
night in these rooms they were all a sickly
shade of yellow, this came from the one oil
lamp fixed onto each ceiling. There were no
windows and the air now took on a smell
derived from human excrement. All of Lilly's
being repelled the truth, this was fact and an
undeniable urge to be sick came over Lilly.

At last the journey through was over. Lilly
was taken up close to a heavy door and a grid

*was opened for her to look through. The
escort said*

*"Here is your husband Mrs Baines, we
cannot take you into the room as he has
violent spasms, at the moment although you
see him calm it is due to a sedative he has
been given but at any moment he could
override that medication and become very
hard to handle."*

*Lilly peered into the gloom and saw Harry.
He had only a white hospital gown covering
his wretched body. Hunched into a corner
liked a trapped animal. Lilly was aghast. The
walls of the room had padding on them and
not a stick of furniture in sight. This then is
what Harry had come to for the conclusion of
his life Lilly said to Annie*

*"Please Annie will you look and verify that
this person is indeed Harry, I am not sure
that it is. How could Harry with a splendid
aptitude towards figures even applying his
mind to be an accountant for many years
come to this sad end?" Lilly shuddered from
head to toe. Annie took her place to look
through the grid. At once she knew it was
Harry and turned to Lilly saying*

*"Yes Lilly it is Harry and I am so sorry."
Annie went to stand closer to Lilly putting her
arm underneath Lilly's for support Annie*

spoke to the attendant saying
"What does Lilly have to do now may we
simply go home?"
"There are a few papers for Mrs Baines to
sign and if you are both related to Mr Baines
we must make an appointment for you to be
examined. Annie quickly replied
"I am not related but Lilly has a one year old
daughter is she at risk?"
"Yes she is both wife and daughter must be
examined. If Harry's disease is present we
have one or two medications we can
administer, and our Doctors are searching
daily for a cure. This is Syphilis we are
dealing with it comes in four stages it is
according to which stage our patient is at, as
to what we can do. Caught early the diagnosis
is easier to deal with, we have our ways of
treating early cases that is why it is
imperative to get the examination done as
soon as possible." Lilly was taking this all in
and realised in an instant that this Syphilis
infection was within her and in baby Rosie.
How she despised Harry bringing into her
home nothing less than a deadly disease. The
attendant then dropped a bombshell into
Lilly's line of thought saying
"Mrs Baines in his more lucid moments Mr
Baines has been calling out for you, he wants

*you to take him home. Now I think I know
what you are about to say but I must ask can
you accommodate Mr Baines. If not he will
have to stay in the Asylum until he passes
away. There is a fee for this, the Asylum
counts on this money to keep wretched people
that have no other family and to pay the
many fees that have to be met. You can let us
know when you attend your examination
appointment, which we shall treat as urgent.
We will see you again in two days time and
baby Rosie. Lilly was utterly taken aback,
bring Harry into her and Annie's home in the
state he was in, it took no time at all to make
that decision Lilly said*

*"I can tell you right now I cannot have Harry
back for me to nurse, we haven't lived
together since he knew I was pregnant with
Rosie, which he said was not his child, I
never knew anything about his private life or
how he spent his days and nights. I have lived
with my friend Annie. I do jointly own the
house that Harry has been dwelling in and I
could settle any fees after that was sold.
Would it be good if I put that in writing? The
money I have at my disposal at the moment is
not enough to pay for Harry's needs here
with you."*

"I think you have to speak to the Hospital

committee and the Doctors in charge of Mr Baines will answer your question. Something could surely be arranged. I will make appointments for your examination and a separate one to speak to the Hospital committee then yes for today you may go home."

 Back through the deadly corridors Lilly and Annie could not get away quickly enough. Before leaving, the said appointments were made and at last the huge wooden door was unlocked to let them through, only the heavy gate now to arrive in the main thoroughfare. Annie said

"I thought that visit would never end I can't wait to get home and put the kettle on. I am so very sorry Lilly my dear, I expect you have a lot of thinking to do to weigh this situation up? Come on I am going to get a cabbie to take us straight home, or rather to pick up Rosie, she is in her perambulator so we will have to walk the last few steps, poor little mite she also has to be examined, good job she is not old enough to be bothered about it."

Chapter Thirty seven

Annie called a horse driven cab from the ones that were passing by and gratefully Lilly stepped up into it. They made quick work of picking up Rosie. The last thing they wanted was to stand talking to Hettie although they gave her many thanks for looking after Rosie. Hettie said

"Rosie has been as good as gold I didn't have to tend to her at all. Anytime you want to leave her with me just bring her round I am always here." Hettie smiled and Lilly forced a smile too. Annie was waiting to be off enough was enough for one day. They left Hettie and speedily went home.

Stepping into the living room they were pleased to see the fire that they had left banked up with slack and tealeaves had burned steadily through, it was warm and had a delightful gleam Annie was pleased she said

"As soon as I have taken off my coat and hat I will put the kettle on, the fire is just right for making toast. Rosie must be getting hungry too." Lilly's head was in a spin and the last thing she wanted to think about was food she sat quietly by the fireside wringing her hands and trying to stop the tears that filled her

*eyes. Annie came in with the tea tray holding
a pot full of tea and china cups and saucers.
Turning her attention to Rosie she toasted a
crust of bread and buttered it one end, putting
a bib on to Rosie she was pleased to see Rosie
enjoying her tea, she would see to her
properly later on for now Annie wanted to
attend Lilly. Going back to where Lilly sat she
said*

*"Now come on Lilly we are home and now I
shall pour this tea it has had plenty of time to
mash, You should have sugar today Lilly it
will help your system to get back to even keel.
This is just what you need Lilly a nice hot cup
of tea." Lilly didn't answer she couldn't
because tears were choking her. At once she
could hold on no longer, her whole body was
racked in sobs tears run down her face and
her nose, her shoulders shook in the agony of
the moment. Annie comforted her sitting on
the arm of the soft chair and folding her arms
around Lilly*

*"Come on now Lilly my dear don't take on so
I know it has been such a shock but I am
here beside you and of course together we
will find a way." Lilly had to have this bout
out so heavy was her burden, disbelief still
haunted her practical thoughts. This was a
situation you only read about in a book, or in*

the local newspaper never did it happen for real. This was all too real and not only Harry had this dreadful disease Rosie and herself were in the first stages of it. Dearly Lord how was she going to get through this and ever be the same? The answers would surely come but how Lilly did not know. Annie shouted at Lilly catching her shoulders and shaking them Lilly was becoming hysterical Annie had to bring her back to solid ground it was for her own good. Finally Annie slapped Lilly's face and in the jolt stopped Lilly getting deeper into the frenzy. It served its purpose and Lilly was quiet once more Annie said

"Sorry Lilly I just had to bring you back to earth. Now we will drink a strong brew of tea. I have had the cosy over it, hot and strong eh?" Between the few sobs Lilly couldn't dispel she accepted the tea but what good it could do other than appease Annie she couldn't imagine. Nothing was going to change the facts she had to face and no-one could relieve her of this terrible burden, the truth had to be met and dealt with there was no other way, she and Rosie had to suffer alongside of Harry. A feeling of pure hate came over Lilly. Harry had sold her and Rosie short and he was in too much mess

himself he couldn't even try to rectify his evil ways. It was dreadful to feel like this towards the man she had loved and indeed married. Lilly had turned and she swore she would never ever forgive Harry he had brought his filthy disease back to Lilly's bed and the straw that broke the camel's back was the fact that she had passed it on to her beloved Daughter dear Rosie. How was Lilly ever going to reveal to Rosie these facts? Annie interrupted Lilly's thoughts saying

"If you don't want to talk about the subject I will understand but your appointment is the day after tomorrow so don't you think we should get a few facts straight?"

"Of course you are right Annie but where to start I am right out of my depth slung in at the deep end you could say. Well for one thing I am definitely not having Harry home. I fear I would strangle him if I did. I just would not be able to handle the situation Annie so that is one decision made and as regards Rosie and me having the examination I fear we have no choice."

"Lilly what makes you think you have this disease?"

"If you put your mind back to the weeks before Rosie's birthday I told you I needed to see a doctor, remember?"

"Yes but that does not mean you not feeling well has anything to do with Harry's disease don't jump to conclusions Lilly. I realise how you feel about having Harry back, he made his own choice about that when you fell pregnant he didn't want to know did he? He had other paths to follow. What is more it would take more than one person to handle Harry in his present state so that would mean the cost of a Nurse. According to the time Harry has left to live the costs could mount up into a fortune."

"Anyway Annie that will not happen I would sooner pay the hospital fee. I don't really know at what stage Harry is in. We will learn that when we see the hospital Doctor. Oh Annie I really can't say another word on the subject tonight, I am so weary, when I have given Rosie her bedtime feed I want to go to bed myself. I just can't take anymore this news has spoiled everything the future looks bleak, that is if Rosie and me have a future. Please Annie no more questions my heart is breaking."

"You go and get yourself into bed Lilly, there is no need to worry about Rosie I will see to her needs. Do you want me to help you in any way before I disturb Rosie?

"I can see myself upstairs Annie, if you will

attend Rosie and put her to bed I will be very grateful."

"Off you go then Lilly I will bring you a hot drink and some biscuits you have to keep your strength up for all our sakes? My God Harry what a blow you have dealt us." Lilly dragged up the flight of stairs and Annie went to see to Rosie.

The day for the appointment had arrived Lilly was full of fear and apprehension. Annie tried to lighten Lilly's load and talk about anything other than Doctors, it couldn't be done. Lilly was anticipating an ordeal in a situation that she had never had the misfortune of dealing with, she was wishing Annie would just be quiet Lilly's dear friend but at this moment in time Lilly stood alone with dread in her heart. Thankfully Rosie didn't know what this was all about and was her usual playful self. The clock ticked on and it was time to leave the security of home and commence their journey to the Asylum placing herself and Rosie at the mercy of the unknown Doctors they must face. Annie would be with them this afforded Lilly a small measure of comfort. Annie was trying to shoulder some reality of Lilly's pain this time though she felt useless.

Chapter Thirty eight

Standing at the outside gate of the Asylum Lilly couldn't stop herself shaking. The day was dirty the air hung in swathes and clung to the Asylum walls. Lilly held Rosie tightly to her bosom as slowly they approached the heavy wooden doors...as Lilly saw it the gate of hell was standing before her. Annie held Lilly with her arm around her feeling the burden of Lilly's shame Lilly turned to Annie and said

"Annie I am terrified the humiliation and the degradation. All my life I have tried to be clean and keep healthy now Harry has brought me to this and I am here with the lowest of the low and not understanding any of it. I am ashamed. I chose the man that is Rosie's Father and this choice has led us to this awful and unavoidable state of affairs."
Overnight it had changed Lilly the awful introduction to the Asylum, its corridors and padded rooms. Now she had to surrender her own body to inspection and her Daughter Rosie. Where was the path that Lilly now had to agree to and live by, a formidable task for any-one? The clean and dutiful life that Lilly had lived doing daily what she considered to be a good backdrop for her husband who

being an accountant at the bank was a person to be looked up to. Lilly had found pride and prestige reflected upon her due to Harry's envied position. Lilly's head drooped where once it had held high. Annie had just stood beside her ready to listen and said

"No Lilly I protest, I must say this is none of your doing and God willing you will cope and survive, keep your chin up dear and let the Doctors know you are putting your welfare and Rosie's into their hands. We will get through this together Lilly I will do all I can to be by your side. If Harry wasn't already dying I would kill him."

They had reached the second great door and Annie reached up to bang the wrought iron knocker. The door was opened and a grim looking lady with a board in her hand said "Name please and the purpose of your visit."

"I am Lilly Baines and this is my friend, my little girl is called Rosie we have come to keep the appointment for an examination."

"Yes I have you on my list step inside please." As soon as Lilly had stepped inside the cold air and the cement floor adhered to the already damp clothes that Lilly had on, she shuddered wanting to run, and cancelling these appointments came to mind but already their escort was ahead and down the grey

*corridors they again went following her lead.
Branching off before they came to the
patient's cells they were shown into a room
that absolutely stunk of carbolic and
disinfectant the air was laden. Lilly couldn't
stop heaving but kept the vomit down with
great effort so she could face the Doctor with
some semblance of decorum. They waited.*

*It seemed ages sitting there forming words
Lilly wanted to say, how should she present
her cause she knew nothing about this illness
at last a Doctor approached Lilly saying
"Now let me see you are the wife of Harry
Baines and the child was conceived by him is
that correct?"*

*"Yes Doctor, there is one thing I must ask
you to do?"*

"What is that Mrs Baines?"

*" You must believe me when I tell you I had
absolutely no knowledge of my husband's
condition when Rosie was conceived and no
knowledge before of being sent for to advice
me of his present condition, you see we did
not live together. He denied the paternity of
the baby and didn't want to give his daughter
his name. I was so stupid, I had never ever
slept with any other man all my married life,
I was dreadfully hurt I wanted this child, all
the years of early married life had never*

given us a baby and now late though it was I was pregnant. I could not give up my baby although I was asked many times by Harry to get rid of it even as early as the first few weeks. I was distraught and cried many tears but nothing would change Harry's mind. My friend here with me today…Annie took me in and gave me a place to live and birth the child, I don't know what I would have done without her. I had no idea that Harry was ill, he showed no visual signs and he seemed to want his freedom. I would not give up Rosie and he did not want Rosie it was as plain as that. I didn't want to know how Harry spent his days and nights, I had money of my own inherited from my own Father so I have used that not taking a penny for Rosie's upkeep from Harry and when I broached the subject on the odd occasion I did see him, he dismissed his parental duty with a gesture of the hand, oh yes Harry Baines didn't want to know Rosie and I existed. Until I was notified of today's overwhelming situation I was utterly ignorant, that is as far as Harry is concerned. It is just of late I have noticed one or two things I don't understand happening to both myself and Rosie. To this day he hasn't seen Rosie and I have only contacted him if there was something I needed to know about. There has been no contact sexually either."

"It is good that you have told me all of that Mrs Baines, it may have a bearing on the treatment you will need. Please relax and sit comfortably dear lady, we are not accusing you of anything, we are not in a court, far from it we want to help you in any way we can." Lilly sighed, a sigh of relief at least she had told this Doctor her worst fears, spluttering out the facts, hoping this was the right thing to do. Now there was the physical examination to face."

"Now Mrs Baines show me on what part of your body you suspect there is something not right and that you have particularly noticed."

"For one thing Doctor I keep getting what I call cold sores on my lips extending to the tongue and then disappearing all together after a few weeks. Another one on my chest, it hurts."

"Are these the only two places you can show me?"

"In all propriety it is, I do have what I think is one developing on my Vulva but I could not possibly show you that it is in such a private place."

"Come now I am a Doctor, you have to let me see or else how can I treat or prescribe the

right treatment. I don't know what I am treating unless I can see clearly. Now Mrs Baines I must ask you to slip off your pantaloons and don't be silly I must see for myself." Lilly coloured up she had never let another man see her let alone touch her she said

"Can't you diagnose this complaint from the lesions that you can readily see without taking my drawers down Doctor?"

"Indeed not, this is a very serious report I must make, it cannot be based on a guessing game Mrs Baines. Get on with your undressing or you will anger me." Lilly knew then the gravity of the situation and that she had to comply with the Doctors request. The Doctor could see the anxiety building in Lilly so he said

"Mrs Baines you have brought your friend with you and she can come and stand beside you. There will be the examination and nothing more does that satisfy you?" Annie knew it was against all Lilly's reason to let another man go anywhere near her most private parts, she spoke quietly to Lilly.

"I am here beside you Lilly and will do as Doctor suggests. I will see that everything is conducted in the proper manner. It will be all over very soon. Rosie then has to have her

turn and then we can all be on our way home. Don't delay the agony anymore it has to be done it is for the best Lilly." Lilly did as requested covering her face with her two hands in shame. Lilly now on the examination couch felt her body go stiff, to allow a Doctor to touch her was beyond her comprehension. Doctor felt the reaction in Lilly and said

"Please dear lady again I ask you to relax" immediately he went to work saying

"Ah ah! Yes as I suspected this sore is not at all like the other face sores. Are you finding it difficult to pass water?"

"I have to admit I am it is stinging when the urine passes the sore."She pleased the Doctor.

"That is one thing I can help you with Mrs Baines, I have mercury ointment that you can use quite liberally several times of day. Nothing is going to procure healing but we can try to halt the procedure so that it gets no worse. Doctors are talking about a cure they are working on it as we speak, if I can slow down the onslaught that is alive within you now it would be a good step to take, every day is a new day and lessons are encouraging. Of course this is Syphilis and mistakes will undoubtedly be made. I will help all I can.

This does not mean I can help your husband, he is still being assessed we will talk about that at a later date. Syphilis comes in stages; it is highly desirable to catch it in its early form. As for yourself and Rosie I think you have a fair chance, living clean has been in your favour and so it is with a good diet. Easy living, no sexual contact these are all in your favour. We must see just how far down the road Harry is and judge from there. I believe he is in the fourth stage their maybe nothing we can do, I will give him my most urgent attention. Now let me look at this little charmer, Rosie is it? A lovely child you may slip off the couch and dress now Mrs Baines." Relieved Lilly soon was on her feet again and dressing. Annie following instruction placed Rosie on to the couch, Rosie looked at this strange face before her and began to wriggle away Lilly stepped forward and assured her that all was well. Holding Rosie's hand Lilly signified to Doctor the rash on Rosie's back
" I do see this rash is nothing like my sores but it may have significance don't tell me I am worrying over nothing? I would sooner it be nothing! I need your reassurance Doctor." "Indeed you do Mrs Baines, Syphilis is a terrible disease and I will help all I can.

"Come on Rosie I am not going to hurt you."
He lifted the back of Rosie's dress up to see
the rash saying
"I could do with this dress off I need to see
where this rash has already travelled."
Immediately Lilly took off the dress saying
"See Doctor it has gone under her arms and
it makes her skin tender, I haven't treated it
with anything for fear of doing the wrong
thing."
"Yes you can make things decidedly worse if
you don't understand what you are doing. I
will prescribe a lotion that will help, I will
prescribe ammoniated salicylated. It is in fact
very new and not easily available. I think we
must all pray for a cure whilst I try to halt the
ongoing symptoms. Seeing me today Lilly will
not cure you or your sweet Rosie she is in the
very early stages of Syphilis poor little mite
the ulcerated patch on her back is sore and
that is why Rosie is fidgety it will give you
some peace of mind knowing that you are
being given the very latest medicine and that
the disease is in a very early stage.
Also a cure is being worked on. This is a
filthy disease with little discretion as to who it
attacks. Nevertheless it is more than obvious
Mr Baines infected you Mrs Baines and you
in turn infected Rosie. Let us hope all will be

dealt with and comes right eventually. In the event of Mr. Baines being sent here indirectly by his own Doctor, the act has done you a favour at least we have caught this evil disease very early in you and Rosie. Have you another partner now?"

"No I live with Annie as I said there is no sexual contact at all."

"There are many good points in your history I can at least give you hope. I also want to talk to you about your husband, a strange thing has occurred, come sit in the waiting room it will be vacant by now and away from the examination room. Lilly Annie and Rosie followed Doctor Lynn into a pleasant room which was much warmer. They sat down as Doctor Lynn said

"This is very private information Mrs Baines do you wish to discuss these facts while your friend Annie is present?"

"I trust Annie in all that I do, she has been by my side since day one so go ahead Doctor feel free to talk to both of us."

"Well you have seen…may I call him Harry? To continue, you have seen Harry in such a terrible state but suddenly he has quietened down. My male nurses went to give him the injection to keep him subdued. He begged them to listen to him first, as he seemed very

normal they gave him time to speak and this is what he said…

"Please listen to my plea."Harry went on to say

" Doctor Ross who delivered me into this hospital has been taking money off me for the last almost a year, he has not cured me of anything and what is further more he has never mentioned Syphilis, this disease has run on unchecked until the day he had me admitted in here, he promised me a cure but had I known this disease was Syphilis I would have realised there was as yet no cure. My bank balance has gone right down not that I minded that, because I wanted Doctor Ross to make me well again. My point being I am not insane I do not belong in this Asylum, the straight jacket was used to quell my anger, I was hysterical and the hospital I was brought to… the Asylum was chosen so that I would have to be sedated. It fit into Doctor Ross's plan so cleverly worked out; Doctor Ross dealt with aggravations of the mind it was not unusual for patients to be brought in here when he could no longer control them. Yes now I know I have Syphilis a disease of the damned, I request to have my case looked at before other mistakes are made, for my mind is clear and I am able to voice an opinion."

Silence fell in the room Doctor Lynn said "Mrs Baines, your husband has made a serious accusation against Doctor Ross and also a very serious entity against Doctor Ross's character. I have to say upon further examination your husband was quiet and did not need restraint. Of course this is an ongoing procedure and your husband will be dealt with in a different manner. Mr Baines is now stating that he is about to sue Doctor Ross, I must add we have given Mr Baines a thorough second examination and he is not as far advanced as we at first thought with Syphilis." Doctor Lynn had now told Lilly word for word of the indiscretion and awaited a reply.

Chapter Thirty nine

"Doctor Lyn I am at a loss for words, I knew nothing of Harry's life and how he conducted his affairs I had finished with him, now it sounds as though he is giving me the responsibility of his welfare all over again. I cannot do it. He has already crippled my hopes and dreams and given me and Rosie this disease. He brought it to my bed no less, he has denied my right to call Rosie his Daughter oh yes he is her Father although I would willingly have it otherwise. Harry has given me nothing but grief, I can barely look his way without a pang of regret, to live with him and look after all his many needs would be beyond my comprehension." Lilly caught Annie's glance and she knew she had made the right decision. Doctor Lyn said
"Well dear lady it was my duty to tell you of these events, no doubt there will be a short while to help you to adjust to the situation. You need to appraise what has been revealed and if I can help I will. Would you like to see Mr. Baines before you leave?"
"No I would not, it sounds as though he will be able to make his own decisions so let him get on with it and I will get on with my own and Rose's welfare. Do you know Doctor

Lynn Harry has given me many awful states to deal with and if I never set eyes on him again it would suit me! The man is selfish and without morals, how I could have married the man I don't know. All my married life I had to pander to his every whim and he held me in the house until that is what I thought I had to do. Annie has introduced me to the life that now I lead, up until now I have been more than satisfied. Now once more Harry has delivered this new blow. I will not be bowled over by it and with your help dear Doctor I can still live a life, but not with Harry.

"Indeed you can dear lady, now I must say good day to you, perhaps you will have less fear of me when you come again Mrs Baines. Make an appointment for next week we must do all in our power to stop this progress of the Syphilis organism. We have a good chance as long as you do everything by the book. Just one more thing before you leave, you have to know that should anything go amiss with your Husband or should it happen that he is transferred to another hospital you will be sought after and notified as next of kin."

"Thank you for reminding me Doctor, not that I have considered Harry next of kin for a very long time." Lilly and Annie at last said

their goodbye's very glad to be out into the fresh air once more. Annie searched for a vacant cab while Lilly comforted Rosie holding her close. The truth was still hard to believe, Lilly would have to do a lot of thinking, at the back of her mind she knew her first thoughts should be for Annie, maybe Annie would not like Lilly and Rosie living in close quarters, Lilly shuddered at the thought. First opportunity they would talk it all over, for now home and the kettle put on to boil, how the simple things took precedence when the cards were on the table.

The week went swiftly by Lilly had still fought shy of asking Annie how she felt about living in close proximity with herself and Rosie although she had found a way around and now was conscious of keeping away from Annie as much as she possibly could. This was a sexual transmitted disease and there certainly was no contact in that regard with Annie, they fell into a new routine quite easily and the mood lightened. All too soon the appointment for Lilly and Rosie dawned once more. Lilly was a little better as regards anticipation but still loathed the Asylum and all it conveyed to her. Annie was again going with them she said keeping the conversation light

"I hope Lilly you will be a better patient today, the Doctor is only trying to help you and Rosie so keep your chin up and your desire to be well to the fore and hurry up we mustn't be late. Arriving at the Asylum did Lilly's nerves no good at all, it was alright Annie lecturing her but Annie didn't have to show the Doctor her bare flesh, this was still an ordeal for Lilly. They waited to be called into the surgery...

"Ah come in Mrs Baines bit better I hope eh?"

"Yes thank you Doctor, there are no more eruptions on my skin, and Rosie's rash is fading, her temperament has been better also."

"Always glad to hear the good signs my dear. Now Mr Baines is still with us but he has no confinement of movement, he has in all fairness explained his case to us in length. He is extremely angry with Doctor Ross, when Mr Baines arrived at this building he was put into a straight jacket and needed restraint we took this as a patient who had lost his mind and needed restraining. We deal with many such cases, then a drug was injected to keep him subdued, all part of our process rightly so, but now we know it was not because his brain had gone it was resentment and anger

that produced the state we saw him in. Fury overtook his very being and the more he struggled the more we thought we had a mental patient on our hands, now I am not saying he has not got Syphilis but I am saying the disease has not yet reached its power to be a problem to his countenance. In other words he is in control of his faculties and is asking to see you." Lilly drew back saying
"No I don't want to see Harry, he has brought me nothing but trouble, I would go as far as to say I hate him Doctor."
"As far as I can see Mrs Baines you really have no choice, Mr Baines is still your husband and he has rights, we thought if you saw him while we were still tending his needs it would make it simpler for you. I would arrange this meeting in a private room and a Doctor would be in attendance at the other end of the room. You would have your privacy and the Doctor would see to it that sanity would prevail. Think about it while I take a look at your body's appearance and Rosie's rash." Lilly said
"I have used the lotions and the medicinal compound to the letter." Doctor smiled and said
"This disease can come and go for years, it can lie dormant for many years too, but the

Syphilis will stay with you until a final cure is found or death occurs, make no mistake about it Mrs Baines, there will be a cure it is trial and error, with time playing a crucial part. The severity of the disease also plays a crucial part, as I told you I am so pleased to say you and Rosie are in a very early stage and I will try to prescribe the very best of medicines for both of you, and of course hope that the cure is not far away, daily it is being worked upon and in many countries. I am going back to Mr Baines, he insisted on a full physical examination, and he told us a few home truths about Doctor Ross, how he has been treating him for many months without mentioning Syphilis. The fees he has charged your husband must be returned. We in turn have asked Mr Baines to let sleeping dogs lie, we will be talking to Doctor Ross and we will see that some of the money that has been paid by your husband will be returned to his bank. In these circumstances we try to keep a low profile, mistakes are made and sometimes they have to be corrected. No-one wants to see a Doctor in court, their reliability must be depended upon, I am sure you agree. The biggest shock to Mr Baines was when Doctor Ross said he could not treat him anymore and that this disease was Syphilis, A bitter blow and it had dire effects upon Mr. Baines. When he was delivered into our hands he was ranting and raving as we would expect of a man who was brain damaged therefore we put him in a padded cell where he could do no harm. We treated what we saw, that being insanity. I would advise you to speak to Mr Baines so that all is cleared up as soon as possible." Lilly looked blank for a moment then said

"This is awful, I cannot forgive Harry but having listened to your statement I am beginning to understand. Do you know just what he wants of me?"

"No dear lady I don't know so please be explicit when you agree to something or indeed not agree. I do not expect fireworks but then again it depends how the conversation goes, I will make the appointment for you away from your check up appointment. That is twice I will see you in the coming week. Do not worry, all will be well you will see" Lilly wasn't entirely convinced.

All this time Annie had sat in the surgery so there was not a lot she knew of the Doctor's previous encounter with Lilly and she didn't know at all about the appointment with Harry the following week. This was one time Annie couldn't intrude decisions had to be made by Lilly.

As soon as Annie and Lilly were free from the Asylum grounds Lilly began to tell Annie what had gone on during the last hour. Annie said

"Well if that don't beat all, got to see Harry have you? What do you think he will have to say?"Lilly spoke

"I don't know of one positive thing I could talk to Harry about, why he wants to see me goodness only knows but the hospital Doctor seemed to think it was the best to have this meeting. I tried to wriggle out of it but the Doctor was insistent."

"If I were you Lilly I would sift through anything important that Harry might want to know, you know how devious he can be and it is not in his nature to be put off."

"You are right Annie I am dreading the meeting, I have only seen him tied up in a straight jacket writhing in the corner on the floor that was enough for me. Doctor says he is much calmer now and I certainly hope so. What on earth could he want from me?"

The weekend sped by and the time of Lilly's appointment with Harry had dawned. Annie asked Lilly if she needed her company when visiting to talk to Harry, Lilly said

" Well Annie I know the way and I shall take a cabbie to get me there, perhaps if you stayed home with Rosie it would be for the best. I have been struggling to think what he wants me for. I plan to say nothing, he will have to ask me directly so that I know the road he is going down, and I shall be sparse with my replies, to tell you the truth Annie I am dreading this coming encounter."

Chapter Forty

A drear cold and miserable day had dawned. Wet mist hung in the air. Leaves on trees were dripping droplets that looked like glass bauble decoration. Lilly would sooner it be dry and bright, it was a big enough job keeping the appointment lest lone picking her way through moss wet and treacherous on the cobblestones. Finally she reached the huge Asylum door finding her solitude unnerving. Keeping her pride and self worth Lilly used the wrought iron knocker, it resounded around the court yard. Lilly pulled herself into an upright position her pride intact. The door was opened and here again was the ominous Matron. Lilly had to notice the heavy bunch of keys locked around her middle, she remembered the heavy "clang" the noise that they had made when walking as she had taken Lilly in the first time. Not smiling she said

"What is your name and who do you want to see?" Stern faced she looked through Lilly. Lilly gave her detail and was let through the door this area looked familiar also in a courtyard design Lilly had failed to notice this when the previous visit had been made, it was precise dark and foreboding. This time

Lilly was ushered to the opposite corridors. It was quieter here with less of the screaming that had frightened Lilly before. Lilly was shown Doctor Flynn's room and was greeted "Sit down Mrs Baines I think we should have a short chat before I take you to see Mr Baines. Is there anything you would like to ask me especially? Or shall I carry on and tell you the things you really ought to know?" Lilly felt trapped her mouth dry and her hands trembling.

"I would like to hear from you Doctor Flynn. I have nothing specific to ask you or indeed Mr Baines."

"The first thing you must be aware of although Mr Baines is calmer it is partly to do with the sedative we have given him, just a mild dose you understand. He still has a more advanced type of this disease Syphilis than you or Rosie. Although now we know it has not yet affected his brain which in turn will be discussed by ourselves, Doctor Ross and your good self and Mr Baines. I assure you Mr Baines will get part or all the fees he has paid to Doctor Ross returned. Doctors do not like being taken to task an out of court settlement would appear to be the best solution for both Doctor and Patient. Your husband Mrs Baines is a very sick man and

unlike yourself and Rosie has no chance of a cure, the disease is too far established. We can help him for a year or two but it is his own self discipline that will be needed. Does Mr Baines drink Mrs Baines?"

"As far as I know he always has whiskey in the house but I have no knowledge about how much he drinks of the stuff, he would never allow me personal access to that knowledge. Same can be said of the time he is out socialising. No Doctor I never went out with him and I am told he went out far more after I left him. I can't for the life of me think what he wants me for, I have no wish to see him, our ways divided some time ago when he refused paternity rights to my, or should I say our darling Rosie. I tried to make him see that Rosie was his Daughter I of course knew it was the truth as I have never had anything to do with any other man. In fact I have not seen Harry for a long while I didn't know he was ill at all it has all been a very big shock to me. I live now with my friend and Rosie we get along fine and to be quite honest I do not wish to know Harry. What reason can he have to want to talk to me?"

"The reason is Mrs Baines… no I hesitate to tell you he needs to talk directly to you. If you have any further questions after you have

seen your husband you will make another appointment to see me and at that time I will be able to discuss your plans in confidence." Doctor Flynn got up from his chair and said "Follow me Mrs Baines." Doctor ushered Lilly down an ill lit passage then into a room that had no windows and a door that was kept locked. Lilly was invited to sit down. How gloomy was this room, was Harry coming to see her directly? Or had she to wait? Doctor Flynn took his leave and within a few minutes returned with Harry saying "Would you like to be left alone or should I stay?" It was Harry that answered "Please leave us together Doctor Flynn I have leg shackles on so I won't be going very far. I have some very personal things to say to Lilly." Doctor Flynn went quietly out of the room carefully locking the door and silence fell.

Who was going to break the deadly silence that hung in every corner of this austere room? Clearing his throat with a short cough Harry said
"It is good to see you Lilly you look well."
"No thanks to your intervention I must say Harry." Like a little boy who had been told off Harry went into character saying
"Oh dear Lilly don't scold me I am still your

husband." He buried his chin into his chest and looked down waiting for Lilly to reply. Lilly had no time for small talk and she knew all of Harry's ways, she wasn't in the mood for Harry to take his time. This was the time for the truth to be told she said

"No Harry you have no power over me, yes you are still my husband but in name only. I would walk an extra mile rather than risk encountering you on the street. I have absolutely nothing I want to say to you." Harry didn't recognise "this" Lilly she was not the Lilly Harry knew. He was put down and realised he had to say something to win her over Harry went on

"I am sorry for many things Lilly but it is all in the past now. You and I could build a new life together. Annie could look after Rosie and all would be well again. I can't give you this disease because you already have it. I think it is a very good idea. Of course you would have to come home again, I don't mind that." Lilly was fuming Harry had so easily passed Rosie on to Annie and made a place for her to go back home. Lilly thought I am at home you silly man I am content with Annie and Rosie. Lilly choked on the very audacity of Harry. Now yes now Lilly must tell Harry without ifs or butts. Her eyes were glazed over *with temper as she said*

"Listen to me Harry Baines and listen well, I have no desire to come back and live with you and what is more I will never again enter the house which I would remind you belongs to both of us. I don't know what the Doctors have told you but if it is the truth and the same as they have told me you are indeed a very unfortunate man. I don't pity you and I don't love you at all, you are despicable in my eyes. The Doctors say you must have a member of the family's consent to witness your signature and so get you out of this place. Your welfare is not of interest to me. You brought Syphilis to my bed and I in turn have passed it on to Rosie. The Doctors say we have a chance of a cure as the symptoms we show are very early stages, we are being treated, and hopefully there will be a cure found very soon. We could say it is nobody's fault but you and I know whose fault it is don't we Harry? I can't think of words to describe how I despise you. If you want help from the outside don't look my way, never in a million years would I help you." Harry had the expression of the old Harry, his face full of scorn and hate, his brow wrinkled and his cheeks puffed with aggravation. He wanted to hit Lilly. Once more he tried saying

"Lilly it is your fault and has been all along you should have been beside me instead of getting yourself pregnant and in fact keeping the brat. You are my wife and when I need you by my side that is the place you should be. You never would fulfil your sexual duties and things went from bad to worse. If you won't come home and fulfil your obligations I shall sell the house, and I will not be leaving Rosie my half I can assure you, that brat has cost me my life and no mistake."

Lilly stood up she didn't have to listen to Harry whilst he looked for a shoulder to cry on. Words had gone beyond her control and she wanted out of this deadly place, Lilly turned her back on Harry went over to the door and sharply rapped it with the silver knob of her umbrella, immediately the door opened. Lilly said

"We have finished all we have to say please see me to the exit door before I do something I will be sorry for." Doctor Flynn came forward saying

"You seem very agitated Mrs Baines is everything alright?"

"It depends which way you are looking at the situation. I just want to get home and just for your private ear I want you to know I will never go back to the house I lived in with

Harry, neither will I ever be available to look after him. If he needs to speak with me again he must go through you, I don't want my name involved. He needs someone to go to but it is not me. I hope I shall not set eyes on Harry ever again please now show me the way out, my next appointment with your good self I and Rosie will thankfully attend, as far as Harry is concerned I shall not need to know, now take me to the outside door for I am longing to get home." Doctor Flynn knew exactly where Harry stood and it was in a total unenviable position.

Harry was stunned he had imagined Lilly falling into his arms and thanking him for a second chance he called after her as she left but the words said fell on deaf ears and once more the door was locked. Just what did Lilly think she was doing? He must get out of this place by fair means or foul just at this moment he had no idea, the thing he did know he must learn how to put himself forward as an asset and curb his inflammable temper, the Doctors must be certain he was sane so he quietened down and waited. Doctor Flynn came back into the room and Harry did his utmost to appear normal Doctor said

"Well dear Sir your wife did not seem too

pleased with the idea of you and she getting together again. I am thinking she left me in little doubt about her position in relation to the getting back together which I know was what you were hoping for. Is there someone else in your family that would take you in?"

"I must think about it Doctor Flynn, Lilly may change her mind if I wait a while. Lilly has been known to be contrary before now."

"You must realise Mr Baines to stay put in this building is going to cost you. You must contact any other family member who would like to help, write if that is the way to contact them, you have spoken to me of a brother does he live locally? Put a few facts before him and see what he says, I will personally see that your letters are posted."

"He lives down south Doctor I very rarely see him he has a small cottage that overlooks the sea, I doubt if he would want anyone to live with him he has always been a loner. Likes spending time on a small fishing boat he owns. We never did have anything in common I liked the town and my banking career."

"At least send him a letter and see his reaction, for now Mr Baines I must leave you behind locked doors and you must make the place as comfortable as you can." He had left

Harry thinking of his options…perhaps my brother would sign me out? After all I have a house to go to, so a permanent address would be in my favour. I might go for years without the lesions on my body were to an extent as to be seen. My brother need never know I could keep this disease hidden beneath my shirts and scarf's, I have to learn to live with this problem, and I could live very quietly. This disease is not apparent to the eye. The world need not know the absolute truth of the matter. Maybe I could lead a normal life. …Harry thought he wouldn't have to deceive Jack only bend the truth a little. Yes this way needs working out, and with my brain I would soon come to a solution. With paper and pen in hand Harry sat in his small room and started to put words together, he had to think of the right things to say. As he dipped his pen nib into the ink another thought came to him, what about his other brother he hadn't heard from him for years, he argued with himself …but he has a wife, now what was her name? Ah yes "Adi" I don't believe they had children? I will write to both parties. So head bent he started to compose the letters.

It took longer than he thought weaving his way into their daily lives and including his desire to live with them was an awesome task. He rather hoped Henry and Adi would reply favourably, there was a chance of home cooking which appealed. He felt his own importance returning as he carefully strung the words compassionately on to the paper. This was the Harry Lilly had known, still his personality shining through and still able to pull a few heartstrings when the occasion arose. Albeit it was his own family he was addressing.

Chapter Forty one

Lilly's legs couldn't carry her fast enough to be with Annie and Rosie again. Her mind was working overtime she was seething at the core. The audacity of the man! Harry was offering her a place to live which indeed was half her own anyway and as if that were not enough he wanted her to abandon Rosie. He had asked her as though it was a privilege for her to do so. Lilly and Rosie were both ill because of Harry's loose living but he passed that by, dismissing the gravity of the situation. What had he said? Yes he was going to sell the house lock stock and barrel. Then for a short while he could live doing just as he pleased. Lilly would get her half and Rosie? What about Rosie? She was to get nothing from Harry. It hadn't bothered him one bit when he made this statement. How could he think Lilly would look favourably on his plan? Harry was selfish through and through. He was going to get the money back that he had paid to Doctor Ross for his own welfare. Harry never missed a trick but what a tangled undignified mess he was about to encounter.

Lilly turned the corner and could now see Annie's house. A warm welcome would be gratefully accepted.

As Lilly turned the key in her front door, the permeating aroma of fresh bread drifted and softened Lilly's angry mood. This was the entire home that she would ever want. Annie apron on and tea towel in hand came into the Hall to greet Lily

"So glad you are back Lilly, I might as well have gone with you for my mind hasn't stop wondering what Harry had to say to you. I will go and pop the kettle over the fire dear you must be well ready for a cup of tea"

Annie kissed Lilly's cheek then scurried away saying

"Is it a good time Lilly to ask what Harry wanted you for?"

"Tonight Annie, when Rosie has settled to sleep. For now the pot of tea you are making would be more than welcome I too am just too exhausted. The smell of bread baking when coming in the front door has reminded me how hungry I am. What are we going to have for tea?"

"I kept it simple Lilly, we have homemade blackberry jam and best butter hand churned from Cherry tree farm. I took Rosie a walk to get the fresh butter I also bought half dozen freshly laid eggs they won't take long to cook with toast or bread and butter. I thought you

may be hungry or on the other hand wouldn't want anything at all. You can have as much or as little as you want. We will have tea on a tray by the fire cosy like and warm, with a fresh pot of tea of course."

"Thank you Annie it sounds delicious and is in entire contrast to the room I have been sitting in with Harry. No I am not going to speak of it I will say though it has made my flesh creep." Lilly shuddered at the recollection.

Slowly Lilly began to relax even had a half hour with Rosie bathing her and blowing soap bubbles. She went down in her cot readily enough with her favourite teddy bear to cuddle. The very thought of Annie as Harry had suggested bringing Rosie up was out of the question. Lilly loved her little Daughter and no doubt about it. Now Annie and Lilly sat before the fire a tray on each of their laps. The bread had cooled just enough to hold the butter and was a lovely oven baked brown, a spoon soon had the jam spread and was delicious. They had enjoyed a boiled egg and this jam was instead of cake. The fire sent flames half way up the chimney and they hardly needed candles to be lit, the flame flickered, making patterns on the wall. Annie could wait no longer she said

"Come on Lilly tell me what Harry wanted you for." At the mention of Harry's name Lilly heaved a big sigh Annie said "As bad as all that is it?"

"Oh yes Annie he has my future all planned out for me. I hardly said a word, I couldn't believe just what he has been suggesting."

"Bet I know, he wants to come here and live with us am I right?"

"Worse than that Annie he wants me to leave Rosie in your care and take myself off to live as we did before in the household that belongs to both of us. He thinks it is a grand solution, he says I could see to his needs and he could slot in where appropriate. Apparently this Syphilis can be dormant and then rampage again. The only words I can connect with are... diabolical and yet another preposterous! Don't worry Annie it is never going to happen. If I don't adhere to his suggestions he says he will sell the house and live while he is able in rented accommodation. Rosie will not be put in his Will and if Rosie has an inheritance it will be from me and not a penny from him. I tell you Annie I was flabbergasted, words would not come out of my mouth, I sat bolt upright in my chair. I knew Harry had sunk low but I didn't know how low." Annie sat blank faced

as she took in this information she said "Tell me the truth Lilly you are not going to consider going back to live with Harry are you?" Her brow furrowed this had worried her

"Of course not Annie I can't bear the sight of him. Money matters, of course it does but I will be thrifty and make sure there is an inheritance to leave to Rosie, it is not impossible. Do you know Annie he flawed me! What is more he expected me to comply completely. What I say! Never in a million years. He will have to find his own way out of this dilemma. There was absolutely no apology for bringing this horrific disease into my home and now he thinks he is going to benefit by it! Again words fail me."

"Don't worry so Lilly, we will work something out and Rosie will always live here with us. There are certain things Harry cannot touch we will work within the law. This time it will be our decision and Harry will have no say in dear little Rosie's future even if he wants to. It has been this way since Rosie was conceived he gave up his parental rights when he rejected his rightful place as Rosie's Father. Silly man he thinks he can bend the rules to suit himself well we will see to it that he can't…he can think again." The

two of them sipped their tea and ate the bread and jam whilst trying to put the world to rights. The only trouble being in this case there wasn't a straight forward way out of this dilemma. The facts stared them in the face. Harry Lilly and Rosie all were infected with Syphilis. Lilly and Rosie would be tended and their symptoms early enough to be cared for with the hope of a cure but Harry was a different story all he could do was hide his lesions and hope they came where the eye could not readily see them. Lilly said "I wonder if Harry knows the gravity of this situation he can't go on ignoring his body and covering up the tell tale signs. If that is a fact he could infect many other people. Oh Annie it is a net that I find myself and Rosie caught up in and for my own peace of mind I must ask you, will you be comfortable living alongside the two of us? Do you think you can avoid picking up this same disease?" "Now Lilly none of that, in the first place it is carried by sexual contact, body fluid and the like, close kissing for example you and I are good friends our association is based on truth and trust alone I shall not even think about you passing it on to me. You and Rosie must keep all your Doctor's appointments with Doctor Flynn. No Lilly we will take a little extra care and we will see this through together don't worry. Harry has to make his own choice and if he has no conscience he won't be troubled about whoever he passes this illness on to. In my opinion he ought to be locked up, but looking from a lawful point of view he has done nothing to be locked up for, it is about what he plans to do and the suffering it will inevitably cause. Glad that is out of the way Lilly we both know the road we shall take and we will take it together. Now I will make fresh tea I am parched." Annie had said her piece she was very glad to have it all out into the open both she and Lilly understood and was now prepared to go on. A slightly different set of rules but they could handle that. Annie asked Lilly

"How are your lesions Lilly have you had any more new ones to upset you?"

"No Annie I thought I was getting rid of the ones that came, they appear and then disappear all in the space of a few weeks and then it is weeks again before they reappear. I am using Doctor Flynn's potion also on Rosie, she seems to benefit from it too daily I pray for a cure Doctor says it will be soon but then another month slips away. It is hard to keep patiently waiting but I must not lose faith in this Doctor he is our lifeline. Time *for bed now Annie I will pop my head in to see that Rosie is alright, goodnight.*

Chapter Forty two

Harry finished composing his letters there were two to be posted. He had a lot of thinking to do. Somehow he didn't fancy living with his brother, this brother had lived alone all his life and would be set in his ways. This left him with just one option his second brother and Adi his wife. Harry wondered if they had children, although they lived just the other side of town he hadn't paid them a visit for a long time. He rang the bell and a nurse came immediately Harry said
"I have two letters I want posting and the quicker the better have you stamps please?"
"Yes I can provide you with stamps but you must leave the letters open they have to be read by one of the staff before they are sent. Were you aware of that Mr Baines?"
"No I have sealed the envelopes. I will have to address the envelopes again and leave them unsealed." In his educated mind he had discovered showing respect to the nurses paid off. He reread the letter to Adi and her husband...

My dear brother and Adi,
I am in need of your help, I have been involved in a misunderstanding and I find myself in a very awkward position. I am now

in a private room attached to the Asylum.
May I say there was a big mistake when I was
first admitted but nevertheless I was brought
here? Now would you believe! I have to have
a relative to witness my signature so that the
Doctors can release me. All a part of having
things put down on paper and correct. Your
signature will directly follow my own and so
relieve this establishment of any blame there
might be. I have asked Lilly but I have very
little to do with her these days, she has a mind
of her own and doesn't live with me anymore
this rift has occurred since she had her
Daughter, naming me as the Father, bunkum
I say. I would like to see you face to face to
explain, would that be possible?

Yours sincerely,
Harry Baines.

There job done, short and sweet and to the
point. Harry wished Adi would come, he
would charm his way into her heart even if it
was through pity. He was ready to eat humble
pie. He could spend his time rehearsing the
right words to say but first he had to get her
here. Would his brother come too? He hoped
not, he had favourable memories of Adi, his
brother? Well that was a different story they
had not always seen eye to eye also his
brother was quick on the uptake and may

want a lot of explanation.

Adi was surprised by the letter, and even more so because it was addressed to Mr and Mrs Baines, Mr Baines Harry's brother had been dead for the last ten years. Sitting down in a chair by the window Adi carefully read the contents. Reading that Harry was in need of her help also surprised Adi. Harry was a man with dignity. From the time Lilly had married Harry Adi had been jealous, thinking Lilly had made such a good match. Harry was then an accountant and very well looked up to. Adi had noticed the way he carried himself and his proud manner. The letter conveyed a mistake had been made, what manner of mistake could that be? To leave him housed in an Asylum and paying for a room there was beyond Adi's comprehension. Hmm Adi mused I could take to Harry even after all these years, let him stew a while then I will reply. I need to know what the manner of the illness is, I must take my time.

Time was passing and still Harry had no reply to either of his letters. He made use of his leisure by getting himself spruced up and took on an upright stance he had drooped while drinking whiskey. There was no whiskey on these premises. It had actually done Harry good the enforced rest and the chilling prospect of the Asylum accommodation had made him take account of himself he had practised his form and smartened himself up considerably. The ankle shackles had been removed and to all intent and purpose he was somewhat in control of his own destiny, it had been a long time since Harry could lay claim to this feeling. He felt younger and once more his thoughts turned to the girls who were probably missing him. Do them good he thought. Absence makes the heart grow fonder. Yes he would have to take stock and try to get some semblance in his life. The lesions he had at this time were all hidden underneath his clothes, very fortunate. He must handle his words with care and hope his letters were answered. Still hoping that Adi would be the one to visit him, he remembered her quite distinctly, he would have to allow for the passing years but she would still be an attractive lady. He wanted to be in command of his own destiny and the sooner the better as this room was costing him a pretty penny. He also didn't want to give a chance for any more lesions to appear.

He lay on the bed his hands tucked behind the back of his head smiling and working out details for the future. He built quite a picture of Adi, his mind working overtime. He still had money and also there was money coming to him from Doctor Ross who had landed him with this Asylum problem. Harry was going to insist he received his full costs for the supposedly treatment he had received the previous year from this Doctor false information too. Oh dear no Doctor Ross you will have to pay every penny back and then more. Harry was almost talking himself to sleep when a sharp knock came at the door. Harry was quite startled, he was used to being behind doors with a lock and key only for Doctor's to use. This door had been locked by him and only he had a key. A paid for in advance room where he gave permission for a person to enter. He quickly looked around yes the room was tidy all Harry had on was just a cotton set of underwear. He snatched up his day clothes and called

"Just a minute I am ill disposed." He pulled on his trousers and buttoned up his shirt placing a cravat around his neck covering up a multitude of sins. Shoes were chosen for comfort and he was ready to open the door. Harry opened the door, the matronly nurse said

"There is a lady at the front gate wishing to speak to you, she has given her name as Adi

Baines do you wish to speak to her?"
Yes please bring her in she is my brother's
wife." Ten minutes later Adi arrived at
Harry's door. Harry ushered her in
recognising Adi   he gave her a seat saying
"How are you? I didn't expect you so soon I
am glad to see you Adi." Adi felt flattered he
had remembered her name she said
"Yes I am well Harry and you?" Adi looked
deeply into Harry's face, this was not the
Harry she had in her memory. Of course age
affects everyone so she made no comment.
Harry picked up the conversation saying
"Well first Adi I must tell you the
predicament I am in."Harry settled
comfortably in his chair and told Adi of
Doctor Ross and his devious ways of getting
money under false pretences, and of how he
had sent Harry into the Asylum in a state of
anger. When he found out that Harry had
realised just what was going on it caused a
huge argument Harry made quite a story of it
all never mentioning Syphilis. No that was
his own secret and while he could cover up
mentally and physically he was going to do
just that. Adi's reply gave Harry the benefit of
the doubt she said
"I assume Harry you know your brother died
ten years ago. I can't understand why you

need me I know nothing of your past."

"My dear Adi no I didn't realise my brother had passed on we didn't really have much in common did we? So you live on your own now?" Harry said with a charming smile

"I only want you to witness my signature, I have to have a member of the family to do that you see, hence the letter. Also the Doctor has to sign alongside our signatures"

"Why have you not asked Lilly? The letter gave me the impression you do not approve of Lilly's life style?"

"Lilly and I haven't lived together for a long time, she blames me for her pregnancy and I denied paternity foolish woman. I have my house all to myself now and will go back there to live so I would be no trouble Adi. Please take a little time to think about it if you wish and then if it is a favourable answer we then would make an appointment for you I and the Doctors to attend and get the job done. I would be very much obliged. My mental state is no longer in question. We could make life sweet you and me. That is all I have to say this afternoon. Thank you so much for coming I hope I will hear from you very soon." Adi was duly dismissed she felt there should be other information but nothing else was offered. As she left Adi's

thoughts crowded in on her…Harry had always been a truthful man his position in the bank required it. I must give his request due thought, why do I feel so uneasy?

Harry was glad to have Adi's visit over and he didn't think he had said anything that was off-putting. Next time she comes hopefully it will be to witness my signature then I will be free again. It was strange how Harry dismissed the fact of carrying Syphilis. It was as though what the eye didn't see the heart wouldn't grieve over. He prayed the lesions would appear as they did now, easy to cover up…and go as quickly, before he had to take them seriously. He felt better than he had done for a long while. New ground beckoned him, why if he played his cards right he might even get Adi to take Lilly's place and look after him, being attracted by her helped the illusion. Harry took off his presentable attire and placed his body length on to the couch feeling quite pleased with his outlook. He must try to keep Lilly and Adi apart as he didn't want Adi to know about the Syphilis. He pondered as he lay resting…The odd thing about this disease is the intervals between each onset, and the severity of the bout. I must learn how to hide and control the damned lesions I must have a way to deal with it…. Easier said than done! I must make every moment count this is my aim a little deception will be required yes I can do that. I have no animosity towards Adi in fact I quite like her, a good figure and well dressed, there is just one thing that annoys me and that is her veiled face, is her complexion that bad so she has to cover it up? I know it is fashionable to wear a veil so perhaps it is just that. I am no oil painting myself I shouldn't be so critical but I do like my ladies to look at their best. Enough of these thoughts my brain is tired. I will sleep for a while.

Chapter Forty three

Rosie had been put to bed and Lilly alongside Annie were stitching the embroidery picture each to her own Lilly said "Do you know Annie I am feeling much better in myself and Rosie is quieter too. I believe the treatment we have from Doctor Flynn is doing us good. We are not now blindly following something we do not understand. Doctor Flynn is very caring and tells me what to expect and he has set us up in the right way. We know Syphilis can be experienced without the shocking knowledge of dying from this disease. We talked at some length when last I saw him and he is very optimistic about a complete cure being found, he says it is only a matter of time. Rosie and I must take the medicine he has prescribed and see him each week, patience is the factor as I know little enough, I know he uses arsenic, but he keeps the doses very low. Life has a way of judging the individual if I hadn't caught this from Harry I would never have met Doctor Flynn and he seems a very educated and sincere person I can put my trust in him. If he approves of what he is using who am I to disagree? I only know the result, when he examines me I know from the look on his face just how the treatment is working. It would be grand if Rosie and I could be cured, of course I am forty seven years old now so time is of the element but I am hopeful if I keep Rosie and me healthy in general who knows? We both might be cured!" Annie replied

"You know Lilly I will always be here for you and Rosie you know that. Have you got to see Harry again?"

"I should think not! I have told Doctor Flynn not to send for me again. I was appalled at Harry's request, wanting me to go back and live with him and bless your life look after him and his needs, it is obvious his needs would be at bedtime. Wife he quoted at me, he has the cheek of the very devil. I thought Harry loved me how cruelly deceived was I. No Annie I am certainly off his list of visitors. I never want to set eyes on him again. Saying that but I expect I will have to see him if I want Rosie to have her true inheritance. The house is half mine so he can't argue that one. I am going to see to it that Rosie gets my share that much I intend to do. Oh Annie I never should have started talking about Harry he is a thorn in my side, let me go in the kitchen and make us a calming cup of hot chocolate. Sorry my dear you must be well

sick of me and my problems.
Lilly stood up and put her needle into the top of the canvass the ruby red silk trailing from it.

Bringing two steaming cups of chocolate Lilly returned Annie smiled contentedly when she saw the chocolate biscuits on the tray. Lilly caught her look saying
"Yes Annie I know it is a bit self indulgent bringing biscuits but all that has gone on in my recent past has altered my way of thinking and my attitude towards keeping slim I find myself in a mellow mood that sometimes I can't explain. I take what is offered and I am glad to be alive and need I say Rosie is alive, and you Annie? Well I can't think of a world without you. There will be a time when I can thank you in a material way but I want you to know now what store I set on our friendship."
"You are more than welcome Lilly, and Rosie, what would either of us do without Rosie." They sat in this congenial atmosphere and peace filled the room. The fire glowed although it was almost burned through to its embers, the grey ash and the last of the coals made a shifting sound as they fell to the bottom of the grate. Lilly said
"I am ready for my bed Annie very soon, I have become very tired this last hour yet it

isn't yet our usual bedtime."

"It is your body clock telling you to rest Lilly. These past few weeks have taken their toll, you have not been getting proper rest, you must do as your body dictates and get your strength back, no fault in that as I can see. Appreciate the fact that you see the worth in our friendship we have both been tossed from pillar to post. Perhaps tidying the debris in the garden is something that will bring us back down to earth and I sincerely hope you will be outside with me Lilly we can plan what plants we are going to have this summer. I really believe if we keep things simple and take our pleasures as they are offered all will be natural very soon. Harry well! What can either of us say about Harry? He must go his own way and leave us alone to find our own way. Least said best off I say. Finish your hot chocolate Lilly and we will sit while the fire embers burn out. We will both retire early."

The next few weeks passed without incident pleasing all concerned. Lilly was a little puzzled at not receiving mail from Harry, she had half expected him to plead his case but no, the matter in hand seemed to have been put to sleep. Lilly couldn't help wondering who Harry would turn to next but as soon as the thought entered her mind she dismissed it knowing full well if Harry wanted to speak to her nothing would stop him. Daffodils were blooming in the garden and the spring trees were sending blossom and leaves, a pleasant scene to work with. Soon it would be time to choose the border plants Lilly knew a gardener that had a greenhouse full of small plants, he never charged her very much and his plants were good and strong. About now was time to put in an order so as to be sure of getting the plants of their choice, they would be left in the greenhouse until the weather improved then Lilly and Annie would have the pleasant task of choosing what went where. Annie liked Marigolds they were bright and offered any vacant space strong colour, these plants didn't need a lot of tending and the bright orange flowers came readily after the clumps of bluebells had died back into the soil. It wasn't yet warm enough to stay outside too long but the spring sunshine cast its rays across the garden and gladdened the heart. The winter look of leaves and sticks that the trees had thrown down had been dealt with and all was filled with promise. Rosie had been wheeled outside in her perambulator to watch Lilly and Annie. Just finishing they

*came to sit alongside Rosie on the garden
bench. Annie turned to Lilly and said
"Phew! that took a bit of effort this year Lilly
but now we can sit back and wait for the
bedding plants to be ready, good job we have
old Jack he always has such lovely bedding
plants and is always ready to oblige with any
information we need. I have been meaning to
ask you Lilly is that "it" as far as Harry is
concerned?"*

*"I am dearly hoping so but whether or not he
will come pestering my life out I can't say for
certain. I told him the plain truth and I meant
it. You know him Annie better than anyone,
he has a dark and devious side to him and he
likes his own way. I have wondered myself
who he will find as witness to his signature?
As long as it is not me I don't care. I think he
is still ill and this façade he is playing out is a
means to an end. You wouldn't sign him out
would you?" Lilly fell about laughing saying
"Me? I would have more chance of fetching
down the moon than bringing Harry out of
his unsavoury abode."*

*"He will try you know Annie said please
don't be fooled whatever he says."*

*"I promise you Annie. Harry may ask you for
help."*

" You know how I dislike Harry why should

he ask me for help?"

"He has the gift of the gab Annie he could charm ducks off water and he will stop at nothing until he gets his own way. Do tell me if he tries to contact you he might try getting to me through you."

"Rest assured Lilly that is not going to happen as far as I am concerned Harry is dead in the water and I hope I never set eyes on him again."

"My sentiments entirely Annie, Lilly shivered saying how Harry keeps creeping into our conversation I will never know. Come on Annie I am feeling a chill now that the sun has slanted, time for tea eh? We have the scones we made yesterday and I can't wait for a cup of tea." They wheeled Rosie back to the front door and pulled her pram through the hall into the kitchen. Rosie liked to watch as tea was made, she also liked the buttered crust dipped in sugar she was given. A large bib was tied around her as buttered crust could go a long way especially with sugar!

Chapter Forty four

Harry had lulled himself into a false sense of security. Preening his looks in front of the mirror he thought he had the upper hand once more and ladies would still fall over themselves for his company. Initially the Syphilis had put him down and fear had been his constant companion. Now he felt different about the whole affair, he would deal with it and put the interest back into his life. What did he care who he carried this disease on to? What the eye doesn't see the heart doesn't grieve over. He would disguise the disfiguring lesions and hope that the initial phrase was over. He knew his disease would kill him but he also knew it came in lapses and he had the chance of ignoring the facts for this intermediate span of time. Harry had learned a lot about Syphilis right from the onset, although he had chosen to ignore what was clearly before his eyes. Doctor Ross had not mentioned the word Syphilis! Now Harry realised he could keep it somewhat under control…he hoped. Harry hadn't realised whiskey had added to his sorry situation. This now of course had been denied to him. He was better for that alone, he could think straight and plan ahead. His thoughts at this immediate moment were on Adi and when he would hear from her. A knock came at the door, he thought… oh no not again. This time he flung on a dressing gown and went to answer his caller. It was Doctor Flynn who had to be polite as now Harry was a paying client

"Sorry to interrupt your leisure Mr. Baines but I have Doctor Ross with me to talk of money matters." Harry opened the door and invited his guests to come in and sit down. Doctor Ross had to smooth over and make little of the way he had treated Harry. Money was at stake and no-one likes to part with their money. Doctor Ross wore the cloak of friendship as he said

"Good to see you looking so well Harry, I hope we can resolve the problem of money with as little fuss as possible" Harry replied "We will Doctor Ross that is if you give me what is owed to me, a tidy sum I think." The two men stared at each other or should I say glared at each other.

"Come now be reasonable Mr Baines, you did take up a regular amount of my time. Not telling you that you had Syphilis was because I thought it was the best way to treat your particular case. I always had your best interests at heart."

"My best interests! I relied on you for the truth and for a cure, all you saw in me was the money, you took that readily off me each week and it found its way into your bank roll, while all the time you knew a cure was not obtainable." Doctor Flynn felt the atmosphere turn cold and butted in to say "Mr Baines you must be civil to Doctor Ross he is here to settle the account between you, the whys and the wherefores are as water that has passed under the bridge. Material differences must be agreed on." Turning to Doctor Ross Doctor Flynn said

"Doctor Ross I think you will agree no court case must develop by slinging angry words at each other. I am here as witness as to what is being said and would like it fine if you gentle men would act as gentlemen and get this deed done. Mr Baines what was the weekly sum that you paid to Doctor Ross?"

"I can tell you directly as it were just a year from my first visit to the present day Doctor Flynn."

"That is 52 appointments I presume." Harry looked up sharply saying

"Yes and comes to the figure of £520 pounds. I want that at least doubled. Doctor Ross sent me here in a straight jacket to be treated as insane I have been locked up in a padded

room. You have defiled my character Doctor Ross and delivered me out of your hands into much discomfort and shame. Do not try to offer me less than the sum of £1.500 pounds. Otherwise you will be paying a lawyer and a court who will decide on the damage you have done. Your court costs would be at least the sum I have agreed to ask and then there is your valuable good name to consider what is that worth I wonder? There you have it, and I want it decided today I will not be kept waiting any longer otherwise you will have the cost of this room tagged on to the figure which is in itself costly." Well! Harry without whiskey was certainly a different man he had stated his case clear and precise leaving no room for negotiation. Doctor Flynn was in awe of his words. Doctor Ross now standing was transfixed, he had hoped to get away with a much lighter sum he turned and spoke to Doctor Flynn

"What do you think Doctor Flynn? Am I being robbed or is this amount that Mr Baines has stated correct?"

"You know in your own mind Doctor Ross, it is the price you must pay to satisfy Mr Baines. I don't come into it and will not directly answer your question as to the amount being settled between you. All I will

say is the amount has been stated and the sooner you settle this account the better." Doctor Ross knew he was cornered he might as well pay the cheque right now and stop his sleepless nights worrying about it. Harry's eyes gleamed as he watched Doctor Ross get out his cheque book, write the sum and pass it to Doctor Flynn who seen to it that the cheque was signed and dated. The amount was £1.500 pounds clearly written. He then passed it back to Doctor Ross who gave it into Harry's hands. Turning on his heel he didn't wait for a handshake or a word of thanks, his business was done and he wanted away and home to tend his open wounds.

Harry was jubilant he had expected a much stronger argument he had got his own way almost without a cross word. It crossed his mind he should have asked for more. The cheque he gazed his eyes upon was real and all was above board. Truth known Harry did not want this case to come to court, a few skeletons of his own might have been brought to light.

Two days later Harry had a letter from Adi saying she was going to be calling to sign and witness Harry's signature. As he looked down upon this letter he experienced a moment of content everything was going to be alright at this moment he swore he would have it so. He would treat his life in a proper manner, simplifying and shrinking the fact that he had Syphilis until the time the fact would be undeniable. Syphilis is a progressing disease it would completely take him over before it was done. Making every hour days weeks and months precious to use for redemption of his soul... Was this Harry? Could he endeavour to clean the slate and begin again once more with Adi?

Adi arrived and a small party of people went into Doctor Flynn's office. All went according to plan and Doctor Flynn saw to it that all handshakes were duly made before he shook Harry's hand saying
"I wish you well Mr. Baines the outcome has turned favourable. Make use of your time and be happy." It was strange to Harry walking side by side with Adi they were out of the Asylum walls, into the courtyard with no restraint free and on to the main gates. On setting his feet on the street cobblestones he breathed a huge sigh of relief, he was free and trembling with relief that is with one exception, he had Syphilis!
Adi called a cabbie and to Harry's delight gave the address of her own home. Turning to Harry she said

I hope you don't mind Harry but I have given the cabbie my own address, I think my dear you will be better off staying with me a couple of days while you adjust to your new circumstances, you have been pulled through the mill of late you will be better off with company. As soon as you wish you can go to your own home." Harry heard Adi with no problem and was delighted it was more than he had hoped for. He thanked her profusely taking her small gloved hand into his own and putting it to his lips. He noticed the blush it had brought to her cheeks. Harry's own sexual desires should have been roused but they were not he thought it strange. He consoled himself that there would be better moments than this to put his sexual moments to the test. Adi was good to Harry so he did not want to spoil this very new relationship. Was it possible that Harry was considering someone else for a change?

Chapter Forty five

Adi's house was just as Harry had imagined, quiet and serene with warmth and sensual feeling. Adi sat Harry in an armchair and said
"Tea I think Harry, I shall go and pull the kettle over the fire." Adi disappeared into the kitchen bringing back a tray with china tea cups and teapot to match also milk and sugar. This matching china tea set pleased Harry it was years since Lilly had done this to please him he felt good.
"Now relax Harry you have plenty of time, I will show you your bedroom soon but as the fire is bright and the tea is made we should make the most of the moment." Adi poured the tea. They sat eating scones and sipping tea. The atmosphere closed around them in absolute contrast to the Asylum and contentment settled over the room. After they had finished the tea Adi said
"Now I think it is time to show you your room Harry." Together they went up the very narrow staircase Harry noticed the carpet was threadbare. Adi had a small oil lamp as the light was dim. Walking along the very narrow passage Adi stopped at a door saying
"This will be your bedroom Harry I know it is

small but the chimney breast runs through it so it keeps warm. My room is the other side of this and also has the warmth of the chimney. My occasional guest has the box room. He is very rarely to be seen he spends most of his time at the local collage. I can assure you he will not be a nuisance. I hope your stay with me will be pleasant and will drive away all thought of the dreaded Asylum. Goodnight Harry."

Harry was suitably impressed by Adi and her quest to make him comfortable. It was such a long time since Harry had been properly cared for he sat down on the bed.

The two day stay that Adi had offered turned into two weeks. Harry was changing, his whole life was changing, time he must have time. Adi looked after Harry and found him respectful and organised. She lengthened the offer of him staying with her. There were no children and her husband was dead so from her point of view Harry was company besides she had her own plans. Bed arrangements had never been discussed and it was taken for granted they each went to their own room. From Harry's point of view the attention Adi showered upon him was received and enjoyed. One thing laid heavy on Harry's shoulders was the fact that he had

Syphilis how on earth was he going to tell Adi the truth? Daily the net grew tighter now Harry was paying for his room and his food and he could tell Adi did not want to speed things along, after all Harry had just been through a terrible ordeal it would be wrong to take anything for granted. Noticing Harry's stand offish manner Adi wondered why? She busied herself with cooking, keeping her appearance in order and attractive. It was working as Harry was appearing as if from a cocoon into Adi's world. He had planned nothing of this it just happened, for the first time since marrying Lilly he knew he was in love, only this time it was with Adi, a fine and indescribable feeling. There was nowhere for him to hide his previous life of sex and street girls it was all in his scared past, but that was it, he had no intention of digging up his old "friends" if only he could leave it all in the past. He had to keep Adi at arm's length still harbouring the awful state of Syphilis. This then was his punishment, for Syphilis was not curable. Little did he know that Adi herself had early signs of this disease contacted from her husband Henry and desperately waiting for a cure? Cursing her former husband she went daily about her business and kept her Doctor's appointments on each Wednesday

*saying to Harry they were beauty treatments,
In a way it wasn't a lie because the lesions
had to be continually dealt with as they
appeared. Noticing Adi went out best dressed
but in a sombre mood Harry had wondered
more than once if the beauty treatments were
really kept. Always on Wednesdays they had a
simple meal as if Adi had spent her energies
and wanted to relax more than anything. One
day I will ask her where this beauty parlour is
and why it takes so much out of her. Her skin
on returning looked aggravated. Harry
pondered this fact, should he tell her?
Deciding no this was a step too far Harry
tried to use his charm saying
"Do you always use a hat with a high scarf
Adi?"
"What a funny question Harry does my attire
not please you?"
"Sorry Adi I should not be enquiring about
what is personal to you, it is just that I
noticed that when you come back from your
beauty session your complexion looks angry
and it may be because you wear a hat and a
scarf so much. I am sure your skin would be
so much better if the air was allowed to help
your facial pores to breath. My goodness Adi
what am I saying please forgive this old fool I
am only acting in your best interests."*

*"Sorry Harry if I do not please you, it is a
secret I have had to live with for many years
and a long story indeed, not a pleasant one.
Perhaps one day when we know one another
better I will tell you but not now my dear not
now." Harry thought there was a sinister
reason in the past, he didn't enquire or advise
any further, he had his own trouble to
contend with. A quiet life is what he wanted
and with Adi he might achieve that.
Quietly he tried to find out how much money
Henry had left Adi? Going for walks, tea at
four, helping her with household
accounts...this was the way he chose casual,
soon he would find out the sum Henry had
left to Adi. Harry decided to be bold and
changed the subject saying
"You have helped me so much Adi I would
like to repay you eventually. As a matter of
pure curiosity Adi what did Henry die from?"
"I won't try to cover it up Harry you are
entitled to know, he died from Syphilis. He
led me merry dances going after the company
of loose women that is where he caught this
disease yes I know a lot about Syphilis."
Harry was sure his face had gone chalk
white, should he open up and tell Adi the
absolute truth? He decided not he had only
just found this haven of delight. It would*

surely wreck all his chances if Adi knew the truth. There and then he decided to keep Adi well away from Lilly that is if it was at all possible, he must play his cards right but "oh what a tangled web we weave when we practise to deceive" Lilly was now a bygone entity. Harry considered himself as single soon he would want for nothing. Yes this side of town made him believe he was secure, he planned to live no more the life he had left. Turning his back on whiskey and keeping away from the many brothels he had frequented. A quiet life with Adi is what he wanted and Harry usually got what he wanted!

The weeks went by Adi and Harry were conversing and politely making short term small plans. Yes Harry was still with Adi and yes he still had Syphilis. There had been no call for explanation Adi did not treat Harry any different than she had treated Henry Doctor Flynn was now giving Harry advice and medication. Funnily enough Harry had to see Doctor Flynn once a week and fortune would have it that it coincided with Adi's beauty treatment. Harry fibbed and told Adi he had a friend that wanted him to call each week Adi was pleased as it was so convenient for them both. The fact being that Doctor

Flynn was examining and dosing Harry for his complaint. A low dose of arsenic and a cream containing mercury, Doctor knew that Harry was a hopeless case but it gave Harry comfort to think he was being considered until the cure was announced. When arriving home on Wednesday Harry always felt groggy and retired to bed very early. After many visits Harry found he had a new lesion coming in a very undesirable spot on the back of his hand. How could he hide this from Adi? He almost panicked then he calmed down thinking least said best off. Adi said
"You have a very angry looking sore on the back of your hand Harry, what is it?" Harry passed it off casually saying
"I have been digging deep in the weeds and the nettles, I must be allergic to something."
"As soon as you felt it sting you should have come in and scrubbed it with carbolic soap I keep it under the sink, it looks very angry."
"I didn't know the soap was there Adi and I didn't want to make a fuss."
"Let me look again Harry." Showing this unsightly lesion was not what Harry wanted to do but he offered the back of his hand to Adi
"It looks more like a wart than anything. I don't think it is an allergy. You must see a

Doctor if it persists." Adi knew full well what it was, her suspicions were being justified. Now a trip to see Lilly would have to be made and what was the name of Harry's Doctor? Adi would make a very private consultation and see what she could find out. Adi had been weighing up the situation and had come to the conclusion that Harry had got Syphilis. Adi needed to know…now not later. Being the lady she was she let the matter drop. Henry had died from Syphilis and Adi had the signs of it coming, being treated was a good thing but how long before the cure became the answer was any bodies guess. Because Henry had left her with the certain signs of Syphilis set her mind wondering if Lilly and the baby were also infected the illness being passed from Harry, Adi felt her temper rise, these two brothers had damaged their wives and any offspring all because they wanted to sleep with ladies of ill repute, she thought …if I had my way they would all be hanged. So Harry thought he was playing her for a fool did he? Adi had her cards still yet to play. First she must be certain of her ground and yet maybe have the winning hand.

Chapter Forty six

Excusing her whereabouts for the next day and ensuring Harry a fond goodbye Adi with Lilly's address securely in her handbag went out. Harry did not like Adi out of his company, he needed her within the confines of their home so that he knew Lilly would not cross her path. Lilly would maybe tell Adi all she knew and that would be a disaster!

Finding Lilly's home Adi tapped the door which was duly answered by Lilly, she said "Is it myself or Annie you would like to speak to? Your name is?"

"You don't recognise me do you Lilly? I am Adi Baines your sister in law."

"I am sorry Adi now that I can see clearly I recognise it is you. Please come in." Adi was shown into the sitting room where there was a good fire. Lilly introduced Annie and showing off her Daughter said

"This is my Daughter her name is Rosie..."

Now sitting quietly sipping tea Lilly enquired the purpose of Adi's visit

"It is a long time since we talked Adi, how is Henry?"

"I am sorry to say Henry has passed away. Been gone ten years now."

"Sorry to hear that Adi, I would convey the

message to Harry but we no longer live together."

"I know that Lilly in fact Harry is lodging with me." A look of surprise came to Lilly's face she said

"How has that come about Adi? You hardly knew one another."

"There is nothing untoward going on Lilly, of course we have separate bedrooms and there is only friendship between us. It is Harry I have come to enquire about."

"I know very little about Harry these days Adi and it suits me that way."

"I have to ask you a very straight forward question Lilly, please don't be offended by it."

"Go ahead Adi I will tell you all that I know."

"Lilly has Harry got Syphilis? I believe I know the answer but I must be sure."

"Yes Adi he has and what is more Rosie and myself show the very first signs of it brought to us by Harry. From my point of view Harry has done enough damage and I never wish to see him again."

"Now I must tell you Lilly I am in that very same position, Henry died from Syphilis and I am also affected in the very same way as you and Rosie, of course inherited from Henry, I am having regular treatment and my Doctor says there is strong talk of a cure in

the near future being developed."

"Yes I know, Rosie and I are under a Doctor's supervision and taking medication waiting for the self same cure to be developed but I must say Adi that Harry has had this disease far too long for a cure to be administered . Has he told you about his illness?"

"No but I am the relative that helped him to be released from the Asylum. I was told a few facts by Doctor Flynn but Harry is unaware that I know anything. I shall leave it that way and he will never know I have spoken to you. You needn't worry about him coming to your door in an angry fashion, this meeting is between you and I and must be kept secret, do you understand Lilly?"

"Yes I do and I agree, your secret is safe with me Adi"

"Now I must take my leave my job here is done and I know exactly how I stand with Harry. Thank you Lilly I hope you and Rosie live happily until the cure is found. We are victims, who in fact have done nothing wrong to warrant the disease we carry. Henry liked the smutty ladies and it appears so did Harry. I doubt if I see you again Lilly unless it is at Harry's funeral." The door was closed as Adi left.

Lilly alongside Annie went into the kitchen to make fresh tea, sitting beside the fire to discuss views on what Adi had said

Adi walked along going over what information Lilly had verified …So Harry is in fact playing me as a fool is he? Well I am no fool, I am indeed sorry for him and I shall give him the exact attention that I gave to Henry. We will have to see how things work out. I shall not be in close contact with Harry so I can deceive him quite easily. I must give this much thought and treat Harry as well as I treated Henry. I must take care I don't mention Lilly in any casual conversation, I must keep this secret to myself I already have Harry at my beck and call so it will not be difficult .

Harry sat waiting for Adi he missed her when she went out alone he fidgeted and kept going over to the window to see if he could see her coming. After pacing the floor and peering along the street a dozen times he now spotted Adi in the distance. Harry found himself now in the kitchen having pulled the kettle over the fire to boil. Never in his life had he made tea for a woman but he wanted to stay with Adi and he must give a good impression, he was at the door before she had time to put her key in the lock he greeted her

"Glad you are back Adi, I have the kettle on ready to make tea, you have been gone a long time. Did you walk all the way from town?"

"Yes I did" Adi said pulling off her hat and coat. Harry carried on in the kitchen putting tea and biscuits on a tray. He wondered at himself, Harry had never lifted a finger for Lilly, Adi was different, she carried herself with pride and dignity she commanded respect. She was always well dressed with clothes that followed the latest fashion. Her parasol or umbrella was always tilted at a jaunty angle. Never did she look old or matronly her figure was to be envied by many a young girl. If only...Harry thought and he was reminded of the disease he carried "Blast beggar and drat he whispered under his breath, but he knew he couldn't change a thing. Harry inspected his body daily and knew for certain sure that the chancres and lesions were increasing. He had hoped in changing his Doctor there would be new remedies to try, evidence of that had not been found. Now the lesions were appearing on the palms of his hands, his arms and his wrists. Adi had not said a word about them. She treated him every day alike with courtesy and respect. They sat together after tea this evening and Adi unexpectedly said

"Harry I have a treat for you tonight." This sent sparks flying all over Harry was she going to offer to sleep with him he thought? She carried on

"I know you have always liked your whiskey my dear so I have put a bottle in the cabinet especially for you, it is only there if you want it shall we say a small reward for the things you help me to do, would you like a glass now before we retire?"

"How very thoughtful of you Adi yes it would help me to sleep, my nights have been restless as of late." Harry went to the drinks cabinet picking the bottle up to appraise the strength of the brew he said

"This is good stuff Adi I should pay you for it."

"Nonsense Harry have it as a night cap just one glass each evening is not going to break the bank and it might just do you good."

"Very well then Adi and thank you." He poured the golden liquid into a cut glass vessel especially to be savoured he said

"I see you have the whiskey decanter sitting empty should I put the remainder of this bottle into it?"

"As you wish my dear I only have a tot of that or brandy for medicinal purposes. I don't want to get used to it and the same applies to *you, have just one each evening as I said."Harry sat down in the armchair opposite Adi saying*

"You are so good to me Adi is there anything I can do for you in return?"

"No Harry just stay quietly beside me as did Henry, which will be thanks enough. Harry got up next day feeling jubilant he said

"Adi I slept so well after having my nightcap I didn't want to get up."

"So you believe it will do you good Harry?"

"No doubt about it but you must let me buy the next bottle, the last thing I want to do is become a burden."

"That is a silly thought you know I like having you here. I only give you the same treatment as I gave to your brother Henry. You are company for me, one day we will both know if our arrangement has paid off. Sit down and eat your breakfast before it has gone cold." Harry preened himself it was a very long time since a lady constantly cooked his breakfast. He was in control once more and he must not offend Adi in any way.

Chapter Forty seven

*The days weeks months carried Harry
and Adi forward his only complaint was of
headache and at times an upset stomach
making him feel dowdy and sick he hid that
away from Adi he didn't want her to think he
was complaining or indeed he was weak but
the signs of deterioration were constant and
even though he hid his condition away it was
getting to the point where the only thing that
really pleased him was his glass of whiskey
each night. He casually spoke to Adi about
his symptoms but she cast it off blaming this
or that and consoling Harry that all would be
well very soon. Never once did she refer to
the Syphilis lesions which were by now more
than obvious.*

*It had taken Adi six months to bring Harry
down she was delighted on seeing the results
of her plan working so well. It wouldn't be
long now before she could sweet talk Harry
into giving her all his detailed documents
with power over his investments and savings.
As she went around the house with a feather
duster her eyes sparkled and under her
breath she chanted…Dear Harry silly Harry,
stupid Harry, did you think you were any
better than your brother Henry? I have given*

to you both what you well deserved. One more week should see the conclusion of all my plans, only then will I be happy!

Steady on Adi there is yet another week! Time enough for things to go very wrong.

Chapter forty eight

Harry had to take to his bed his legs would not hold him steady. He felt such shame under the clean glace of Adi's eyes. He was constantly saying sorry. Adi took it all in her stride, taking his whiskey up to him at bedtime and in general trying to keep Harry with food he could keep down. Now Adi was offering help with Harry's financial affairs. Adi was very careful saying

"This is none of your own fault you are not to blame Harry. Is there is anything you would like me to help you with to give you peace of mind Banking or personal investments? I could bring a Solicitor to see you here, he would tie in any lose ends and you would be seeing that things were as you wish them to be, it would ease your mind a little dear."

"Oh Adi would you do that for me? You are so kind. My head is not in a fit state to make the right moves but with you beside me explaining each item and helping me to make the right decisions I am sure I could cope. Your opinions would be more than welcome."

"We will arrange it for next week Harry that is unless your health has taken a positive turn for the better. Who is your Solicitor Harry? Where do you keep the copies of your

documents and important receipts? I will make it my business to go through them the best I can and I will be sure to be here when the Solicitor arrives. This is the first step towards getting back your health and strength Harry." Adi kissed Harry on his forehead and comforted him he said

"Adi I know it is early in the day but do you think I could have just one glass of whiskey? I want to close my eyes and relax and I know the whiskey will help."

"Of course Harry you may, a little indulgence when you need it is fine. I will go and bring the decanter back with me and I will replace the bottle while I am out shopping, there is not a lot left." Harry breathed a sigh of relief knowing he could trust Adi's willing hands and the whiskey's powerful intoxication. To himself he whispered... Hell's teeth if this affliction had not suddenly got worse I would have been able to bed Adi what rotten luck!

Mr. Jones, Harry's solicitor came the following week. He and Harry went through all the pile of papers. Adi stood by to agree or disagree, things needed clearing up she made sure her own name came into focus when big decisions were being made. It was Harry's fault, she wasn't being pushy it was the way Harry wanted it to be and he had signed for

Adi to receive a very generous lump sum. Adi had overwhelmed Harry right from the moment she walked out of the Asylum with him. Now she controlled his every thought. Their relationship was nothing at all like Harry had envisaged, he had fallen head first into his own trap and Adi was standing by just to close the trap door!

It was a few days later and Harry's condition had worsened considerably. Adi pleased that her plan was working out so well tended him constantly. Harry couldn't do a thing for himself if he tried to eat it made him want to vomit. His only solace was the whiskey that Adi generously poured for him. Adi held Harry up to sip the drink. Harry tried to protest saying

"Adi I have not been much good to you have I? Believe me I did not want to burden you and now I have no choice." He sipped and groaned as the fiery liquid burned his throat Adi said

"Now Harry don't drink too much." Adi cushioned his top weight sitting at the back of him and holding his head, he asked her to lay him down and as she did so she said

"I always told you Harry I would give you the same consideration and attention as I gave to Henry and you see my dear you have been

receiving that every moment you have stayed in my home. Now I will kiss you goodbye in the exact same manner that I kissed Henry goodbye. Harry's eyes met Adi's and he read the meaning behind the look! He then knew now just what she was conveying, he opened his mouth to speak but Adi interrupted giving him the last of the whiskey in the glass with purpose. Harry flopped forward Adi said "Goodbye Harry my dear, justice has been done and Lilly myself and Rosie might be able to live until the cure has been found. Oh! Yes Harry I knew all along you had Syphilis you didn't think I was so much a fool did you as not to notice your chancres and lesions. Sleep tight my dear. Harry tried with all his might to sit up, but dropped forward as a dead weight Adi caught his body she heaved his head back on to the pillow, still he stared at her his eyes glossy and dark. Don't worry Harry I will see that you have a decent funeral and I will follow you to your graveside. Harry's body began to shake and tremble he had heard all that Adi had said and terror struck him in his last few moments. Adi felt his pulses. He was already growing cold and grey. Harry's journey in this life was over, just as Henry's life had been over. Adi's plan had worked to the last detail. Harry's own Doctor had prescribed Arsenic as part of his medication. All Adi had done was lace the whiskey with rat poison containing Arsenic. Harry and Henry both loved their whiskey and rat poison was right, both Henry and Harry had behaved like dirty rats, bedding with many other women until they had become ill with the dreaded Syphilis. Passing this disease on to Lilly and Rosie was unforgivable. Just as Henry's deed in passing his Syphilis on to Adi. Henry and Harry had behaved like rats so it was fitting that they should die like rats. If a post mortem was required of course both Henry's blood and Harry's blood would contain Arsenic it was part of their cure wasn't it?... Kill or cure they were both now very dead.

Dear Reader, yes there is an epilogue, turn to next pages. Hope you have enjoyed this story, I have enjoyed writing it, although I must say some of the more graphic passages have been a trial, but this is life, and life has many sides to it. A peep in to a different way of living should make you realise just what you have achieved. Enjoy all that you have, and the people who are sharing it with you. Nearly time to put the kettle on, read the epilogue before you leave me in these pages.

Epilogue

Adi had done her work and was smiling with satisfaction. Now it was Lilly she had to inform. Adi stood at Lilly's front door and tapped it in a lady like fashion. It was Lilly that answered Adi went straight into her pitying mode saying

"A most unfortunate affair my dear. I am afraid Harry has passed away. A look of shock and surprise sprang to Lilly's eyes. Lilly headed straight for her chair, feeling her legs would not support her, finally she spoke

"I need not ask you the cause of his death I know it only too well. There will be a lot to do now and quite quickly too

"Don't worry about that Lilly, I had a Solicitor come to the house to see Harry and his affairs are now all in order. I must make you aware that Harry left me a lump sum of money in return for looking after him. I told him I was only looking after him in the same way as I did his brother Henry, but he insisted I had my reward

"Dear Adi do you think I begrudge you that? I was at my wits end and didn't know how I would cope, you did me such a favour I will never be able to thank you enough

"Thank you Lilly I am glad you see it like that. I will make all the arrangements and see that the funeral is carried through with dignity. There is no need for you to attend, you have dear little Rosie to consider, just tell me what flowers you would like to pay your tribute with?"

"White Lilly's please Adi and of course I will pay the funeral costs, you have taken a great weight off my mind Bless you Adi. Seeing Adi to the door was Annie's job she said

This will bring Lilly peace of mind she has worried about Harry for a long time, not that in my mind he was worthy of it, Lilly thought she would be able to put matters right and I knew she never would. Thank you Adi for all you have done I will look after Lilly.

Adi left, all was satisfactory and she had delivered her news without causing upset. All would be well now and Rosie Lilly and Adi could patiently wait for a cure. It would come and all of their lives would be whole again. Adi had done just as she intended to do and Harry would be buried with Henry where they would trouble no-one anymore.

Sylvia Jackson Clark ©
June 16.th 2016

Made in the USA
Charleston, SC
13 December 2016